A Journey to Joy

by Nancy I. Young

 FriesenPress

One Printers Way
Altona, MB R0G 0B0
Canada

www.friesenpress.com

ISBN
978-1-03-917001-8 (Hardcover)
978-1-03-917000-1 (Paperback)
978-1-03-917002-5 (eBook)

1. FICTION, CHRISTIAN, HISTORICAL

Distributed to the trade by The Ingram Book Company

Table of Contents

Dedication vii

Chapter 1 1

Chapter 2 26

Chapter 3 73

Chapter 4 105

Chapter 5 123

Chapter 6 138

Chapter 7 166

Chapter 8 182

Chapter 9 198

Chapter 10 220

Chapter 11 239

Chapter 12 255

Chapter 13 265

Chapter 14 279

Epilogue 289

End Notes 294

Dedication

This book is dedicated to my 'oldest' friend, Laurie Klassen Robertson. Our friendship has spanned many decades even though we now live half a world apart. Thank you, Laurie, for not only being my friend, but also for reviewing the first draft of this book from a Down Under's perspective. Without your knowledge of Western Australia, I would have made the mistake of having my hero find koalas in the bush of WA. I did not know they were not indigenous to your part of Australia. Thank you again for all your help.

Love you, my friend!

A quokka, the happiest mammal on earth!

Chapter 1

"No."

"No, what?" asked her stepbrother Howard.

"No, you will not be getting any more money today, or any time in the future. The Stillwater bank is now closed to you." Bethany took a step backward as his face reddened.

"What!" He shouted, his face now the colour of a ripe tomato as he moved towards her. "Why?"

"Because I know how you are spending it, and it is not for household expenses." Trying to remain calm, Bethany retreated again.

"You have no right—"

"That is where you are wrong. This estate came to me; it was a legacy from my mother. She brought it into her marriage with my father and so, legally, you have no claim upon it."

"I am your brother." He narrowed the gap between them. "We should have equal shares in the estate."

She moved back a final step. Soon, if he continued to edge towards her, she would call for help from the butler and the footmen. Howard had always had a temper, but today's display was the worst she had ever seen of it. While not panicking about his advancement, she was nervous about what he might do next.

"You are my stepbrother, not my blood brother. If my father had owned the estate, then yes, I agree you should have your share of the estate. But as I just said, that is not the case, and you will not be getting any more handouts from me. You need to earn your own way in life and not expect me to finance your habits."

Then he was only an arm's length away. "You will regret this action, Bethany. I guarantee it. When I have full control of your late mother's land, I will sell it from underneath you and use the profits for my happiness. You have crossed me to your detriment, and nothing will save you now. You'll pay the price for what you've done. Good day, little sister. Until we meet again." Taking his hat from the butler Kingsley, who had appeared in the doorway, he spun on his heel and headed out the open door. A satisfied Kingsley quickly closed the door behind him, almost hitting him before he cleared the doorway.

Bethany found herself shaken in the aftermath of Howard's threat. "Thank you for your aid, Kingsley. I didn't know he would get so angry."

"No problem, Miss Bethany. I have wanted to do that many a time. It gave me great pleasure to show him out in such a manner. Are you all right?"

"I will be fine, thank you. Perhaps I need a cup of tea to settle my nerves. I will withdraw to the Sunshine room now, if you don't mind bringing my tea there?"

"Of course not, and I will see if Mrs. Kingsley has any sweet treats for you. I will bring your tea shortly."

"Thank you again. I don't know what I would do without you and your wife."

"Well, we don't have any plans to leave you, Miss, so not to worry. Now, let's pray Master Howard's words are just a lot of blustering and nothing else."

"I hope you're right."

Bethany left the foyer and headed down the hall to her favourite room in the manor, sending a prayer heavenward as she walked.

***

Kingsley strode to the kitchen to fetch Bethany's tea and have a word with his missus. How dare that pompous little man threaten his mistress. It had given him a great deal of joy to shove Howard out the door after what he had said to her. She was right. Howard had no right to the estate or any of its proceeds. It was hers, and hers alone, a legacy from her mother. Bethany's father had understood this, and even after the passing of his beloved wife and his remarriage a few years later, he had never tried to wrest the estate from his daughter. Instead, he had managed it well, so when he died it was a profitable inheritance for her. If Howard got hold of it, it would either be sold or in ruins within a year of his possession. Kingsley prayed that never happened.

Arriving in the kitchen, he found his plump, silver-haired wife putting out a tray of scones to cool on the table. Coming up behind her, he put his arms around her and gave her a big hug.

"Mr. Kingsley, you startled me," she said with a smile, turning and returning his embrace. "What are you about, scaring me like that? I could have dumped the entire tray of scones on the floor, and we would have none left for tea."

"Just wanted to let you know I love you, that's all."

"And I love you, too. I presume you are here to take a tray of tea to Miss Bethany, although is it not a bit early for her?"

"Yes, but she had quite a set-to with Mr. Howard just now, so she needs her tea early to help settle her nerves."

"A set-to? What about?"

"The usual." Kingsley described what he had observed only moments previous to his coming to the kitchen.

"Good for her. No wonder she needs her tea early after such a scene. I'll put the kettle on and have tea ready for her in a few minutes. I will take it to her myself and congratulate her on a job well done. No need for you to wait here for the tray. You can go back to your duties and come for tea with me later."

Satisfied with that arrangement, Kingsley headed out of the kitchen and back to the front foyer, hoping they had seen the last of Mr. Howard Stillwater.

***

Mrs. Kingsley headed down to the Sunshine room to deliver the tea to Bethany. The Sunshine room was so named because it was at the end of the hall and had windows facing in three directions: east, south, and west. It filled with sunlight most days. Bethany had named the room when she was very young, and the name had stuck.

"Here you are, Miss Bethany. Some hot tea and warm scones with clotted cream to settle your nerves."

"Thank you. The scones smell wonderful, as does the tea. I suppose your husband filled you in on what happened earlier this afternoon."

"Yes, he did, Miss. Of course, he was not gossiping; he would never stoop to do that, but he thought I should know why you were requesting your tea earlier than usual today."

"You and Kingsley are family, so I don't mind him telling you such things. I also know you will keep it close and not spread the word around about Mr. Howard's visit."

"Definitely not. But I wish I had been there to give him my two cents when he started threatening you."

"That may have made things worse, but thank you for the support. I hope he cools down before he gets home, or he may take his anger out on Cassandra."

"That poor young woman. I don't know how she endures life with him."

"I don't either. But she has no other choice."

Cassandra had been forced by her father to marry Howard because of the outstanding gambling debts owed to him. And now, with their four boys, she had nowhere else to go.

"Gambling can wreak such havoc on families, can it not?" said Mrs. Kingsley.

"Yes, it can. I fear that is happening to Howard and his family, especially now that he has run through Cassandra's dowry. I think he will be back to seek more funds from me when his debts mount up again."

"You do not think today's words will keep him away, Miss?"

"No. Gambling is a sickness with Howard. It's in his blood. I understand his father was in a similar situation before he passed away."

"Let us hope he sees the error of his ways before it is too late. Much as I dislike the man, I will pray for him."

"I will pray as well. After all, he is my brother, and I have many fond memories of him from my childhood. I would like to have that Howard back in my family someday."

"Perhaps that will come to be. But for today, drink your tea and eat your scones while they are warm. I will be back to pick up the tray later."

"Thank you. I feel much better already." She poured herself a cup of the fragrant tea before reaching for a scone.

"Any time, love, any time." She exited the room, leaving Bethany to her tea and solitude.

***

Bethany would not have been so comforted if she had known Howard's thoughts as he bounced back to London in a poorly sprung hired hack. Every time they hit a hole in the road, a nasty piece of metal jabbed into Howard's backside, increasing his anger. Once he had control of the Stillwater estate, he would never ride in a hired carriage again. He would have his own carriage with well-padded seats, a driver, and a couple of footmen to cater to his needs. He would sell the estate so he would never have to travel this way again. He did not know what possessed people to purchase, or build, country estates. There was very little to do here, except watch the grass grow. No entertainment, no ladies, no nothing. Of course, when he went to sell the estate, he would feature all its virtues so he could get the highest price possible for the sale. Why . . . he might even consider a tour of the continent after he disposed of the estate. That would depend on whether there was enough money left over after paying off his creditors. Perhaps he could sneak away and leave Cassandra to deal with his gambling debts. The idea of just stealing away from his responsibilities brought on a twinge of guilt which Howard quickly squelched. He had no time to dwell on thoughts of how his actions might affect his family. His father certainly never had. He'd drank away all his money and left his wife and children in poverty. No, Howard had learned the hard lesson from his father. Look out for yourself, and don't let guilt shame you into straying from your path. Howard had only married Cassandra for her dowry, but now that money was gone. No matter. Howard gave his head a shake to clear away any remorse. The money from the estate would set him up financially for the rest of his life. Cassandra would have to find another way to pay the household bills, even if it meant she had to sell her prized jewellery. He would leave the jewels for her; it was the best he could do.

In the hour it took to get back to his rented townhouse, Howard contemplated what he could do to wrest the estate out of Bethany's hands. He knew she was right in claiming he had no rights to the estate. But he did not care. When his mother had married Bethany's father when Howard was eighteen years old, he had dreamed that his stepfather would leave the estate to him one day. He had walked and talked with his stepfather daily, trying to persuade him that Bethany, as a woman, would be better off if he, Howard, became heir to the properties. He had assured the senior Stillwater that he would always look after Bethany, and that she would want for nothing. But his stepfather had held firm to his promise to his first wife, from whose hands he had received the estate. Bethany would inherit the entire estate, and he, Howard, could, if he desired, manage it for her, receiving a healthy wage for his efforts on her behalf. But that arrangement did not satisfy Howard. The wage they paid him was scarcely enough for him to live on, especially when he started playing cards with the high rollers. That was when he had married Cassandra, to satisfy her father's debts and to receive the bulk of her dowry. The jewellery she brought with her was not a part of the contract. It was Cassandra's security, in case she needed it in the future. Howard occasionally pawned pieces of the collection when he was hard up for cash, but he always bought them back as soon as he could so Cassandra would not know what he was doing. For that, and to pay for his gambling debts, he relied on extra handouts from Bethany. He hated having to go her to her and beg for money. He never told her it was to pay gambling debts; instead he always claimed it was to buy food and clothing for Cassandra and the boys. Howard knew Bethany would not give him any more funds if she knew where the money was truly going. She was a *good Christian woman* with strong morals, and he knew gambling was unacceptable in her eyes. But he could not help himself; it was in his blood. Time and time again he had tried to resist the lure of the card tables, but it was no use. As soon as he had a bit of cash in his pocket, he was off to the gambling dens. He seldom made any money, but if he did it was used as a stake for his next game. If only he could quit . . . but that was an impossible dream. No, he just needed more money before he would put the cards aside. Once he got what he wanted, and needed, he would quit. He wasn't addicted to the rush of winning like his father had been. No, he only needed the money for another stake. At some point his winnings would be enough, but not now . . . not until . . .

And that was why he needed control of the estate; to sell it and play with the high rollers. Then he would have it made.

His father had been a gambler and died one night when he was discovered cheating at the table. Extra cards had been found up his coat sleeve. Outraged, his card playing buddies demanded he surrender all his winnings, but he refused. Instead, he gathered them up, stuffed them in his coat pocket, and prepared to leave the table. But the others were having none of it. They pulled out pistols, first to scare him into dropping the cash, and when that did not work, shots rang out. Howard's father dropped to the floor with three bullets in his heart. His body was dragged out into the alley and the card game continued without him. No money was left for his wife or son, so Howard's mother hired herself out as a nanny. That was how they met the Stillwaters. Mr. Stillwater was looking for a nanny for Bethany. He hired Howard's mother for the position and even gave them a cottage on the estate grounds. Within a short time, he saw the potential in the nanny as a mother for Bethany and asked her to marry him. After accepting his proposal, she and Howard had moved into the manor, and from then on Howard was treated like a son, and became a loving older brother to Bethany. Howard assumed that when his stepfather died, he would inherit the estate, while Bethany would receive a large dowry and marry well. At that time, he would be a somebody, not just Mr. Howard Stillwater. He would walk, with his head held high, among the upper class in Hyde Park and attend their snobbish parties. People like the Duke of Yardley and his sons would pay their respects, not just a simple nod, when they passed on the street. But those dreams all died along with Mr. Stillwater. Bethany inherited all and dwelt in society, while Howard remained the estate manager. Howard fumed when the will was read, and he realised where he stood in relation to his stepsister. She was his boss and he hated that. Soon his hatred for his position turned into rage against Bethany herself. He no longer doted upon her but was constantly looking for ways to deprive her of her wealth.

Fudging the estate books became a method of retribution and extra income for Howard. When that was not enough to pay his mounting gambling debts, and his wife's dowry was drained, Howard used the card of poverty to get more money from Bethany. That, too, had worked, until now. Somehow Bethany had heard about where the money was going and was cutting him off. Well, Howard was not going to have his easy money cut off. Bethany was going to pay, and pay dearly, for her words.

But how was he going to achieve his objective? What if Bethany committed a crime that had her transported to the colonies to serve out her prison sentence? He would be in full control of the estate and could do whatever he wanted to do. She would have no say in the matter, and if statistics were correct about the number of prisoners who died, either on route or in the colony prisons, she would never come back again. The more he thought about it, the more he liked the idea. But how to get her tried and convicted? She was of the lesser nobility, but she had friends within the upper class. It needed to be a significant enough crime that her connections would not save her. Howard thought of murder, but that was too messy, and he did not want there to be a chance of him being implicated in such a crime. No, theft was a better idea. But what could she steal that would convince a judge to send her away? Fine jewels, that was the ticket. And he knew just where to find them and how to get his mousy little wife to agree with his plans. If she did not, she would bear the consequences of a divorce and losing her sons to his custody. If there was anything that Cassandra valued above all else, it was her sons. The thought of losing them would make her do precisely what Howard wanted, for her to perjure herself in a court of law. She would lie about the theft of her jewellery, and being an upstanding woman from a good family background, who would doubt her story?

Knowing how the justice system worked, Howard needed an accomplice within the system to make sure they convicted Bethany of theft. He knew just who to call. Frank Walden was an old acquaintance from Howard's school days. They had kept in touch throughout the years. Frank was now a barrister with the Queen's Court. However, Frank also had a problem with gambling, and lived on the edge of the law. He could keep his private life secret from most, but Howard had discovered his secret and now exploited it whenever he needed a legal favour. Howard knew he could convince Frank to do his dirty work and have Bethany convicted of the crime. He was sure his plan would work and Bethany would be out of his life forever, as he had Frank and Cassandra securely in his pockets. Nearing London, Howard sat back with a satisfied smile. Tomorrow, he would start putting the pieces in place for Bethany's downfall.

***

Howard began the workings of his plan the next morning. He saw Cassandra sitting with their sons when he came down for breakfast. They looked up when they heard his footsteps with varying degrees of wariness. As it was not usual for him to appear at this time of the morning, they were uncertain why he was there.

"Good morning, my dear," said Howard as he walked over and gave his wife a kiss on her upturned cheek. "How are you this morning?"

"Fine, thank you, Howard. And you?" replied Cassandra, raising her eyebrows at his kiss. What was he up to now?

"Isn't it a lovely morning? What are you boys up to today? Playing with your friends?"

"No, Father," ventured Peter, the oldest boy. "We have school today."

"Oh, that is right. It is a school day. How foolish of me to have forgotten. Well, you had best hurry and finish your breakfasts and then be off to school. You don't want to be late, do you?"

"No, sir," replied the boy, looking at his brothers. "It is time we got ready to leave, isn't it?"

They pushed back their chairs and started to get up when Cassandra said, "Boys, you have not finished your breakfasts. You need to eat before you go to school."

"We don't have time, Mama," said her middle son, Wendell. "We have to get to school."

"Don't fuss, Cassandra. The boys will be fine. When I was their age, I never ate breakfast prior to leaving for school. And look at me now." Howard pushed out his massive belly, barely restrained in a tight waistcoat. "I am fit as a fiddle."

"Yes, Mr. Stillwater, but your circumstances were such that—"

Howard interrupted her. "We don't need to discuss the past now, do we, my dear?"

Recognising his anger and what it could lead to, Cassandra said, "No, of course not. Boys, do as your father says and get ready for school."

With that dismissal from their mother, the boys turned as one and ran up the stairs, leaving only their youngest brother at the table with his parents.

Howard looked at him before saying, "And what are you going to do this morning, young man?"

Arthur thought for a moment. "Play with Mama."

"You and Mama are going to play together?"

He nodded.

"Where?"

"In the playroom."

"Then you need to go up and sort out the toys you want to play with, don't you?"

Looking down at his still full plate, and then at his mother, he said, "I'se still hungry, Papa. Want to eat breakfast."

"You are done, boy. Go up to the playroom now."

"Yes, Papa," he said, getting out of his chair.

Before he left the room, Cassandra said to him, "I will be up soon. Pick out your favourite toys and we will play with them."

He nodded and headed towards the stairs. After one last look at his uneaten meal, he turned around and slowly ascended the steps to the upper landing.

When he was out of sight, Cassandra turned to Howard. "What do you mean by depriving the boys of their breakfasts? You know you would have given anything to eat breakfast every day, and now you are starving your sons for no reason."

Howard growled. "They will not starve if they miss one meal, Mrs. Stillwater. And mind your manners with me. You might find your household funds substantially decreased if you carry on like this."

Cassandra shut her mouth. It did no good to argue with Howard. As he said, he held the purse strings in the family and felt no remorse about cutting her household spending, even if it meant harming his sons. For the umpteenth time, she wished her father had never met him and sold her to him in marriage. It had been a disaster since their wedding day. The only good thing that had come out of this marriage were her four little boys, and she would die before she let anything happen to them. In a more contrite manner, she said, "Why did you join us for breakfast today, Howard?"

"I needed to speak with you and knew you would be here with the boys for breakfast, as you are every morning. I have commitments this morning, so could not wait until later to have this discussion."

"What about?"

"I need you to do me a favour."

"A favour? What kind of favour?" Cassandra wrung her hands. Howard never asked normal favours, and it bothered her that he was asking one of her now.

"I need you to lie for me."

"Lie, as in, tell a lie?"

"Yes."

"Why?"

"For money."

"Of course, it is always about money with you."

"Cassandra," he warned.

"I'm sorry. What am I going to lie about?"

"The theft of one of your necklaces. It is going to go missing soon."

"Not if I can help it, Howard. My jewellery is my only security."

"I know. You are not going to lose it. You only have to say that it has gone missing."

"And who do I say this to?"

"The police."

"A bobby?"

"Yes."

"Why would I tell a bobby that a piece of my jewellery has gone missing when it has not?"

"So someone will be accused of stealing it and be prosecuted for the crime."

"And this someone would be . . .?"

"Bethany."

"Bethany! Your sister Bethany?" She dropped her teacup to the table with a crash.

"Yes."

"No one would accuse Bethany of such a crime, or any crime. She is too honest and—"

"Yes, I know all her virtues, Cassandra. I spent many years living in the same house as her, hearing how wonderful and sweet she was."

"Then you know whatever you are planning will never work. Even if I consented to your plan, which I will not, no court would ever convict her of stealing a piece of my jewellery."

"They will, and you will, too, if you know what is good for you."

"No, I will not. I will tell the police what you have just told me, and they will arrest you for planning such a thing."

"If you go near the police and tell this story, you will be out on the street with no means to support yourself, and you will never see your sons again."

"You would take my sons from me?" she asked in horror, the blood draining from her face.

"In a minute."

"I don't believe you. You are lying."

"Try me and see, Mrs. Stillwater."

"But why Bethany? What harm has she ever done to you?"

"I need her money. It should have been mine, but she stole it out from under me, just like she stole my mother's affections. And now she is going to pay."

"Ah, now I understand. The loan sharks are nipping at your heels, aren't they, Howard?"

"That is none of your business."

"When thugs are knocking at my door day and night, demanding money, and frightening my sons, it becomes my business."

"If you do this for me, they will go away."

"But for how long?"

"Forever."

"I wish I could believe you, but I don't. What guarantees do I have that they won't come back?"

"After I pay off their boss, I will leave the country, perhaps never to return. So they will have no reason to bother you any further."

"You are leaving? Without us?"

"Yes."

"When?"

"I just told you, after I get the money from the estate to pay off my creditors. Are you not listening to me, woman?"

"How will we survive?"

"You will find a way. That is not my concern."

"You do not worry about your sons' survival?"

"No. I have no use for them."

"No use for them? What a terrible thing to say about your sons."

"Don't be so dramatic. It does not become you. I gave you children so you would have something to do with your life. You, and they, have outlived their purposes for me."

"I will not miss you if you leave, but I cannot believe you can say such things about your boys. Thank goodness they have no real attachment to you."

Her words of dismissal caused a pang in the region of Howard's heart. When they were first married, even though they had not married for love, they had been considerate of each other's feelings. And now they were using words to hurt each other. When had their marriage gone wrong?

"That will make things easier for them when I depart. Now, back to my question. Are you going to cooperate with me, or do you want to lose your darling sons to me?"

"After what I just heard from you, I would rather consign them to a workhouse than have them live with you, Howard. So, yes, I will lie for you, to the police and to the judge, if need be."

"Good. We understand each other. Now, here is what I need you to do . . ."

***

One week later, Bethany left the estate and headed for town for two reasons. First, to speak with her solicitor and make sure Howard had no way to access funds from the estate without her knowledge and approval. Then, to attend a charity ball. The former, she was looking forward to doing, whereas the latter she faced with a great deal of trepidation. She had to attend such parties because as a member of society, even a minor one and the chair of the sponsored charity, it was obligatory for her to show up. Bethany would go, greet the right people, have a glass of punch, and then leave. The gentlemen seldom asked her to dance, but if they did she refused.

Her parents had never taught her the proper art of dance and so it was to her embarrassment, and her partner's discomfort, whenever she accepted a dance invitation. Knowing this, most men avoided her and only nodded in her direction when their eyes met at a party. There were some she wished would ask her, but they never did. One was at the top of her list: Samuel E. Yardley, the second son of the Duke of Yardley. However, being a duke's son, he spent his time with the higher nobility. If they met at the punch bowl, he was always polite and poured her a glass of punch before going back to join his family and friends. His greeting would often be the highlight of her evening, and soon afterward she would leave the party. She wondered if he would attend next week's event.

Bethany laughed and shook off her foolish dreams. That was all they were, fantasies and not reality. She was here on more important business, and she needed to focus on those items. If not, Howard might abscond with more estate funds. No, Samuel E. Yardley was out of her realm, and she needed to put him out of her mind as well.

She reached her London townhouse later that afternoon and was surprised to find an invitation for tea from Cassandra. Whenever Bethany came to the city, they would get together, but Bethany had not sent a notice to Cassandra of her impending arrival. How had she known Bethany was coming to town? She surmised Cassandra must have heard about the upcoming gala and known Bethany would attend the event. That had to be it. Bethany immediately penned a note to Cassandra, accepting her invitation for the next day, and sent it off. She also sent a note to her solicitor, advising him she was in town and would like to meet with him as soon as possible. Bethany settled in for the rest of the day after accomplishing her tasks. She told her staff she would not be open to visitors until the next day and headed up to her room to change out of her dusty travelling clothes and into something more comfortable.

***

The next day, Bethany arrived at the townhouse just before teatime, and a subdued Cassandra greeted her. Bethany supposed Cassandra's demeanour was a sign Howard was up to his usual habits, staying out all night, drinking, and gambling. Bethany did not know that Cassandra's only care was how it might reflect upon her sons, to hear stories about their father's activities from their schoolmates. Other than that, she had long ago given up worrying about what Howard was doing. She lived her life, and he lived his. She was quite happy with that arrangement.

No, Cassandra's facial expression revealed her silent sorrow. When Bethany mentioned her appearance, Cassandra brushed off her concerns, pasting on a fake smile to convince her that everything was fine. Seeing the change in her, but not knowing what it was about, Bethany decided not to probe and instead settled into a conversation about Cassandra's favourite topic, her sons. Cassandra brightened and told Bethany all about their recent antics. Then, towards the end, she brought up the gala, asking if she was planning to attend.

"Yes. It is an annual event and because of my involvement with the charity I am required to attend, even though I would rather not."

"I know how you dislike these parties. Is there no one else who could attend in your place?"

"No, I must be there to represent the charity because I am the chair of the committee. So, I will grit my teeth, paste on a smile, and go through the motions of being delighted to attend once more, even though everyone there will know that I am feeling quite the opposite."

"I wish you could find an amenable husband. You would feel much better about these events if you had someone by your side."

Bethany groaned. "Amenable husband? Someone like Howard, perhaps?"

Cassandra laughed. "I said amenable, not horrible. Oh, forgive me, I should not have said that about him."

"Don't worry, my dear, I won't tell him what you just said. By the way, where is your, uh, husband?"

"I don't know, and to be frank, I do not care. All I need from him these days is money for the household expenses and nothing more."

"I am sorry you have to endure such a miserable marriage. Looking at what you have to put up with, I am uncertain I ever want to get married."

"Don't use our marriage as an example. I am sure there are plenty of pleasant marriages. I just happened not to wed a good man. Oh, there I go again, and he is your brother. Please forgive me for saying such things."

"He is only my stepbrother, but at one time he was kind to me. But since my father died, Howard has changed. I don't know him anymore."

"Let's not talk about Howard. I would rather hear what you are planning to wear to the party."

"Wear? Cassandra, you better than anyone should know I only have one gown suitable for such an event, my blue dress. It hangs in my townhouse wardrobe and only comes out once a year, on this occasion. It is a bit out of fashion and everyone at the gala will have already seen it, but I refuse to buy a new gown only to wear it once a year."

"What will you wear with it?"

"My pearls, I suppose. Why the interest?"

"Because I have a sapphire necklace that would look perfect with that gown. Would you like to see it?"

"I'd love to, but I don't need any new accessories; my pearls will do."

"Come with me up to my room and see if I can tempt you otherwise, my friend. You need something new to dress up your old gown."

"Very well, I will look at it."

Upstairs, Cassandra pulled up the rug beside her bed, loosened a board, and pulled out a small box. Getting up from her crouched position, she came over to Bethany and opened the box. There, on top of the pile of jewellery, lay a beautiful sapphire necklace. Taking it out, Cassandra handed it to Bethany. "What do you think? Would this not go well with your dress?"

"It would go very well, but are you sure you want me to borrow it for the party? It looks quite valuable. What happens if I lose it, or heaven forbid, someone steals it from me? I would feel terrible about its loss."

"Have thieves ever stolen jewels at the gala, Bethany?"

"No, but . . ."

"And knowing the class of women who will attend the gala, will they not be wearing more expensive jewellery than this necklace?"

"You are right. I am sure the Duchess of Yardley will wear diamonds and emeralds, and others will show off their finest as well."

"Then you shall wear sapphires, my sister. Come, won't you try it on and see what you think?"

Bethany agreed. They walked over to the mirror on the dressing table, and Cassandra fastened the necklace around Bethany's neck.

"Oh, Cassandra, it is beautiful," said Bethany, reaching up to touch the sapphires.

"No, you are, my friend. It brings out your beautiful blue eyes," said Cassandra, her own eyes filling with tears.

"Are you crying? Is it too much for you to lend me the necklace for this one night?"

"No, I am just thinking you look like a princess. Now, if only we could find you a prince."

The word "prince" called to mind Samuel Yardley's face. She did not need a prince, but the son of a duke . . . that she could envision. Shaking her head to clear her thoughts, she turned. "If you are certain that you don't mind lending this necklace to me, I would love to wear it. I will take excellent care of it and return it to you the very next day."

"Oh, I am so glad. I cannot wait to see it on you that night."

"You and Howard are attending the gala?"

"Yes, he has agreed to escort me to this party. Of course, I doubt I will see much of him; he will almost certainly be in a back room playing cards most of the night. But I don't care. It is a chance for me to get out and enjoy myself, even if I have no one to dance with."

"You can dance with me, my sister," laughed Bethany, "if you do not mind me stepping on your toes all evening. It will be so nice to have someone to talk to for once in my life."

"That would get the old biddies gossiping, would it not? You and I dancing together? No, I will be content to sit with the other matrons and watch the festivities from the side lines."

"I will be there with you. This is the first party I am looking forward to attending. Now, I must get home and shake out that old blue gown to make sure there are no rips or stains on it. You are certain I can borrow the necklace?" she asked a last time, before reaching behind her neck to unclasp it.

"Absolutely. Seeing you in that necklace will bring me a great deal of joy." Searching the small box, she found a cloth bag to put the necklace in.

Bethany took the bag from Cassandra's outstretched hand before giving her a hug. "I am sorry for what you must live with, my friend, but I am not sorry Howard married you. You are the best friend I have ever had."

To stop the tears from starting again, Cassandra said, "Enough of that. You know it goes double for me. Now, get out of here before I end up in a puddle of tears on the floor."

Bethany laughed before starting out the door and down the stairs. "I will see you at the ball, my friend. Save a seat for me, won't you?" she called back over her shoulder before heading out the door.

Cassandra sank to her bed. Yes, I will see you there, Bethany. But after that, if things go as Howard plans, I might never see you again except in a courtroom. And how I will miss you.

***

Bethany arrived at the gala one hour after it began. That was the fashionable time to arrive. She had committed a faux pas the first time she had come to one of these events. She had arrived at the designated time, eight o'clock. But to her horror and embarrassment, she was the first one there. The footmen had not even taken up their posts when her carriage arrived at the door. She had thought about going back to her carriage and going home, or at least having her coachman drive around the block and wait for thirty minutes before coming round to deposit her again at the grand entrance. But instead, she sat on a chair inside the ballroom and waited, and waited, and waited. Finally, about an hour after the party was to begin, the hostesses arrived. Bethany shocked them when they saw her sitting there. They were quick to inform her that even though the invitation said eight o'clock, no one arrived before nine. Soon, others started trickling into the ballroom and by ten o'clock they packed the room to capacity. Now Bethany never arrived before nine.

There were a few others in the ballroom when she arrived, but she did not know them. She saw a row of chairs set up on the far side of the room, ready for wallflowers such as herself. Not seeing any sign of Howard or Cassandra, she crossed over to the chairs. She sat on the one second to the end, then untied her shawl and draped it over the back of the end chair, wanting to keep it for Cassandra. Even though that left her feeling exposed, especially with the sapphire necklace on display, she sat up straight and smiled. The smile stayed frozen in place until one matron who sat on her charity's committee spied her and came over.

"Bethany, how lovely to see you, my dear. Why, what a beautiful necklace. Is it new?"

Bethany nodded in a noncommittal way. How was she to explain that the necklace was not new, but was new for her, and only for tonight? She accepted the compliment with a smile and nothing more. The matron, puzzled by her lack of a proper response, turned away to greet another of their committee who had just arrived. They left Bethany out of the conversation, and she wished she had never worn the necklace. But it was too late now to go back and change. Oh, where was Cassandra? She needed her here now.

An hour later, Cassandra and Howard entered the ballroom. The room was now crowded with guests, and Bethany was tired of warding off questions about her necklace. As soon as Cassandra came in the door, Bethany was going to give her the necklace to put in her reticule. She would wrap her shawl around her shoulders to conceal her lack of jewellery until she could gracefully leave and go home. Never again would she let Cassandra talk her into wearing any of her jewels. Seeing Cassandra in the room, Bethany reached up, undid the clasp of the necklace, and let it fall into her hand. Reaching for her reticule, she placed the necklace in the bag and pulled the strings tightly to close it.

Instead of waiting for Cassandra to join her, Bethany got up and took her leave of the other women. She started walking away, knowing full well that as soon as she was out of earshot, if not before, they would start talking about her. And she was right. She was only six feet away when she heard her name being bantered about by the matrons. She shrugged and carried on, instead of turning back to confront them for gossiping about her. After all, that was one reason for this event, to get out and talk about everyone else in the room. As she made her way around the room, she nodded to the Duchess of Yardley and her companions as she passed them. The duchess acknowledged her nod with a smile; she was a very kind woman and never put on airs like some of her peers did. Bethany noticed that there were no men in the duchess's entourage. Perhaps they had already left for the gaming rooms, although that would have been unusual for her husband and sons. They did not gamble, choosing instead to spend their social evenings dancing or visiting with their friends and family. Bethany passed the large punch bowl but did not stop to get a drink. This, too, reminded her of the Yardley family and of the kindness Samuel had shown to her at the last party she had attended. Too many reminders of him, she thought. It was time to give the necklace back to Cassandra and leave, pleading a headache coming on. That would not be a lie, because she could feel the tension in her temples and knew she would have a painful night. She hurried to where she had last seen her brother and sister-in-law. Then she saw Howard standing by the door, watching her. Cassandra was nowhere in sight.

Bethany hurried over to his side. "Howard, good evening. Where did Cassandra go? I saw her standing with you only moments ago."

He looked her up and down as if he had never seen her before. "She has gone to the ladies' retiring room, I believe. Is that a new gown, Bethany? Something is different about you tonight."

"No, you have seen this gown many times before tonight, Howard. The difference is my lack of jewellery. Cassandra loaned her sapphire necklace to me, and now I want to give it back to her and go home. I feel a headache coming on."

"Ah yes, the necklace. When we arrived, I saw you across the room and noticed the necklace. When I asked Cassandra about it, she burst into tears and ran to the ladies' room to compose herself. According to her, you stole it from her on the day you came for tea. She let you try it on, but you would not give it back before you left. I am surprised to see you wearing stolen jewellery, Bethany. I would not have thought such a thing of you, being so *Christian* in your attitude."

"Stole it? I did no such thing, Howard Stillwater. Yes, I tried it on, at Cassandra's insistence, but she loaned it to me for this occasion.

Where is Cassandra? I would have the truth from her. I cannot believe your word, so I want it verified by her."

"I lied," sneered Howard.

Bethany heaved a sigh of relief until she heard his next words.

"She has gone to get the bobby standing outside in case there was any trouble tonight."

Bethany paled. "Gone to get the bobby? Surely you jest."

"No. In fact, here he comes now, with my wife," said Howard.

Bethany turned towards the entrance and saw Howard's words were true. Cassandra was walking towards them, accompanied by a bobby. When they came close to Howard and Bethany, the bobby said, "Is this the woman, Mrs. Stillwater?"

"Yes," mumbled Cassandra, not looking up at Bethany.

"Cassandra! What is going on? You know I did not steal your necklace. You loaned it to me. In fact, I was looking for you to give it back." Bethany opened her reticule to retrieve the necklace. "It has caused too many people to stare at me tonight, and you know how I hate that kind of attention. Here, take it back, and let's be done with this nonsense." Bethany, having difficulty withdrawing the necklace, thrust her entire reticule at Cassandra.

Instead, the bobby intercepted it. "I will take that bag, Miss." Turning to Cassandra, he said, "Mrs. Stillwater, if what you say is true, we will need to keep your necklace as evidence for the trial."

"Evidence? Trial? What trial, bobby?"

"You are being charged with a felony, Miss Stillwater, the theft of a valuable necklace from your sister-in-law. You will need to come with me now to the station."

"Howard, say something. You know this is not true. Cassandra, please! Why?"

Cassandra kept her head down and eyes averted. Howard smirked as Bethany struggled to release herself from the bobby's firm grip.

"Miss, if you do not come peacefully, I will have to handcuff you," he warned.

Handcuffs, in a room full of high society? Bethany calmed. She would find a way out of this mess once she was at the station. Taking a deep breath, she nodded and turned towards the entrance, with the bobby still holding her arm. Her head held high, she walked past all the whispers and out the door. As soon as she was outside, she heard the room erupt. They had arrested Bethany Stillwater!

Chapter 2

The metal door clanged on Bethany's cell, and she heard the lock click. She was in prison. It was unbelievable. They had accused her of stealing Cassandra's necklace, but she had done nothing wrong. Had it all been a setup to trap her? But why? She had never harmed either Howard or Cassandra, other than refusing to continue paying his debts. And she did not see how cutting Howard off was harming him; she hoped it would help him get his life back in order. And Cassandra . . . she could see Howard doing something like this, but not Cassandra. She was a sweet, loving woman who had never said a cross word to Bethany, let alone conspire to put her in jail. No, Howard must have threatened her. She would not put it past him. Knowing Cassandra, it had to have been a threat to her sons; she would not care about her own welfare if her boys were safe. Perhaps her solicitor would come and free her once he got her message that she was in prison. She would ask him to investigate the situation with Cassandra and the boys to find out if Howard had threatened them. Then, threats aside, perhaps Cassandra would back away from her accusation.

Bethany eyed the single piece of furniture in the cell, a metal bed with a very thin mattress atop it. The mattress was filthy. She wondered when it had last been cleaned, if ever. There was no place else to sit except on the grimy floor, but she decided that was better than the mattress. She sank to the floor, her blue ball gown floating out around her. One thing was for certain. When she left here and went home, the ball gown was going to be thrown out. After tonight, she would never wear it again. It was time for a new gown. Pulling her shawl more closely around her shoulders, Bethany bent her head to her knees and closed her eyes. She tried to pray, but the words would not come. Then she remembered the verse that said the Holy Spirit would convey her unspoken requests to the throne of God when you cannot pray for yourself. This was one of those times. She lifted her head up and looked at the ceiling, saying, "Holy Spirit, help me." She bent her head down again and waited for God's deliverance.

The next voice she heard, although not God's, was still a welcome one. Mr. Edwin Brown, her solicitor, stood on the other side of the bars of her cell. Bethany immediately got up and rushed over to him, grasping his outstretched hands through the narrow bars. "Oh, thank goodness you have come, Mr. Brown. Have you spoken to the officer in charge of the station? Are they going to release me?"

Her solicitor, a slight man with a receding hairline, said, "Miss Stillwater. I cannot contemplate why you are here. What a terrible travesty of justice to put you behind bars. I do not believe for a moment that the charges against you are real." He shook his balding head.

"The important question for me is whether you can get me released from here so I can go home."

He hemmed and hawed for a moment before saying, "Unfortunately, Miss Stillwater, that may not be possible this evening. The charges against you are serious enough that only a judge can release you. And the judge for this district is at the gala. He would not take kindly to having his evening disturbed to review the charges against you. You may have to stay here until morning when you, and I of course, can plead your innocence before him."

"Stay here all night? I cannot. I would be happy to appear before the judge tomorrow morning, but not after spending the night here." Bethany swept her arms around to show him the size and condition of the cell.

"I am afraid my hands are tied for the moment. I am only a solicitor and not even a barrister. Perhaps he could find a legal loophole to get you released tonight, but I cannot."

"Do you have any suggestions for a good barrister to represent me, in case I need one?"

"I do, and I will contact him first thing tomorrow morning."

"Thank you for that. Also, would you, or the barrister, please contact Mrs. Cassandra Stillwater, my sister-in-law, and find out if she is being coerced by anyone to lay these ridiculous charges against me? I cannot see why she would do such a thing unless she or her sons were being threatened, perhaps by her husband. I cannot speak with her, but I was wondering if you would on my behalf."

"I will attempt to see her, Miss Stillwater, but in cases like yours, sometimes the accusers refuse to talk to the defendant's solicitor, especially if, as you say, her life or the lives of her sons is being threatened."

"Cases like mine," repeated Bethany. "I never thought I would hear those words in relation to myself."

"Never fear. You only need to stay here tonight. Tomorrow morning, we will get you out and back home."

"Thank you for your confidence and thank you again for coming. I appreciate your diligence on my behalf."

"Not at all, young lady. I am appalled that an upstanding young lady like yourself is treated in such a manner, and I will do everything in my power to help you out of this situation. Now I must head home so I can send off a note to the barrister I spoke of and ask him for an early morning meeting to apprise him of your situation.

Goodnight, Miss Stillwater. I will be back first thing in the morning to escort you to the judge's chambers."

"Goodnight, Mr. Brown," said Bethany to his retreating back. "Have a good rest. I know I will not. I will see you tomorrow." She turned away from the bars of the cell and looked at the bed again. No, the floor was better to rest on than that filthy bed. She would curl up in a corner of the cell until daybreak. There was nothing else she could do.

***

Cassandra was also reviewing the events of the evening. After seeing everything unfold at the gala, she was having second thoughts about her participation in Howard's scheme. Perhaps she could go to the police and ask for protection for her sons. Then she would confront Howard and he would have nothing to hold against her. Immediately after the scene in the ballroom, she had fled home in a hired carriage. She did not know where Howard had gone, and she did not care. She never wanted to see him again if that was possible. But that was before she had come up with this plan of her own. Tomorrow, or whenever he staggered home again, she would be ready to call his bluff.

She went to bed but could not sleep. Bethany's face, when the bobby arrested her, was in the front of her mind. The worst image was her look of surprise and utter disbelief when Cassandra accused her of the theft of the necklace. Cassandra would never shake that image from her mind, either. She would have a lifetime of seeing Bethany's trust in her disappear in that instant. If only she had told her what Howard was planning on the day she came for tea. Bethany would have helped to get her and the boys away from him. Cassandra knew she would have; she was just that kind of sister and friend. But instead, she had served her up to Howard like a sacrificial lamb. What kind of horrible person did that to their best friend?

Clearly, she was one of those people, and she would have to live with it for the rest of her life. After that, she would have to face God and His judgment of her actions. Would He still accept her into heaven, or would she end up going to hell? Right now, hell's fires did not seem strong enough for what she had done to Bethany. She would deserve everything meted out to her for giving Bethany to Howard. Tossing and turning, she could not sleep, so she got up and sat in her favourite chair in front of the dying fire. It was tempting to put her hand in the flames to see what hellfire would be like, but she resisted. Soon enough to feel the heat when her life was over.

***

Howard, unlike Cassandra and Bethany, was feeling on top of the world. His plan was working. Bethany was in jail and hopefully spending the night there. Cassandra had followed his plan without another murmur. He imagined she had gone home after Bethany's arrest. Howard did not care. He did not stay around either, he needed to see Frank to talk about his upcoming role. Not wanting to be seen together, the two of them had agreed to meet in a seedy little tavern on the banks of the river, and that was where Howard was heading now. He had left his carriage at the ballroom and was taking a hired hack to his meeting. That way they would think he was still inside, enjoying a game of cards, when he was far away planning the next step of Bethany's downfall. Howard laughed. The look of horror and disbelief on her face when the bobby arrested her would stay with him for many days, perhaps forever. Now he was the one in control, and she was his puppet. He would keep her dangling on strings until her day in court. Then he would pull them up tight, just to see that look again, when she was tried, convicted, and sent away to the colonies for many years. Yes, that would be another highlight of his life. But first they needed an ironclad case no defence barrister could refute. Frank would come in handy to create just such a case.

Reaching the tavern, Howard pulled the collar of his greatcoat up and brought his top hat down around his ears. It never hurt to be cautious about concealing his identity, although he was almost certain that none of his associates, or any of the upper class, would frequent such a lowly establishment. It was an excellent meeting place for these kinds of situations. Paying the driver of the hack and asking him to wait until he re-emerged, Howard made his way into the one-room pub. Almost immediately, the smell of unwashed bodies and stale beer overwhelmed his senses. He staggered a bit and the taste of the sour punch he had consumed at the gala threatened to come up again into his throat and mouth. Pulling his silk scarf up around his nose and mouth, he took a deep breath of scented air. That was enough to settle his stomach, and he looked around the tavern. Finally, he saw Frank sitting at a table in a far corner. Howard made his way over to him and sat down beside him, keeping his back to the wall.

"Glad to see you could make it, Frank," he said.

"Did I have any choice?"

"Keep your voice down. I don't want us to be overheard."

"Fine. I will ask again. Did I have any choice but to meet you here tonight?"

"No. But our meeting, if things proceed as I hope they do, will benefit you as well as me. Don't I always come through for you?"

"Yes."

"And this time will be no different. Now, here is what I need of you, my friend . . ."

**

Frank listened to Howard, only asking occasional questions of him before agreeing to assist him once again. He had reservations about Howard's plan, being that Bethany was a member of society. But it was worth his while to try, as he was needing extra cash to pay off his loan sharks. He wished he could quit gambling and not have to jeopardise his career by associating with people like Howard, but alas, it was too deep in his blood for him to stop now. He was hooked and did not think he could ever overcome the habit that was ruining his life.

"How soon do you want me to work on this?"

"Right away. We do not know when Bethany's case will come to trial, but we need to be prepared."

"Very well. I will do what I can to make an airtight case against her. I have to say, though, it pains me to be involved in hurting someone with Bethany's excellent reputation. She has done a lot of good in the community in the past couple of years."

"Yes, I know," sneered Howard. "Bethany is perfect. Bethany is beautiful. Bethany is so kind. I tire of hearing all her wonderful attributes, especially from you, Frank. You are my friend, so I thought you would support me, not her."

"I am, but I was just expressing my opinion. The community sees her in a very positive light, so we may have a hard time finding an impartial jury."

"I plan to ask for a trial by judge alone, not a case tried by her peers. Do you think I am stupid? We will have no chance of convicting her if she has a jury of her peers to decide her fate."

"Whether to try the case by judge or jury is the prerogative of the defendant, not the accuser. If Bethany wants a jury trial, how will you override her wishes?"

"By saying we are wasting time and money waiting on a jury trial. I found out the next convict ship leaves for the colonies in a few months. If we delay, they may not transport her for a year, and for that whole time the British taxpayer will have to pay for her room and board at Millbank. Whenever you mention money, the court always wants to expedite things."

"You have thought this through. I have no more questions for now. I will start to work immediately."

"I thought you would. And as always, this is to be kept between us. It cannot get out to the public what we are doing."

"I know.

"Indeed. Now, just to be cautious, I will leave first, and you can follow in about five minutes. Agreed?"

"Agreed."

"Fine. Once again, it is a pleasure doing business with you. I will be in touch soon." Howard got up from the table, adjusted his scarf and collar, and took his leave. It had been a good evening all around.

***

The next morning, all of London was abuzz with the news of Bethany's arrest. Although she was only a minor member of society, they all knew of her good works and charity. The society women gathered their friends together for tea and a *chat* about what had occurred the previous evening. They all wanted to share what they had seen and heard. From there, the news rapidly travelled to the servants' quarters before heading to the streets. Even the laundresses and char women heard the news. Many of them wept when they heard of Bethany's arrest, as they had benefited from her compassion. And finally, the women who profited most from Bethany's kindness heard the news and wondered if she would ever be free to continue her work among them again. By evening, almost everyone in the city knew that Bethany Stillwater was suspected of being a thief.

The one household where there was no gossip about Bethany was the Duke of Yardley's townhouse. Although the duke and his sons were away inspecting their flocks of sheep and their mills in rural England and Scotland, the duchess's authority was absolute. She did not believe in gossip, knowing that it was not a positive thing. Not only did she not take part in such an activity, but she did not condone it amongst her staff. Of course, she had been there to witness what had happened to Bethany the night before, but she was reserving judgment. First, because as with the rest of society, she did not know all the details that had led to Bethany's arrest, and because she held to the words of the apostle James, who said there was only one Judge and that was God the Father.[1] The previous night's events saddened the duchess as she had been observing Bethany over the past couple of years, hoping to introduce her to her son Samuel as a potential bride. Bethany had the demeanour and the graces that the duchess embodied in her children and their spouses. Her oldest son, Rupert, had followed her guidance in choosing his wife several years ago, and they were now producing several little Yardleys to fill all the rooms of the main ducal townhouse and estate. Now it was Samuel's turn. As he appeared to be in no hurry to follow his brother into wedlock, his mother had given him a bit of a nudge in Bethany's direction. It did not bother the duchess that Bethany was of a lower societal status and only had a modest dowry. They, as a family, had all the wealth that they needed and more, and Samuel was planning to add to that wealth by establishing trade with the sheep farmers in Australia within the next year. No, Bethany would have been the perfect wife for him, but with the scandal that would accompany her now, from just the accusation of theft, deleted her from the duchess's list. She treated everyone with kindness, but she had to protect the virtue and integrity of her family, meaning that Bethany no longer qualified as a future daughter-in-law. She shook her head sadly before attending to other duties of the day.

Knowing the scandal would be old news by the time her husband and sons returned home from their trip, the duchess decided not to mention it to them upon their return. It would be in the past and that is where it should stay.

***

Bethany's morning began as her evening had ended, with a visit from her solicitor. He informed her there would be a judicial review of her charges at ten o'clock that morning. He had not been able to convince the judge to release her. The judge was reserving judgment on that action until after he had seen her today. Mr. Brown had also contacted the barrister, who would represent her in court if needed. He would join them this morning in the courtroom.

Bethany thanked him for his work throughout the evening and this morning. Looking at the clock in the station, she realised she only had about an hour before her appointment with the judge. She had already had breakfast, if one could consider a slice of hard bread and old cheese, food. She had nothing with her to freshen up her appearance, so she shook and straightened her skirts as best she could after sitting on them all night, and finger combed her hair. Even without a mirror, she could tell it was a mess, so she straightened it as best she could, braided it, and wound it in a coronet atop her head. She knew a coronet was not appropriate for her age, but at least it tidied her hair for the morning. Perhaps, after her visit to the judge, she could go home, take a nice long bath, and wash her hair. If not . . . no, she would not even allow such thoughts into her head. She was going home today, and that was final!

Soon, she and Mr. Brown were in a courtroom waiting for the judge to appear. Mr. Brown's associate, Mr. Steven Damon, the barrister, accompanied them to the tables at the front of the courtroom. Appearing to be in his mid-thirties, with thick sandy hair and a medium build, he presented well to Bethany. He told her he had already heard the gossip on the streets about her arrest when he stopped at a local coffee shop for his breakfast. It would be hard to find an impartial jury of her peers if the judge proceeded with arraigning her for the crime and she had to go to court. If that was the case, she might think about a trial by judge alone. But, said Mr. Damon, he hoped it never came to that and that the judge today would dismiss the case altogether and send her home. Bethany agreed with his statements; she could not wait for that moment of dismissal.

The judge appeared in his robe and white wig. He took his seat behind his desk, far above them. Once seated, the others in the room sat as well. That included Frank Walden, who, Mr. Damon informed them, was the people's prosecutor. Bethany had taken no notice of him prior to Mr. Damon's words. Then she looked over at him and found him staring at her. His weasel-eyed stare made her very uncomfortable, so she pivoted her head back to look forward at the judge.

The judge said, "Bailiff, will you please read the charges against the defendant?"

"Yes, Your Honour," he replied. "'The people of London, represented by Barrister Frank Walden, hereby charge that Miss Bethany Stillwater, the defendant, on the night of 15 September 1853, did steal one sapphire necklace from her sister-in-law, Mrs. Howard Stillwater. They found Miss Stillwater at the gala event with the necklace in her possession. Mrs. Stillwater will testify that it was taken unlawfully from her home and not loaned to the defendant for the event, as the defendant claims.'"

"Thank you, Bailiff," said the judge. Then, looking at Bethany, he said, "And how do you plead to this charge, Miss Stillwater?"

"Not guilty, Your Honour."

"I see," replied the judge, looking down at the document on his desk. "So, they found you with the necklace in your possession, and your sister-in-law, Mrs. Howard Stillwater, states she did not give, nor loan, it to you but you stole it from her. Who am I to believe?"

"Your Honour," said Bethany. "May I have permission to speak?"

"You may."

Bethany recounted the previous day's activities and what led up to her arrest by the bobby. She ended her story by restating her innocence and asking the judge to dismiss the charges against her.

"I see," said the judge once more. "So, now you are accusing your sister-in-law of lying instead of owning up to your crime?"

"Your Honour, there is no—"

"Silence," interrupted the judge.

Bethany shut her mouth and waited. She did not have to wait long for the judge's pronouncement.

"Miss Stillwater, there is ample evidence to try you for the crime of theft. We will proceed to a trial in due time. In the meantime, the court remands you to Millbank Penitentiary until your trial begins. Any questions?"

"Your Honour," said Mr. Damon. "Miss Stillwater is an upstanding citizen with a spotless reputation. We ask the court to allow her to go home on her own recognisance until her trial begins. We do not see her as a flight risk."

"Your Honour," said Frank, standing to his feet. "As a representative of the people, I do not agree with Mr. Damon. Miss Stillwater has ample resources to leave London and England if she is free. I would ask the court to remand her to the prison until her trial."

"Agreed, Mr. Walden. I have heard much, both last evening and this morning that would lead me to believe that Miss Stillwater would leave the country if not placed in prison until her trial. Therefore, we will escort her there this day," said the judge, while nodding to the bailiff.

"One more thing, Your Honour," said Mr. Damon. "It is the matter of the trial and who will prepare the verdict."

"Yes, I forgot. Thank you for reminding me, Barrister. Miss Stillwater, as the defendant, which would you prefer, trial by jury, or trial by judge alone? How say you?"

"Trial by judge alone, Your Honour."

"So be it. Bailiff, please take Miss Stillwater back into custody and make immediate arrangements to transport her to Millbank Penitentiary."

"Yes, Your Honour," said the bailiff before walking over to stand beside the table where Bethany and her companions stood.

"Court dismissed," said the judge before getting up and leaving the room.

Bethany collapsed back into her chair. Not only was she not going home today, but she was now remanded to a penitentiary until her trial. She looked up into the sad faces of Mr. Brown and Mr. Damon. "What happened here? Why did he not believe me?"

"Circumstantial evidence, Miss Stillwater," replied Mr. Damon. "That, and nothing else."

"Please, please, talk to Cassandra. She knows the truth and can free me from this horror. Will you do that, Mr. Damon?"

"I will, Miss Stillwater. I will sort this out as soon as possible."

"Excuse me, Mr. Damon," came Frank's smooth voice as he walked over to them. "I could not help but overhear your conversation. You may speak to Mrs. Stillwater, but only if I am present as her counsel. You may not approach her when she is alone."

"I will do whatever the law allows, Mr. Walden. Nothing more and nothing less."

"Good. Then we understand each other. Good day, Miss Stillwater, gentlemen."

The men tipped their heads, acknowledging his farewell, while Bethany mumbled a farewell to him. Then Frank left the courtroom with a spring in his step; he had won the first round. Now onto the second, and more crucial, stage.

After he left, the bailiff stepped up to Bethany. "Time to go, Miss Stillwater."

Bethany looked up at him and then over at the other men. They shook their heads but did not refute the bailiff's words. Bethany got up and walked away from the table. When she reached the door, she looked back at the men and said, "I will see you soon, will I not?"

"Without a doubt, Miss Stillwater," said Mr. Damon.

"Of course, Bethany," replied Mr. Brown. "Let me know if there is anything you need, and I will bring it to you."

"Only my freedom, Mr. Brown," said Bethany. "Only that." She turned away and preceded the bailiff out the door.

***

She was immediately processed into the system at Millbank when she arrived there from the courthouse. A female guard stripped her down and gave her a shapeless brown gown to put on. Then, to her dismay and horror, she approached Bethany with a large pair of scissors.

"What are you going to do with those?"

"Cut your hair."

"Why?"

"It's prison regulations. Women get their hair cut short and men's hair is shaved off."

"I'll look after myself. Please don't cut it off."

"It's prison regulations," she repeated.

"I have no choice?"

"No."

"Then do your worst," said Bethany. Her days of being in control of her life were over.

The guard came over, and without another word, unbound Bethany's braids to let the hair fall loose. It came almost to her waist. The next thing Bethany heard was the *snip, snip* of the scissors while she watched great hunks of her hair fall to the ground. Soon, her hair was cut to chin length, and even that was uneven. The guard was not skilled in hairdressing; either that or she did not care about Bethany's appearance whatsoever. The guard stepped back and said, "That's done. You will thank me later when you lack the water to wash your hair. It is better this way."

Bethany dared not run her hands over her shorn scalp. She feared if she did, she would fall weeping to the floor. She needed to stay strong, so she held back the tears and waited for the guard's next command.

"Follow me now to your cell."

"What about my undergarments and gown?"

"We will deal with them."

"What do you mean?"

"As of now, you have no personal items, only those that the prison provides to you. If the gown and undergarments are of any value, we will sell them for extra funding for the prison. If not, we will throw them away."

"Everything?"

"Yes. Now, I have no more time for your questions. Be quiet and follow me."

"Yes, ma'am," replied Bethany, getting up from the stool to walk behind the guard.

"Oh, and one more thing: you have a number sewn into your gown. Remember that number; it is now your name."

"They have taken my name away, too? What more can they want?"

"Be thankful it is not your life. Many do not leave here alive."

"I intend to walk out of here alive and with my head held high. I am innocent of the crime I am accused of, and I intend to prove it."

"Good luck with that. Now, here is your home for the next while." She handed Bethany a blanket, a bowl, a small length of towelling, and a sliver of soap. "I'll be back later to give you some water to drink and for washing." After the guard left, locking the cell behind her, Bethany turned to survey her new home.

This cell was larger than the one at the police station. Three sides were solid cement, while the wall facing the hallway was comprised of iron bars. There was a narrow plank bed in one corner of the cell, and a necessity pot in another. That was all the furniture. No place to hang the towelling or put the pan for water, except on the bed. This was her home for the next few weeks, or months, until her trial. Bethany could not believe it. How was she even to survive in here?

Then she thought of the women she helped in the workhouses. Their living conditions were not much better than this. Many of them were one step away from being jailed, especially if they snatched an extra piece of bread at mealtimes. Perhaps God was using this to help her more deeply understand their plight. If so, she was learning fast, and she hoped the lesson did not last too long. She was almost at the end of herself, and her trial had not even begun yet.

Bethany spread the blanket over the board bed and sat down. The hard surface revived the pain from having sat on the police station floor all night. This board was no softer than the floor had been. And there was nothing she had to remedy the situation. When she got home, she was going to thank God over and over for the softness of her feather mattress. She would never take the amenities of her home for granted again. Never again.

She wondered what one did all day long in a cell such as this. Bethany longed for some reading material; perhaps Mr. Brown would bring her some. Looking up at the small window high in one wall, she realised she would not have much light to read by during the day. Perhaps they would allow her to have candles in her cell. That would help to chase away the shadows. Were there vermin in the cells? She shivered at the thought. Kingsley and the footmen kept the estate manor free of any vile creatures. Here, there was no Kingsley to chase away the rats. How she longed for her dear friends. Did they know what had happened to her, and if so, how were they coping with the news? She hoped they stayed away and did not visit her. She could not bear their pain when they saw her shorn hair and shapeless gown. She did not want any visitors while she was a resident at Millbank except for Mr. Damon and Mr. Brown. No one else should see her like this . . . no one but God.

***

While Bethany was wringing her hands in anguish, Howard was clapping his in joy. He had just received a note from Frank stating that the first part of their plan had gone well. The judge had dismissed Bethany's claim of innocence and remanded her to prison. He had taken Frank's suggestion seriously, that Bethany, with her ample resources, could flee the country before her trial if she was allowed to go home. Now Bethany was in Millbank Penitentiary and would be there until her trial. The note said Bethany had opted for a trial by judge alone, so Frank had not had to speak to the judge in that regard. He would inform Howard as soon as he knew which judge would preside over Bethany's trial. In the meantime, he would continue working to present a solid case to the judge, one that would see Bethany convicted and transported far away. At the end of the note, he cautioned Howard that Bethany's barrister was hoping to speak with Cassandra soon, to poke holes in her story. He had told the barrister he wished to be present when he spoke with Cassandra, but he was not sure if the barrister would abide by his wishes. Howard needed to be aware of this and prevent Cassandra from speaking to the man.

Indeed, I will, thought Howard. If Cassandra was alone with the barrister, she might have a moment of guilt about her participation in Howard's plans and tell the barrister all. He needed to put the fear of God once again into her and remind her of the consequences of any poor decisions on her part. And he needed to do it now. He set out to find her.

***

Howard found his wife in the playroom with Arthur. He swore she spent more time in there than she did in the rest of the house. Perhaps if she had spent more time with him instead of the boys, they would have had a happier marriage. But the time for reconciliation was past. Now they were almost strangers, spending less and less time together. Not that Howard minded her inattention to his life. He would have had more complaints if she nagged him about his drinking or gambling. No, they had reached an unspoken agreement in their life together; she would not interfere in his and he would stay out of hers. But on this issue, he needed to interfere. She needed to be reminded what it would cost her if she spoke out of turn.

Howard stepped into the playroom and walked across the room to Cassandra and Arthur. Crouching down, which was an arduous task these days because of his massive belly, he said, "What games are you playing with Mama, Arthur?"

Surprised at his father's appearance and his question, Arthur looked at his mother for support. "It's all right, Arthur," she said with a smile. "You can answer your father."

"Trains, Father," he mumbled. "Mama and I are playing trains."

It irritated Howard that his son looked to his mother for agreement before he answered him. What kind of sons was she raising that they could not speak for themselves? But instead of voicing that opinion, he said to Arthur, "Trains? Where are they taking you, son?"

"Far, far away, Father. And we are never coming back."

"Really? You are leaving me here alone with your other brothers?"

"No, they are coming too. You are the only one not coming."

"Why can't I come too, Arthur?"

"Because you are always busy. You don't play with us."

"I see. Did Mama tell you that?" asked Howard.

"No."

"I am here today, so perhaps we can spend some time together later. But right now, I need to speak to Mama. Can you take your train to your bedroom and play alone for a few minutes?"

"I suppose so, if it does not take too much of Mama's time. I like playing with her."

"We won't be long, Arthur. Now run along like a good boy."

"Yes, sir. I will see you later, Mama?" he asked.

"Yes, of course, darling. I'll come and get you as soon as I finish talking to your father. Do as he says and run along to your bedroom."

"All right." He gave her a big hug before he ran out of the room.

Howard was fuming. "What kind of boys are you raising, Cassandra? Arthur would not even speak to me without checking with you first. And just now, he waited for your instructions before leaving the room. I've a good mind to discipline him for not obeying me right away."

"Don't you dare, Mr. Stillwater. You spend so little time with the boys, they scarcely know you. So of course they are going to look to me for permission and support. Arthur is only four years old, for goodness' sake. You cannot expect him to respect you as an authority figure in his life when he does not even know you."

"I'll let it go this time, but you need to remind the boys that you are not the head of the household. That is my position in this family. I expect them to obey me instantly when I give them an order, or they will suffer the consequences."

"I will. Now, what did you want to speak to me about?"

"I just heard from my associate that Bethany's barrister may come round asking to speak with you. If I am not here, I want you to refuse him entrance to the house. I also want your promise that you will not even speak with him if I am not present. Do you understand?"

"Yes, Howard. You are afraid that if I speak with this man, your scheme will come to naught, and the police will be after you. I understand."

"Your promise, Cassandra?" he warned.

"I promise I will continue to lie about my involvement in your scheme."

Howard thought for a moment about her words. Was there something there that she could use against him? He shook his head and decided not. Cassandra did not know how to outwit him. That was why he had married her. "You do remember what will happen if you don't obey me, don't you?"

"I do."

"Then keep your mouth shut, and all will be well."

"For both me and Bethany?"

"I don't care about her!"

"Keep your voice down, Howard. Arthur may hear you."

"Perhaps he needs to until he learns who the boss is in this household. Now, I am going out and will not be back for a while. Remember this conversation, Cassandra. Keep it close to your heart."

"I will, Howard. Have a delightful time. Don't hurry home on my account."

"I won't. You can be sure of that. You lost your allure for me many years ago."

"Funny, you never appealed to me at all. If it had not been for my father, I never would have given you the time of day."

"Glad we understand each other. I'm off and leaving you to explain to your son why his father had to leave."

"He won't mind. He is wise to your ways, husband, as are his brothers. They expect nothing from you, nor do I."

"You can all expect trouble if you don't obey me," was Howard's parting shot as he left the playroom and headed down the stairs.

When Cassandra heard the front door open and then close, she collapsed in a heap on the floor. She needed time to compose herself before facing Arthur. Unfortunately, he was too quick for her. A moment later she heard the playroom door open and his little voice saying, "Mama, are you all right? Has Father left?"

Summoning up a smile, she turned to him and said, "Yes to both questions, my darling. Come back in and we will continue playing trains. Where would you like to go now?"

"Anywhere Father is not, Mama," replied her wise little boy. "Anywhere but there."

"So would I, son, so would I," was Cassandra's response as she gathered him close to her breast.

"If only that were possible, Father God," she whispered, "but I am in too deeply to ever escape."

***

The first thing on Steven Damon's mind was to contact Mrs. Stillwater and interview her, hopefully without an audience. He might know if she was lying by watching her body movements and facial expressions, even if her words said otherwise. Of course, he could not use the former things in a court of law, but they might be enough to convince a judge the key witness was lying, and Bethany's case would be dismissed. It was worth a try. He had nothing else to go on.

He headed over to the law court and got the Stillwaters' address from the office clerk. Summoning a hack, he then proceeded to their townhouse, which was in a more modest part of the city than he had expected, considering the value of the necklace Bethany had allegedly stolen from Mrs. Stillwater. After alighting and paying the driver, Mr. Damon opened a rather rickety wooden gate and proceeded up the path toward the front door. On his way, he noted toys in the front yard, toys that showed young children lived here. Filing that message in the back of his mind for further consideration, Steven walked up the steps and onto the porch, again noting peeling paint on the porch and door. These things did not add up to the Stillwaters being a wealthy family. They depicted a family in need of money. He must look deeper into Howard Stillwater's finances to see if that would be reason enough for him to frame his sister for theft. He lifted the iron knocker, let it clang upon the wooden door, and waited. Then he heard little footsteps running to the door, with heavier ones following closely behind.

"Arthur . . . do not open . . ."

The door opened, and a small boy's face peered out at Mr. Damon, before a woman raced up behind him.

"Hello," said Mr. Damon to the little boy. "Is your mother at home?"

"I am his mother, Cassandra Stillwater. And you are?"

"Steven Damon, at your service, ma'am."

"I'm Arthur Daniel Stillwater. Pleased to meet you, sir," said the little boy while sticking out his hand to shake Steven's.

"I am very pleased to meet you as well, Master Stillwater," said Steven, smiling, before looking back up at Arthur's mother.

"What can I do for you, Mr. Damon?"

"I was wondering if I might have a few minutes of your time, Mrs. Stillwater."

"For what purpose?" Cassandra twisted her hands together.

"To discuss the case against your sister-in-law, Bethany Stillwater. I am her barrister."

Cassandra paled. She looked down at her son. "Arthur, I need to speak with this gentleman for a moment. Why don't you go into the kitchen and ask Mrs. Dowder for a snack? Tell her I sent you. I will come and join you in a few minutes."

Arthur grumbled. "Adults, always telling you to leave the room," he said before heading off back into the house.

Steven smiled. "A wise little boy you have, Mrs. Stillwater."

"Too wise for his age, Mr. Damon, I'm afraid. Now, I don't know what else I can tell you about Bethany's case. I have given my statement to the police. Is that not sufficient?"

"Sometimes we remember things later that we forgot to tell the authorities. May I come in? You do not wish your neighbours to overhear our conversation, do you?"

"I do not mind, Mr. Damon, for I have nothing to hide." Cassandra's hand-wringing and pale face belied her words. "You cannot come inside. My husband has given me strict instructions about that. And, as he is not here now, I must abide by his wishes."

"I see. Would there be a more convenient time to call, perhaps when your husband is at home?"

"No. My husband's hours are quite irregular, so I can never accommodate you. I am sorry, but I have nothing further to say to you. Good day to you, sir." Cassandra moved to shut the door.

Steven's manner changed. He said, "Mrs. Stillwater, you know the penalty for perjury, do you not? If you have lied in your statement to the authorities, and especially if you lie under oath during Miss Stillwater's trial, you could go to jail yourself. Perhaps you would like to visit her and see her present living conditions. It might help you recall certain details you have forgotten?"

Cassandra trembled. She remembered Howard's threat. It would be worse than being put in prison. "I am sorry, Mr. Damon, but we have finished our conversation. I have nothing more to say to you. Good day." She shut the door and Steven heard the lock click in place.

This is not the last time we will speak, Mrs. Stillwater. And the next time, you will be under oath in a courtroom of law. I look forward to our conversation at that time. He turned and left the property, again noting the boys' toys in the yard. Something did not add up, and he was determined to find out what it was, and why her hands shook when she was speaking to him. He also needed to take a good look at Howard Stillwater and his finances.

***

Cassandra sagged against the door as she heard Steven's footsteps leaving the porch. Why could she not have told him the truth? Howard was not here, and she could have confessed all. Instead, she had lied again. Not even the threat of jail time for perjury had loosened her tongue. What held her back?

She heard a little boy's laughter drifting from the kitchen and had the answer to her questions. This was for Arthur and his brothers. That was her focus. Nothing else mattered except the welfare of her sons. Nothing. Re-establishing that fact, she straightened her back, shook out her skirts, and headed to the kitchen to join her son.

***

On his return to the business district of the city, Steven headed for Mr. Brown's office. As a solicitor he might have more access to the financial aspects of life than Steven. Perhaps he would have more insight into Howard Stillwater's finances, and if not, would know who in the banking world to contact regarding this matter. It was just after one p.m. and Steven found that Mr. Brown had no appointments until two o'clock, so he was free to discuss Bethany's case with him.

"Good day, Mr. Brown," said Steven, entering the office and extending his hand.

"And to you, Mr. Damon," replied Mr. Brown, accepting the handshake. "What can I do for you this fine afternoon?" Then he laughed. "As if our interests were not the same at present. Have you discovered anything new in Miss Stillwater's case?"

"Nothing substantial, but I had an interesting conversation with Mrs. Cassandra Stillwater just before lunch."

"Oh, what did she say?"

"It is not what she said. It is how she was acting while we were speaking."

"What manner did she present?"

"An attitude of extreme nervousness."

"Are you sure she was not just intimidated by your presence and your questions?"

"No, she would not allow me to ask her any questions. Her husband has forbidden her to speak to anyone without him being present, and he was away when I presented myself in her doorway."

"Not unexpected, from what we heard from Mr. Walden this morning."

"No, but I was hoping because he was not there, she would open up and tell me the truth. But she did not."

"You said her manner was suspicious, though, Mr. Damon. In what way?"

"She was wringing her hands together, she was very pale, and she was leaning against the door jamb to keep herself upright."

"Again, nothing we could use in a court of law to prove she was lying."

"No. At the end of the conversation, I reminded her what the penalty for perjury was, but it did not convince her to change her statement. I am wondering if she is being threatened by someone to keep her mouth shut. I saw several boys' toys out in the yard and a sweet young lad opened the door for me on my arrival. He was quite charming, but very put out when his mother told him to go to the kitchen and get a snack while we talked." Steven smiled at the memory. "I think perhaps either Mrs. Stillwater, her sons, or both are in danger of harm if she speaks with the authorities. Maybe the threat, especially to her boys, is what is keeping her from telling the truth."

"You may be right. But if that is the case, she will not readily change her story."

"No, so I am hoping to approach this case now from a different angle, and I hope you can help me."

"I will do what I can. What is it you need?"

"I noticed almost as soon as I arrived in the Stillwaters' neighbourhood some things that did not fit with the profile of a woman with such expensive jewellery."

"What were those things?"

"First, they live in a working-class neighbourhood, not somewhere you would find members of society, even the lowest strata, living. The yard and house are ill-kempt, in desperate need of repairs. One board on the porch was missing; someone could hurt themselves falling into that hole. When I knocked on the door, Mrs. Stillwater and her son opened it. I could see no servants in the foyer while we spoke. Also, she had on an old cotton gown, nothing stylish, something you would expect to see on a servant, not the lady of the house. So, if this all adds up to the Stillwaters living on the edge of poverty, where did the necklace come from and why was it not sold to finance a better lifestyle for the family?"

"That is odd. You are very observant. Here is the situation . . ." The solicitor then went on to explain what the situation was with Stillwater Estate, and the present relationship between Bethany and Howard.

"So . . . we have to find a link between Howard's lifestyle and his financial needs. Do you know who I could contact to find such a link?"

"As no banker will deal with Howard now because of his bad credit, you need to go into the underbelly of London to find such information. But be very careful. These fellows are very nasty to deal with."

"I understand. However, I have a link to those men from other cases I have dealt with in the past. I will contact him and see what he can find out for me. Thank you for your help. I will be in touch as soon as I know anything more. Good day to you, sir." Steven picked up his hat, doffed it to Mr. Brown, and left the office.

"Be careful, Mr. Damon," whispered Mr. Brown to Steven's retreating back. "Be very careful. Howard will stop at nothing to get that estate. I guarantee it."

After leaving the solicitor's office, Steven headed for his own. When he got there, he penned a note and sent it to his contact in the other London world. Having completed that task, he leaned back in his chair to contemplate all he had seen and done that day. He chuckled when he remembered little Arthur. He was quite the character, the son he would like to have some day. Some day in the distant future . . .

***

Frank, too, had been busy. After lunch, he went back to the court's office to see if he could find out who would preside over Bethany's trial. Once he knew, he could put pressure on the judge to hold the trial sooner rather than later. Usually, in a trial for theft, the perpetrator could languish in Millbank Penitentiary for months before he or she came to trial. Frank could not afford to have that happen with Bethany. He knew of Steven Damon's reputation and that he would do a good job of defending Bethany. Perhaps even now he was trying to interview Cassandra Stillwater. It was a good thing Frank had given Howard an early warning about the barrister's plans. If not, Cassandra might have caved and told the truth, and Frank and Howard would be looking at the judge from another spot in the courtroom—the prisoner's box. Cassandra was their key, and she needed to be kept quiet.

Inside the office, he found things as he had expected. Bethany's case was not on a docket for the near future, nor was it likely to be. Frank pleaded his case about needing to speed up the trial so if she was convicted and sentenced to transportation to the colonies, it would happen this year. Then the British taxpayer did not have to pay for her room and board while she stayed at Millbank. He did not mention that the British people funded the colonial prisons, so it did not matter how long it took Bethany to go to trial. No, let the clerks think that once prisoners had left Britain, the good people of England were no longer responsible for their welfare. Only people like Frank knew differently.

His strategy worked. The clerk agreed with him and started looking for a date on the court calendar. He found one, two weeks hence, which Judge Owen Henley could preside over. Only two weeks would give Damon very little time to mount a proper defence for Bethany. Frank also knew Judge Henley, a no-nonsense man who had little time for the airs of the upper society. He had come from a working-class background and made his way up the judicial ladder. Because of his background, he gave lighter sentences to those in the lower classes of society and maximised the sentences of the rich and powerful. Judge Henley was perfect for Bethany's trial.

Thanking the clerk for his time and effort, Frank walked out of the courthouse with a light step. He and Howard were on their way to a victory. He needed to send him this news right away.

***

When Steven received the date of Bethany's upcoming trial, it shocked him. Two weeks? How had Frank managed to get a court date two weeks from today? After this was all over, he and the law society needed to check into Frank's practice. Had Frank bribed the clerk to get such a favourable date for the prosecution? Had he gone so far as to also bribe the judge? These were unknown factors for Steven, but one thing he knew, he needed to work fast to bring this to a just ending for Miss Stillwater. He sat down and wrote another note to his contact, stressing the need to swiftly find the facts about Howard and his gambling. There was no time to waste.

***

Howard received Frank's note and whooped with joy. The men at his poker table looked at him. "Received good news, Howie, old boy?" asked one.

"The best, gentlemen, the best. Soon I will be rolling in money and living my life the way I want to."

"Someone die and leave you their entire fortune?" asked another.

"Something like that. I can scarcely believe it."

"Well, I will believe it when I see hard cash on the table and not a stack of IOUs, Howard," said the first man. "You are in deep, man, and need to pay up."

"I will, I will. I just need a little more time, that's all."

A deep voice from the shadows behind Howard said, "You're running out of time, Howie. My boss is getting antsy. They want their money back now, not next year."

Howard squirmed in his chair. He knew that voice. He had heard it many times before, in different locations. They always seemed to find him whenever he joined a game. How did they do it? Were they following him? Cassandra said they had showed up at the house looking for him and money. Fortunately, he was seldom there. She could look after herself. He was not about to stay home and protect her. No, he was looking out for number one. But if the thugs were following him from gambling parlour to parlour, he needed to come up with some cash fast to satisfy their boss's appetites. If not from game winnings, then it would have to be Cassandra's jewellery. There was no more money in his bank. Frank's note brought him hope that soon he would roll in cash. Perhaps that would be enough to put off the loan sharks for a little while longer.

"Yes, yes, I know," said Howard, waving his hand backward while concentrating on his cards. "Just need a little more time . . ."

***

It was a good thing Bethany was not aware of the speed at which her future was changing. Not having anything to do but sit on a hard bed or floor, she spent her time envisioning what she would do when she was released from Millbank. She determined she would work to improve the lives of those forced to live here, having now seen and experienced the living conditions in the cell. They were deplorable. Perhaps, when Mr. Brown or Damon came, she would ask them to bring her a writing tablet, quill, and ink. She would write to her fellow committee members about what she was experiencing and what the prisoners needed to make life bearable. Comfortable would be too much of a stretch for some of the high society ladies who trusted in the law and believed every criminal deserved to be punished. Bethany was not of that mindset. She saw many, especially women and children, who committed crimes of theft just to survive. Some stole for themselves, but many were slaves of street masters who forced them to steal for their master's profits. Some criminals, perhaps, needed to be taught a lesson, but not those who were living hand-to-mouth. Those were the women Bethany would champion now and for the rest of her life.

As she pondered these things, a guard came to her cell. Putting her key in the lock, she opened the cell door and said, "Come with me."

"They have released me?" asked Bethany.

"No, you have a visitor. You need to come with me to the visiting room."

Disappointed in her answer and wondering who her first visitor was, Bethany accompanied the warder down the hall to the visiting room. Before she opened the door, however, the guard put shackles around Bethany's ankles and handcuffs on her wrists. Entering the room, Bethany saw Mr. Damon sitting on the far side of a table that was set in the middle of the room. There was one chair on Bethany's side of the table and the guard pushed her towards it. When Bethany sat down, she attached a length of chain from her ankle bracelets to the table leg. After doing that, she moved back to lean against the wall, while keeping a close eye on Bethany and Steven.

"How are you doing, Miss Stillwater?" Steven asked. "Are you being treated well?"

"Well, Mr. Damon? I don't think that word applies to my situation anymore. But they are not abusing me, if that is what you mean."

"I suppose you are right. None of this is fair to you."

"Mr. Damon, have you spoken with Cassandra yet?"

Mr. Damon relayed his brief meeting with Cassandra. "I met one of her sons, Arthur, I believe his name was. He is a cheeky little fellow, isn't he?"

"He is, and smart, too. I love all the boys, but I must admit Arthur is my favourite."

"He seems to be quite wise for his age. How old is he?"

"About four, I think. I can barely believe he is that old. It seems like only yesterday he was a tiny baby in my arms. Why do you mention his wisdom?"

"He made a comment that struck me when his mother told him to go to the kitchen and wait for her there. He said something about *adults* in a quite derogatory way before he obeyed his mother and left the room. What do you make of that, Miss Stillwater?"

"Only that they have most likely sent him away whenever his father wants to speak to his mother. Howard has no time for the children and their questions, and he would not want them around if he were chastising Cassandra for something."

"Does he do that often?"

"Criticize Cassandra? Yes, much of the time."

"What about?"

"Her expenditures, her clothing, her looks, everything . . . he seems to find fault in all that she is and does."

"Why did he marry her? Forgive me for asking these personal questions, but I am trying to get a picture of their family life."

"For her money. Her father sold her in marriage to Howard to cover his gambling debts."

"So it was a gambling transaction? Did Mrs. Stillwater have no say in her future?"

"None."

"She is to be pitied then."

"Yes, I try to do what I can to help her and the boys without Howard's knowledge. Otherwise he would take the money I give her for household expenses and use it for his vices."

"Does she have any other resources that she can dip into for funds?"

"Only her jewellery. It had been her mother's and so her father could not pawn it off for cash. She keeps it hidden from Howard, although I suspect he knows where it is and would pawn it off as well, if he could get his hands on it."

"The jewels are real?"

"Yes."

"That helps me understand how a woman living in a rather run-down townhouse, in a poorer area of the city, can have such expensive jewellery. It's a wonder she still has them."

"I know. I have offered several times to keep them for her, but she refuses. They are her security blanket."

"Now to a more sensitive topic. Mr. Brown told me you support your brother with a quarterly allowance from your estate. Is that correct?"

"I do." Bethany continued to fill in the gaps in the story he had heard from Edwin Brown about the will and the fund management for the estate. She expressed sorrow that Howard was not content with his role as estate manager and his salary but reiterated that he made a good living. He had no need for more funds.

"You believe he is responsible for you being here?"

"Definitely."

"And his wife? Why would she lie for him?"

"To protect her boys from him. There is nothing Cassandra loves more than her boys, and if she thought they were in danger, she would do anything to keep them safe."

"Including perjure herself?"

"Yes, even that."

"My time with you is almost up. Thank you for speaking with me, Miss Stillwater. I have a much better picture of the situation now."

"You are welcome, Mr. Damon. Anything to shorten my stay here and get me back home."

"Uh, about that . . ."

"Yes?"

"The prosecutor, Frank Walden, got a court date set for your trial."

"That's good, isn't it?" asked Bethany, perplexed at the frown on his face.

"Not exactly. The court date is two weeks from today."

"Two weeks from now? Isn't that rather sudden? I thought I might be here for weeks or months before my trial, but only two weeks?"

"Yes, and that does not give me much time to prepare a proper defence for you. I will do my utmost for you, but . . ."

"I have faith in you, sir, but more than that, I have faith in God. He will work out everything for my good, so do your best, and I will pray for our success."

"Thank you for your trust. I will work and you will pray. Sounds like an excellent combination."

"Is there anything else I can do to help? I admit, my resources are limited," she said, giving her restraints a little shake, "but I will assist you in any way I can."

"No, I have a plan; I just need to execute it. So, I will bid you farewell, and keep in touch. Good day to you," he said, picking up his hat off the table, setting it on his head, and nodding before heading to the outside door. It was opened by a guard, and he left. Bethany pondered his words as she waited for her guard.

The guard came and released Bethany's chain from the table. She shuffled over to the door and through it, accompanied by the guard. They walked down the hall to Bethany's cell, and once inside, the guard removed her restraints and then left the cell, locking the door behind her. Bethany headed over to the bed and sat down. Two weeks! Could Mr. Damon find enough evidence of her innocence in that time? She remembered she had promised to do her part by praying, so she closed her eyes and poured out her soul to her Heavenly Father, asking that His will be done in her life—which in her mind meant she would soon be free again.

***

The next day Steven's contact came through with a name, Teddy Soller. Teddy was a known loan shark who lived on the edge of high society. Because of his situation, he could move around in the higher classes and offer solace, and funds, to the gentlemen who had empty pockets in the gaming rooms. Of course, he did this for a price and expected repayment with interest within a reasonable period. When the gentlemen did not meet his deadlines, he sent his thugs to them with gentle reminders that payment was overdue. If that encouragement did not work, the thugs were authorized—by Teddy of course, not the bobbies—to use greater force to get Teddy's money back for him. And so it went. Teddy was very disappointed that even after all the encouragement he gave his customers, some still did not pay him back. As a result, they often had an accident which sometimes resulted in their death. That never satisfied Teddy, because after all that, he never got his money.

Steven knew of Teddy and his thugs. Because Teddy was a "gentleman" of sorts, he agreed to meet Steven at a well-known and well-respected restaurant in central London. Steven arrived at their appointed meeting time to find Teddy already seated at a back table. After his guards had patted Steven down to make sure he was not carrying a weapon, they escorted him to Teddy and then took up their stances guarding the table.

"Mr. Damon, I presume," said Teddy, reaching out to shake Steven's hand.

"Yes. Thank you for agreeing to meet with me, Mr. Soller, especially on such short notice."

"No problem. I think we have similar interests to discuss."

"What makes you say that, Mr. Soller?"

"Please, call me Teddy. All my friends do."

"Teddy, then. What similar interests do we have?"

"Why, Howard Stillwater and his gambling debts, Mr. Damon. Is that not why you asked to see me?"

"Yes."

"What would you like to know?"

"Exactly how deep into debt is Mr. Stillwater and are there other *lenders* out there holding some of his IOUs?"

"To my knowledge, and I know everything that goes on in the gambling parlours, I am in sole possession of all Mr. Stillwater's IOUs."

"How much does he owe you?"

"Mr. Damon, I do not disclose client information with other parties. Mr. Stillwater and I have a gentleman's agreement between us."

"Would you give me an approximate figure, Teddy? I need to know if Howard would be desperate enough to send his sister to prison in Australia to gain full access to her estate."

"Howard Stillwater would sell anything and everything, including his sister, if he thought he could make one pound sterling from the sale, Mr. Damon. And without disclosing the sum, let's just say that Mr. Stillwater had better make an enormous profit from the estate to pay me back for all I have loaned him in the past few years."

"If he owes you that much, why have you not called him on it yet?"

"Because a live client is worth more to me than a dead one. You get my drift?"

"I do, and I thank you for your time and information. It has been most helpful to me."

"You are welcome. Would you like to stay and have a drink with me, or perhaps a meal?"

"No, thank you. I must be off."

"Pity. I have enjoyed our little chat. Perhaps we can do it again someday."

"Perhaps," said Steven while getting up from the table. "Good evening to you, sir."

"Good evening, Mr. Damon. Best of luck with your case." Teddy signalled his guards, and they moved to the side to allow Steven to pass them before moving together again to protect their boss.

When he got outside, Steven heaved an enormous sigh of relief. Even though he had been certain he was in no danger from Mr. Soller, he had still felt very uncomfortable in his presence, especially with his two guards standing watch over them. He was glad he was not a gambler and never had reason to associate with men like Teddy Soller. One meeting was enough to last a lifetime.

***

The next day, Steven met again with Mr. Brown. He had paled the previous day after receiving the message from Steven stating that Bethany's trial was only two weeks away. They needed to work swiftly and efficiently to prepare their defence case. Steven informed Mr. Brown of what he had found out from Teddy Soller. It concurred with what he knew. But even with that information, how could they prove Howard had framed Bethany so he could gain control of her estate? The only people who knew the facts were Howard, Cassandra, and most likely Frank Walden, but none of them were talking. Circumstantial evidence was against Bethany, as they had found her with the necklace in her reticule. She testified she had received it from Cassandra but with her consent. Could they use Howard's words of anger at Bethany's home as a motive for revenge? It was about all they had right now as a defence. It was only Bethany's word against Howard's unless they had a witness to his outburst that day. Then Mr. Brown remembered that Bethany's butler, Kingsley, had been present when Howard threatened her. They needed to interview him and get him to testify on her behalf. Mr. Brown said he would get on that right away.

Damon decided they needed some character witnesses as well; men and women who would testify to Bethany's impeccable character and the impossible notion that she would commit such a crime. He said he would go back to Millbank that afternoon and get a list of possible character witnesses from Bethany.

Armed with their tasks for the day, the men split up to go their separate ways, with a plan to meet the next morning to discuss what they had found out and what needed to be done next.

***

Mr. Brown headed out to the Stillwater Estate. Kingsley met him at the front door when he got there. He invited him to come to the kitchen when he heard the purpose of Mr. Brown's visit. Kingsley wanted his wife to hear the news along with him so he did not have to retell it later. Mr. Brown agreed and accompanied Kingsley down the hallway to the kitchen, where Mrs. Kingsley was preparing tea.

"Mrs. Kingsley, we have a visitor," Kingsley announced as he entered the room.

Looking up, Mrs. Kingsley recognized the solicitor and said, "Mr. Brown, how delightful to see you again. What brings you out our way?"

"I wish it were to taste your delectable baking, ma'am, but unfortunately, it is not. No, I have come on a matter of great importance."

"Great importance. What might that be? Miss Stillwater is the only one to deal with such things around here, and as you know, she is still in town."

"Yes, I am aware of that fact. And it is on her behalf that I am here today."

"On Miss Bethany's behalf, Mr. Brown? Whatever has happened? Is she ill?"

"No, nothing like that."

"Then—"

"Mrs. Kingsley, my love, give the man a chance to catch his breath. So many questions, my dear."

"You are right, Mr. Kingsley. Please forgive me, Mr. Brown. Sometimes my tongue runs away with me. Won't you have a cup of tea and tell us your news?"

"Thank you. I would love a cup of tea."

"Then sit yourself down at the table and I will bring it straightaway." She indicated the table with a wave of her hand. Mr. Brown and Kingsley took seats there while she bustled around making tea.

Mrs. Kingsley also sat down once the tea and scones were on the table. After helping himself, Mr. Brown said, "Now back to our conversation. Miss Bethany is neither ill nor injured, but she is in a bit of a predicament and needs our help—especially yours, Mr. Kingsley."

"What kind of predicament?"

"She is in jail," Mr. Brown stated.

"In jail?" gasped Mrs. Kingsley, bringing a hand to her chest. "Whatever for?"

"They have accused her of stealing her sister-in-law's sapphire necklace."

"Theft? Of Mrs. Cassandra's necklace? I don't believe it."

"Believe it, ma'am. The judge did, and now Miss Stillwater is in Millbank Penitentiary awaiting trial."

"Oh, poor Miss Bethany. Kingsley, we must help her," said his wife as she reached out to grasp his arm.

Patting the hand on his sleeve, Kingsley turned back to Mr. Brown and said, "Sir, you said Miss Bethany needs our help. What can we do for her?"

"We, her barrister Mr. Damon and I, believe her stepbrother, Howard Stillwater, is behind the charge of theft, Mr. Kingsley. He was the one who brought the charges against her. I understand he was here a short time ago and had a heated conversation with Miss Stillwater. Am I correct?

"Yes. I was privy to their entire conversation and the threat he made to Bethany before he left."

"That was my understanding, and that is why we need your help. We need you to testify in court what they said, especially Mr. Stillwater's threat to Miss Bethany."

"Of course I will. It will be my pleasure to testify against that scumbag."

"Mr. Kingsley, your language," gasped his wife.

"I am sorry, my dear, but that is what he is, the scum of the earth."

"You might want to keep that to yourself while testifying in court. It might not help our case, even though I totally agree with your description of Mr. Stillwater."

"When do you need us to come to London, Mr. Brown?"

"As soon as possible. Miss Stillwater's trial is set for two weeks from yesterday."

"Less than two weeks from now?"

"Yes."

"But why the rush? I would like to see Miss Bethany home soon, but I am surprised they arranged her trial so quickly."

"So were we, Mr. Kingsley. Frank Walden, the prosecutor, arranged the date with the court clerk yesterday. We do not know why he is rushing the trial, but he must have a reason he is not sharing with us. We can only abide by the court date and hope our defence strategy is ready to refute the claim of theft."

"Is their case strong, Mr. Brown?" asked Mrs. Kingsley.

"Bethany had the necklace with her when she was arrested. That is fairly convincing evidence. And both Cassandra and Howard will probably be testifying against her, their word against hers. We need to find a way to refute their testimonies. That is why I came out today."

"I am sure Howard has threatened her with something nasty if she does not cooperate with him," said Kingsley. "I would not put it past the scu—" He stopped just in time.

Mr. Brown and Mrs. Kingsley laughed. Then Mr. Brown said, "Thank you for the tea, and for being willing to come to London to testify. I must be on my way back to the city now. There is much to do in so little time." Pushing back his chair, he stood up.

Mr. and Mrs. Kingsley also rose. "I'll see you to the door," said Kingsley.

He nodded and, after thanking Mrs. Kingsley again, the two men headed back to the front entry.

Arriving there, Kingsley assisted Mr. Brown with his coat and hat, before saying, "Is there anything else I should know that you did not feel comfortable sharing in front of my missus? Is Miss Bethany all right?"

"I have not seen her since she stood before the judge yesterday morning, Mr. Kingsley, but my colleague spent an hour with her yesterday afternoon. He said that she is holding up as best she can in the circumstances. That is all we can hope for."

"Yes, of course. And your colleague, Mr. Damon, I believe you said. Is he a competent barrister? Will he get Miss Bethany out of this mess?"

"He is very good. If anyone can free Miss Stillwater, it will be him. But the prosecutor has a powerful case, what with Bethany holding the necklace and Mrs. Stillwater's testimony. We will have to wait and see who comes out on top."

"Mrs. Kingsley and I will be praying. God is always victorious."

"Prayers are always appreciated. Now, good day. I will see you soon."

"Yes, we will come in tomorrow and stay at the townhouse. You can reach us there. Safe journey, Mr. Brown." Opening the front door, Kingsley stood back as the solicitor walked past him and down the steps. He entered the waiting carriage and waved to Kingsley as it rumbled off down the drive.

Kingsley closed the door and headed back to the kitchen to make travel plans with his wife.

***

Attempting to get character witnesses for Bethany was a long and frustrating process for Steven. After a quick visit with her at the jail, he was going door-to-door to visit society women on Bethany's list of potential witnesses. The butler often asked him to wait on the steps while he informed the lady of the house of the reason for Mr.

Damon's visit. Often, the butler came back with a message. While his lady sympathized with dear Miss Stillwater's plight, she could not be a character witness for her. On the rare occasion that Steven was invited into the foyer of the home, and the lady of the house came and spoke with him, she would gush on about what an unfortunate situation this was for the dear young lady, but as she did not know her that well, she could not see her way to be a character witness for her. After all, perhaps Miss Stillwater had fooled them all into thinking she was an upstanding young woman when she indeed did harbour criminal thoughts. Maybe she made a habit of stealing from the wealthy and that supported her lifestyle. You never really know a person, do you?

Steven headed to the home of the final lady on his list. It was Mrs. Hayward, the vicar's wife, of Bethany's church. Walking up the path to the manse, he wondered if she, too, would reject the idea of being a witness for Miss Stillwater. He knocked on the door and a young female servant opened the door.

"Good day," he said, while doffing his hat. "My name is Steven Damon. I am here to see your mistress. Is she in?"

"Yes, she is, sir, as is the vicar. Please step in and I will tell them you are here." She stepped aside and motioned him to come in.

"Thank you." Steven smiled at the young girl.

"Please wait here and I will fetch Mrs. Hayward."

Steven nodded, and the young girl turned and walked into the interior of the house. Within a couple of minutes, both the vicar and his wife came towards him.

"Mr. Damon?" asked the vicar.

"Yes."

"I am Donald Hayward, parish vicar. This is my wife, Harriet. You wished to speak with her?"

"Yes, but I am happy to speak with both of you, if you wish it."

"Please, come into the parlour and have a seat, Mr. Damon," said Mrs. Hayward. "May I offer you anything to drink?"

"No, thank you, but I appreciate the offer. Our conversation will be brief."

"Then what can I do for you, sir?"

"Before I answer that question, let me introduce myself more fully. As I told your girl, my name is Steven Damon, and I am a barrister in the city of London. I am currently employed in that capacity to defend a Miss Bethany Stillwater in her upcoming trial."

"Bethany. Oh yes, that poor dear. How is she doing? I feel sick about what has happened to her."

"Are you quite familiar with her, Mrs. Hayward?"

"Very familiar, Mr. Damon. She is a regular guest here in our home, is she not, Donald?"

"Yes, my dear. We love having Bethany here. She is a sweet young lady."

"Then you do not feel that the charges against her are legitimate, Vicar?"

"Legitimate? Huh! Anyone who knows Bethany would know she could have not committed such a crime. Why, I am surprised the judge took the route that he did; I expected he would have claimed the charges false the moment he saw her."

"I agree, but unfortunately he saw things differently, perhaps because she had the necklace on her at the gala."

"We were there, Mr. Damon," said Harriet. "The hosts invited us to the gala because I am a member of the charity committee. I was heading over to sit by Bethany when she got up and walked away. Next thing you know, her stepbrother and his wife were accusing her of theft and having the bobby take her off to prison. Disgraceful, that is all I can say."

"Did you see her with the necklace around her neck, ma'am?"

"Yes. Just before she got up, she unclasped it and put it in her reticule."

"Can you think why she would have done that?

"Probably because the necklace attracted attention to her, and if there is one thing Bethany hates, it's attention upon herself. Why, whenever she does something charitable, she always wants to keep it very hush-hush so they do not single her out for praise. She is very humble and not one to have airs about herself."

"Do you also know her stepbrother and his wife? I know they do not live in your parish, but I wondered if you had ever met them?"

"I have never met her stepbrother, but I have met his wife, Cassandra. She is a shy woman with not much to say for herself. I have gone with Bethany occasionally to deliver needed things to their home and have also met Cassandra's little boy, Arthur. He is a delightful child."

"I agree. When I went to speak with Mrs. Stillwater, I met him. He is the type of son I would love to have some day."

"Are you married, sir?"

"No, not at present."

"Do you have a special young lady?" asked Harriet, a gleam in her eye.

"No, ma'am."

"Now, Harriet," said her husband while shaking his head. "Please forgive my wife, Mr. Damon. She is forever trying her hand at matchmaking."

Steven laughed. "I am afraid that I am too busy at present to be looking for a wife, ma'am, but when I do, I will come to you for help. But getting now to the purpose for my visit. Although the necklace is powerful evidence for the prosecution, I am building my case around Miss Stillwater's impeccable character and her stepbrother's rather shady reputation. I am looking for women who will testify in court to her fine character, and thus the impossibility of her having committed such a crime. Would you be willing to testify for her?"

"Absolutely, young man. And I would like to tell that stepbrother of hers a thing or two as well."

"That would have to be outside the courtroom, I'm afraid, ma'am. I would like your testimony to focus on Bethany and not her brother."

"Of course. I will be discreet and answer only the questions put to me, Mr. Damon. Would that be sufficient?"

"More than sufficient. Thank you very much. You are the first lady to agree to witness for Miss Stillwater, and I have gone through a long list of them."

"Well, if they are ladies from our committees who are of high society, I am not surprised. Most of them look out only for themselves. This kind of activity would not serve them well in their image making."

"So I have discovered, ma'am. Now, with your permission, I must be off. I will send a message when I need to see you again to review your statement." Steven got up from his chair and walked with the couple to the front door. Mrs. Hayward gave him his coat and hat while the vicar opened the door.

Just before he stepped out the door, Harriet asked, "Has a trial date been set yet? I know that sometimes it takes a long time before one goes to court, but I was just wondering how long I had before the trial begins."

"I should have told you as soon as I arrived. Forgive me for forgetting. Yes, the date is set for two weeks minus a day from now."

"In two weeks? So soon?"

"Yes, that was a surprise for me as well. Not much time to mount a good defence for Miss Stillwater, but I will do my best."

"I am sure that you will. I am glad Bethany has you on her side. But she has God on her side, and He will prevail. Let us know if there is anything else we can do in the next couple of weeks, besides being in constant prayer for her."

"I will. Thank you again for agreeing to be a character witness for her. I know she will appreciate it. I will be in touch. Good day." Steven doffed his hat before heading down the path to the street.

Well, at least his effort had not been a total loss. He had one character witness for Bethany and perhaps others would reconsider their refusals in the next few days. The vicar's wife was an important one; if you could not trust the word of a woman such as Harriet Hayward, who could you trust? That thought lightened Steven's step as he headed for his boarding house and supper.

***

While Mr. Damon and Mr. Brown were working feverishly on a defence for Bethany, Frank Walden was working just as hard to prepare a solid case against her. Cassandra grew tired of having him always underfoot, but she could not refuse him entrance. He was Howard's friend, so she welcomed him whenever Howard was home, which of late seemed to be all the time. He had forsaken his vices for the time being to make sure Cassandra stuck to her word and learned her lines for the trial. The boys hid out in their bedrooms and the playroom most of the time to avoid their father. But they needn't have worried. Howard had no time for them; all his attention was on the upcoming trial.

On the last day before the trial, Frank said to Cassandra, "Now, Mrs. Stillwater, I am going to pretend to be Mr. Damon, Bethany's defence barrister. He will ask you very hard questions, so you need to be prepared to answer him with no hesitation. Do you understand me?

"Yes."

"Very good. Now, first, what is your name?"

"Cassandra Stillwater."

"Wrong answer. You are Mrs. Howard Stillwater. Howard is a recognized member of society, and it will give your testimony more credence if you name yourself as his wife. Please remember that fact."

"I will."

"Very good. Now, where do you live?"

"At twenty-six Wellington Street."

"And whereabouts is that address, Mrs. Stillwater?"

"In mid-London."

"Wrong again. You want to impress upon the judge that you live on the edge of the fashionable district of Hyde Park. That, too, will elevate your status in the judge's opinion."

"But we live in a rented townhouse. How can that be fashionable?"

"Never mind that fact. Just do as I ask, please?"

"Very well," said Cassandra, while trying to keep all these facts straight in her head.

"Now, this is very important. Pay close attention, please. What is your relationship like with your sister-in-law, Bethany Stillwater?"

Thinking this was a simple question, Cassandra replied, "Very close, sir, we are very close."

Shaking his head, Frank said, "No, you are not. She is constantly over here wanting to borrow things from you, your gowns, your jewels, your shoes. You grow weary of seeing her all the time."

"That is a lie. I love Bethany, and it is she who brings things to me when I need them, not the other way around. And because she lives in the country most of the time, I seldom get to see her. She is not a frequent visitor in my home."

"Mrs. Stillwater," piped in Howard. "You are to answer the questions as if you hated Bethany, not this way. You are hopeless, Cassandra. Frank, do you think we can trust her to speak correctly on the witness stand?"

"We must, Howard. Our entire case rests on her testimony and the fact that Miss Stillwater had the necklace in her possession at the gala. Without your wife's testimony as to how she got the necklace, we have no case."

"You hear that?" warned Howard, moving over to Cassandra. "If you mess this up and Bethany goes free, you will bear the consequences of your testimony. You are aware of what those are, aren't you?"

"Yes, Howard. You have drilled them into me. I just have such a terrible time saying such things about Bethany when I know they are not true."

"Lose those feelings of compassion. They will do you no good."

"Yes, Howard."

"Very good. Now, let us start over again . . ."

At the end of an hour-long session with the prosecutor, Cassandra was limp with exhaustion, and the men were grinding their teeth. But there was no time left to practise; the trial started the next morning at nine o'clock. Cassandra was as ready as she could be for the ordeal ahead of her. As soon as the men excused her, she headed upstairs to her bedroom to lie down.

Howard and Frank headed out to a local pub to get a drink or two. While now uncertain of the trial's outcome based on Cassandra's shaky responses to Frank's questions, they could do no more. They needed a drink to bolster them for the days to come.

***

Bethany spent the last evening of her confinement praying. She knew Mr. Brown and Mr. Damon had done their best to prepare a good defence, but she was uncertain if it was adequate to disprove Howard and Cassandra's lies. Knowing the One who was in total control, she came to Him with her plight, asking that His will be done in the coming days, hoping that would be to her benefit. She could only wait and see.

Chapter 3

The courtroom was packed. It seemed everyone in society needed some entertainment, and Bethany's trial was the focus of the week. The ladies who had refused to act as character references for Bethany were all out in force in the seats and galleries of the courtroom. They were more interested in gossiping with their friends and showing off their finery than they were in the fate of one of their own. One would think they were at a ball rather than in a courtroom. Their husbands, mostly, were not in attendance. They were taking this opportunity to pursue their own activities. So, whether it was horse racing, or cards, or just a drink with a friend at their club, they kept their distance from the courthouse and its proceedings.

One lady of the highest ranks, the Duchess of Yardley, was also not present. While sympathizing with Bethany for what she must be experiencing, the duchess did not see that her support would be of any value to Bethany. Her husband and sons were still away in Scotland, so she did not have his guidance to assist in her decision. But she did not want to involve herself with the gossipmongers who would be sure to be in attendance, so she stayed home.

A few minutes before nine o'clock, Steven Damon and Edwin Brown came into the crowded courtroom and made their way to the front table on the left, facing the judge's chair. Steven looked around in disgust at the crowd. "Look at this crowd, Mr. Brown. It is sickening to see how many women of the upper class are here, not to support Miss Stillwater, but just to see what happens to her."

"I agree, Mr. Damon. If I had my way, I would clear the courtroom and only allow those who are involved in the case to remain."

"That is an excellent idea. As soon as the judge comes in, I will make that request of him. Miss Stillwater should not have to bear this spectacle."

Just then, the rear doors opened again to allow Frank, Howard, and Cassandra to enter the room. Frank was wearing a black robe with the customary white wig. Howard, however, had dressed to impress. He was wearing a white shirt with a starched high collar under a gold vest. His jacket was a peacock blue colour, as were his trousers. To complete the outfit, he had a pair of highly polished black shoes. Carrying the requisite cane, he strutted down the centre aisle with his head held high, waving a white handkerchief to acquaintances as he passed by them. As he moved forward, one could almost hear the whispers about his appearance.

Cassandra, in contrast to her husband, was all in black. She wore a simple dark black gown, covered by a black cape. She clutched a black reticule, and her head was covered by a simple black bonnet. The colour choice suggested she wanted to blend into the woodwork. Once she reached the first row of seats on the right-hand side of the courtroom, she slid in, and over, to the far side of the bench. If she could have, she would have slid out of the bench and onto the floor so no one could see her. But she knew that would not be proper, so she sat down and hunched over, looking at the floor.

The next pair to enter were Mr. and Mrs. Kingsley. They had arrived in town a week ago, and had wanted to visit Bethany at Millbank, but she sent word through Mr. Damon that she was not seeing anyone other than her barrister and solicitor. Understanding her need for privacy, the Kingsleys did not press the matter, but instead spent their time in prayer for her. Mr. Kingsley also worked with Mr. Damon on his testimony. Seeing Mr. Brown up at the front, they hurried down the aisle and seated themselves behind him.

Then the Haywards arrived. It appalled them to see many of the members of high society crowding the benches of the courtroom. *If only I could get that many into church on Sundays,* thought the vicar. It would serve them a lot better than sitting here gawking at poor Miss Stillwater. The Haywards made their way up to the first bench on the left side of the courtroom and slid in beside the Kingsleys. The couples smiled at each other and exchanged greetings, Mr. Brown and Mr. Damon turned and acknowledged their presence.

Then a hush came over the room as a side door opened, and they ushered Bethany into the prisoner's box. That hush was followed by a loud gasp that echoed throughout the room at her appearance. Instead of seeing a neatly, appropriately gowned, and coiffured young woman, they saw a woman in a shapeless brown gown with jag-gedly cut, chin-length hair. Her face was pale, and she did not look up as she followed the warder into the box. Once there, and before sitting down, she looked up and over at Mr. Brown and Mr. Damon. They each gave her encouraging smiles, which she acknowledged, before looking at the Haywards and Kingsleys behind them. Seeing her dear friends sitting there almost broke her composure, and she quickly looked down again to hide her sudden tears. She could hear the noise of the crowded room but, not wanting to observe the audi-ence, she kept her eyes to the floor.

The clock struck nine, and all eyes turned to the door beside the judge's seat. That door opened, and the bailiff called, "All rise, Judge Owen Henley presiding." Then the judge climbed to his bench and settled himself on the chair behind his desk. The bailiff then motioned the crowd to be seated, and the trial began . . . but not quite. Remembering Mr. Brown's comment about clearing the courtroom, Mr. Damon stood and waited for the judge to acknowl-edge him. When he did, Steven said, "May I approach the bench,

Your Honour? I have a request to make of you before we start the proceedings."

The judge nodded, and Steven went forward. The judge leaned forward and listened to Steven's request before motioning Frank to also come forward. Upon hearing Steven's request, Frank frowned and said, "Your Honour, this is a public trial, therefore the public has a right to be here. I do not support Mr. Damon's request to clear the courtroom of all spectators."

"I agree, Mr. Walden. Request denied, Mr. Damon."

Frank smirked as he and Steven returned to their respective tables. "One point for me, Damon, and many more to come."

Mr. Damon did not comment and returned to his seat beside Mr. Brown. Frank, while taking his seat, whispered something to Howard, which caused him to laugh out loud.

"Order in the court," called the judge. "This is a court of law and not a jester's court, sir. Please restrain yourself from such jocularity."

"My apologies, Your Honour," said Howard. "It will not happen again."

"I hope not, sir. Now, let us proceed. Bailiff, if you would read the charges against Miss Stillwater."

"Yes, Your Honour," said the bailiff. Bringing out a parchment and holding it high, he read, "'The people of this great nation living under our glorious mother, Victoria, Queen of England, and all her colonies, do hereby charge Miss Bethany Anne Stillwater with the theft of one sapphire necklace, valued at £500 sterling."

The judge turned to his left and looked at Bethany in the prisoner box. "Miss Stillwater, you have heard the charge against you. How do you plead?"

"Not guilty, Your Honour," said Bethany, raising her eyes to look at him.

"So be it. Clerk, please record that the defendant, Miss Bethany Anne Stillwater, has pleaded not guilty to the charge of theft over £100," the judge said, looking down at the prosecutor and the barrister. "Gentlemen, you may proceed. Mr. Walden, your first witness, please."

"Thank you, Your Honour. I wish to call Mrs. Howard Stillwater to the stand."

Cassandra got up and came out from around the far side of the bench. She walked over to the witness stand, keeping her head down and not making eye contact with anyone. After climbing into the witness stand, the bailiff extended a Bible for her to rest her left hand on, before asking her to raise her right hand. "Do you solemnly swear to tell the truth, the whole truth, and nothing but the truth, so help you God?"

"I do," she said in a faint, whispery voice.

"What is your name?"

"Cassandra, I mean, Mrs. Howard Stillwater."

"Thank you. You may be seated."

Cassandra sat down, knowing she had already fumbled once, and her testimony had only begun. She began to twist her hands together out of the sight of Howard and Frank.

Frank got up and walked over to stand about three feet in front of the witness box.

"Mrs. Stillwater, you are the wife of the businessman well known in society as Howard Stillwater, are you not?"

"I am."

"And you are here today to testify that the defendant, Bethany Anne Stillwater, your sister-in-law, did steal a valuable sapphire necklace from you on the tenth day of September of this year."

"Yes."

"Please tell us, in your own words, Mrs. Stillwater, what happened on that day."

"Certainly, Mr. Walden," she said. Then she told the courtroom what had happened on the day Bethany came for tea, and then when she saw her wearing the necklace at the gala. After her long discourse, Cassandra stopped and looked down at her hands.

"Thank you, Mrs. Stillwater. That must have been quite an ordeal for you. One last thing, is the person who stole the necklace from you in the courtroom today?"

"Yes."

"Would you please point her out to the court?"

Cassandra raised her eyes and looked over at the prisoner's box, straight into Bethany's eyes. Then she raised her hand and pointed to Bethany. "There she is, sir. She is sitting in the prisoner's box." After saying that, she quickly put down her hand and reverted again to looking at the floor.

"Let the clerk record that the witness, Mrs. Howard Stillwater, has identified the prisoner, Miss Bethany Stillwater, as the perpetrator of the crime." Frank stepped back a foot and said, "No more questions, Your Honour," before walking back to his table.

"Mr. Damon," said the judge, "do you wish to cross-examine the witness?"

Getting up from his chair and carrying a pad of notes he had been writing while Cassandra spoke, Steven said, "I do, Your Honour."

"Your witness, Mr. Damon."

As Steven walked over to stand before the witness box, Cassandra's knees started to shake and her hands trembled. This was the moment she had been dreading. This was when she was going to have to lie like a pro, just like her husband. There could be no slip ups, or she would face the consequences of Howard's wrath.

"Good morning, Mrs. Stillwater," said Steven as he stood in front of her. "How are you today?"

"Fine, thank you."

"That is good, Mrs. Stillwater, or may I call you Cassandra? I understand that is your given name, and such a lovely one at that."

Frank jumped up and said, "Objection, Your Honour. Mr. Damon is trying to disarm the witness."

Steven looked up at the judge. "I was only trying to make her more comfortable, Your Honour. She appears to be quite nervous."

"Overruled. Carry on, Mr. Damon."

"Thank you, Your Honour. Now, again, may I call you Cassandra or do you prefer Mrs. Howard Stillwater?"

"Cassandra."

"Very well, Cassandra. Now, to get to your testimony. I just wanted to clarify a couple of points. But before I do that, I want to remind you that you are still under oath and what the penalty for lying to the court is. Are you aware of the penalty for lying?"

Frank was on his feet again. "Your Honour, Mr. Damon is out of line. He is threatening the witness."

"Your Honour, I am only reminding the witness of the serious-ness of lying to the court. There are some points in her testimony that do not add up for me, so I need to review them again with her."

"Overruled. But, Mr. Damon, you are treading a fine line here. Do not try my patience."

"I won't, Your Honour, thank you. So, Cassandra, I will ask you again, do you know the penalty for lying to the court?"

"I do," she whispered.

"I'm sorry. I did not hear your response. You must speak louder so the clerk can record your answer."

"I do."

"Very good. Now, let us begin. First, you said Miss Stillwater is your sister-in-law. Is that correct?"

"Yes."

"But I understand your husband is her stepbrother. Is that correct?"

"Yes."

"Then, correct me if I am wrong, but would that not make you her stepsister-in-law?"

"I suppose so, but I don't see what the difference is. We are sisters and have been for quite some time."

"I see. So you view your relationship with Miss Stillwater as a close one?"

"It was until recently, yes."

"I can see how accusing your sister-in-law of theft could break a relationship, Cassandra. My sympathies to you."

"Thank you."

"Now that we have established your correct relationship with Miss Stillwater, tell me, who is the owner of the Stillwater Estate?"

"Bethany."

"So your husband, as her stepbrother, has no assets in the estate?"

"No, he only works for her."

Frank roared. "Irrelevant, Your Honour. Neither Mr. nor Mrs. Stillwater are on trial here today. Mr. Damon has no right to continue this line of questioning."

"I am only trying to establish the relationship of the family members, Your Honour."

"Unless this line of questioning produces worthy information immediately, Mr. Damon, I will cease your questioning of the witness. Do you understand me?"

"I do, and I am bringing this to an end soon, Your Honour. I only have one more question regarding the family estate."

"Very well, I will allow it, Mr. Damon, but only this once."

"Thank you, Your Honour. Now, Cassandra, if Miss Stillwater is the owner and controller of what I know to be a very profitable estate, why would she have to steal a necklace from you to accessorise her gown for the gala? Why could she not just go to a jeweller and purchase a sapphire necklace for herself?"

"I do not know, sir."

"Nor do I, Cassandra, nor do I," said Steven before changing his line of questioning. Consulting his notes, he asked, "Would you tell me, please, why you and your husband waited over a week before confronting Miss Stillwater with the theft of your necklace? You said Mr. Stillwater wanted to publicly humiliate his sister in front of her peers. Is that correct?"

"Yes."

"But why? Does he not get along with Miss Stillwater? Does he not respect her authority over him at the estate?"

"Objection, Your Honour," called Frank, without bothering to stand up.

"Sustained. Mr. Damon, Mr. Stillwater's relationship with his sister is not relevant to this case. Please cease this line of questioning."

"Oh, but it is, Your Honour. In fact, I believe it is central to this case. I believe Mr. Stillwater used his wife to frame his sister so he could gain control of the estate and its assets. And I intend to prove it. No further questions at this time, Your Honour."

A gasp went through the spectators. This was not just a theft trial, but one of family intrigue. The news would feed the gossips for weeks to come.

"Order in the court, order in the court," shouted the judge, banging his gavel on his desk.

The chatter died to a whisper, then silence, before the judge looked at Frank. "Do you wish to re-examine the witness?"

"Not at this time, Your Honour."

"Very well. Mrs. Stillwater, you may step down."

Cassandra stood and then walked down the two steps onto the floor. She quickly made her way back to her seat while avoiding looking at either Howard or Frank. Retribution would come later that evening at home, but right now, neither man could say anything to her. For a little while, she had a reprieve. After sitting down, she kept her eyes on the floor as she felt Howard's icy stare upon her. It sent shivers down her spine.

***

Indeed, Howard was furious, but he managed to contain his anger. How dare Cassandra disobey him like that and speak as she had to Mr. Damon. Their carefully rehearsed answers had flown out the window. Howard wanted to take the boys tonight to another place where Cassandra could not find them. Then perhaps she would understand he meant business with his threats. But where to go? He would have to think on that for a while; perhaps at the lunch break he and Frank could discuss it. Howard turned his thoughts back to the trial.

"Your next witness, Mr. Walden?"

"Yes, I now call Mr. Howard Stillwater to the stand, Your Honour."

Howard got up from his seat and moved around the table to cross over to the witness stand. He needed to repair the damage his wife had done and restore his reputation. This was his moment to shine.

He walked up to the stand and stood while swearing the oath of honesty.

"Please state your full name for the court record."

"Howard Peabody Stillwater."

A little titter went through the crowd as his middle name was revealed. To this day, no one in society had ever known it.

"So be it. Please be seated."

Howard took his seat with a great flourish of the tails of his jacket. Once he was suitably arranged, he looked up and smiled at the crowd of onlookers.

Frank walked over to stand in front of him. "Mr. Stillwater, how are you today?"

"Very well, thank you, sir. And you?"

"Very well. Thank you for asking. Now, Mr. Stillwater, I understand you are the husband of the previous witness, Mrs. Howard Stillwater, are you not?"

"I am. We have been married for over ten years now. Ten thrilling years of marital bliss."

"That is wonderful, Mr. Stillwater. Not too many men admit to such a fortunate marriage after that length of time."

"Yes, you could say our marriage has been one long honeymoon, and we have four wonderful boys to prove it."

"Indeed? Congratulations on producing such progeny. I am sure you are very proud of them."

"Proud as a peacock," said Howard, trying to take away the sting of the crowd's laughter at the disclosure of his middle name. He hated that name.

"I am sure you are, sir. Now, moving along, would you tell the court your relationship to the defendant, Miss Bethany Stillwater?"

"I am her stepbrother."

"And how long have you been in a relationship with her?"

"Sixteen years. She was only two years of age when her father married my mother. I was eighteen at the time."

"Quite an age gap between you, isn't there?"

"Yes, but I loved her as a sister from the first time I met her. We got along very well."

"And now?"

"Our relationship has suffered over the past few years. I suppose I am mostly to blame, having not spent much time with Bethany, due to all my business interests."

"You are the manager of Stillwater Estate?"

"Yes, my stepfather assigned me that role once I reached a mature age."

"So it was he, rather than your stepsister, who gave you that position?"

"Yes, with the understanding that when he passed away, I would be granted ownership of the estate."

"And did that happen?"

"No. His *Last Will and Testament* declared the estate was Bethany's inheritance, as it had come with her mother to the marriage."

"I am sure that came as quite a shock to you, Mr. Stillwater, after labouring for the estate for many years."

"Yes, I was very disappointed, I must admit. But, not wanting to cause any problems, I did not dispute the will. I agreed to stay on and manage the estate for Bethany."

"That was very generous of you. I am sure Miss Stillwater appreciated your gesture."

"At the time, she said she did, but now I am not so sure."

"Why is that?"

"Because on the odd occasion I speak with Bethany about the need to increase my wages so that I can properly look after my wife and children, she turns me down. She says that my wage is quite adequate for my position in life."

"Does that anger you?"

"No, I am not a man of anger, but I am saddened by her callous attitude towards my family."

"So even though you are not paid well for the work you do, you have never thought of harming Miss Stillwater in any way?"

"Never! She is family."

"So, moving forward to the recent events, how did you feel when your wife told you Miss Stillwater had stolen her necklace?"

"Objection, Your Honour," called Steven. "The fact of theft has not been established."

"Sustained. Mr. Walden, you will rephrase your question, please?" said the judge.

"Of course, Your Honour. Please forgive me. Mr. Stillwater, when did you discover your wife's necklace was missing, and how did it make you feel?"

"I was angry, of course, at the loss. The necklace and other jewellery pieces are my wife's dowry. To have a valuable piece go missing like that, well, it was almost incomprehensible."

"So, what did you do to find the necklace?"

"I suggested to my wife that, as there was a gala coming up soon, we should attend and see if the necklace showed up there."

"Why did you not inform the authorities right away about the missing jewellery?"

"I wanted to handle its retrieval and not embarrass anyone at the party."

"That was very kind of you."

"I try to live in such a manner, sir, every day of my life."

"How noble of you, sir. Now, when you got to the gala and saw Miss Stillwater, what did you see?"

"She was wearing the necklace. I was stunned."

"What happened then?"

"When she saw me staring at her, she took off the necklace and was heading for the doors when I caught up with her."

"And?"

"I confronted her about the necklace and demanded to see it, to make sure it was indeed Cassandra's. When she pulled it out of her reticule, she handed it to me calmly; she was not remorseful that she had it on her person."

"How did she say she got it, Mr. Stillwater?"

"She said Cassandra had loaned it to her for the evening, but now she wanted to give it to me as she was going home."

"Did you believe her story?"

"No. It differed completely from what my wife had told me, and I believed my beloved wife, not my stepsister."

"What came next?"

"A bobby had been assigned to watch the party for any thefts, as there were a great number of ladies there from the upper class. My wife summoned him and, after ascertaining that Bethany held the missing necklace without permission, he took her into custody."

"Thank you, Mr. Stillwater. I have no further questions for you at this time."

"Mr. Damon, do you wish to cross-examine the witness?" asked the judge.

"I do, Your Honour," said Steven, getting up from his seat and coming to stand in front of Howard.

Howard's hands turned clammy, and he wiped them on his trousers to dry them, but it was futile. The sweat kept returning to his hands and his brow.

"Mr. Stillwater, I am Steven Damon, the barrister for the defendant. How are you?"

"Fine, Mr. Damon," said Howard, wiping the back of his hand across his forehead.

"Forgive me, Mr. Stillwater, but you do not appear to be well. Can I get you anything before we begin, a glass of water, or a clean handkerchief perhaps?"

"No, I am fine, thank you."

"Very well, but if you change your mind, please let me know."

"I will, thank you."

"Now, Mr. Stillwater, I just want to clarify a few points in your testimony. Do you mind?"

"Not at all. What would you like to know?"

"You stated your mother married Miss Stillwater's father when you were eighteen years of age. Is that correct?"

"Yes."

"A young man of that age should already be employed, or at least apprenticing, for a career. Were you doing either of those things at the time of your mother's marriage?"

"No."

"May I ask why not? Did your family have money, so you could live the life of a gentleman?"

"No. My mother worked as Miss Stillwater's nanny before marrying her father. Mother wanted me to be a gentleman, so she paid all our bills out of her wages."

"That was quite a step up for her, and for you, Mr. Stillwater. A nanny becoming the wife of a nobleman. You must have been very pleased at her marriage to such a man."

"I was, Mr. Damon, not because of our status elevation. I liked Mr. Stillwater, and he liked me."

"It sounds like it was a match made in heaven, as they say. Would you not agree?"

"I do, sir. My mother was thrilled, as was I."

"And how did Miss Stillwater react to her father remarrying?"

"She was still very young, so she was happy that her nanny was now her mother. And she loved having me as a big brother."

"And you? How did you feel about Miss Stillwater?"

"I loved her as my sister, sir, and still do."

"I see."

"When did you become the manager of Stillwater Estate?"

"Father, Mr. Stillwater, started teaching me the skills soon after his marriage to my mother. He said it was time I learned how to manage such a large place."

"So he did not actually say that someday you would own the estate, only that you could manage it. Is that correct?"

"No, not in so many words, but he implied it."

"And you never had a written copy of such an agreement?"

"No, it was a gentleman's agreement."

"Did you shake hands on it?"

"No, I don't remember doing so, Mr. Damon."

"A gentleman's agreement requires a handshake, Mr. Stillwater. If none occurs, then there is no agreement. It was only in your mind that you saw yourself as someday being the owner of the estate; Miss Stillwater's father knew he would pass it on to his daughter because of it being formerly her mother's property. He trained you as the estate manager to give you a job, nothing else. You were deluding yourself if you thought differently, sir."

"That is not true," yelled Howard, his face getting red. "He promised the estate to me. He did!"

"No, he did not, and because of that you decided to get the estate yourself, by framing your stepsister for a crime she did not commit so you can gain control of the estate and its profits."

"Objection, Your Honour," called Frank. "Mr. Damon is badgering the witness. Mr. Stillwater is not on trial here."

"Sustained," said the judge. "Mr. Damon, you will refrain from this line of questioning and stick to the case at hand."

"Yes, Your Honour," said Damon, having accomplished his goal to reveal who Howard was, a greedy little man who would stop at nothing to fulfil his own wishes. "No further questions at this time, Your Honour."

"Mr. Walden?" asked the judge.

"Not at this time, Your Honour."

"Very well. The witness may step down. Seeing the time, we will recess for a lunch break. We will reconvene at one o'clock. Court dismissed." The judge rose and exited the courtroom. As soon as he was out of the room, the gossip began again.

***

Bethany left the prisoner's box and was brought to a cell where she could look after personal needs before the warder delivered her a tray of food. The cell had a table and chair, besides a cot with a mattress on it. It surprised Bethany to see the amenities in a holding cell when she did not have them in her current cell at Millbank. She sat down at the table. After blessing the food, she started to eat. It was delicious! It was a beef and vegetable stew with two slices of bread to go with it. There was even a cup of lukewarm tea on the tray. She did not mind that the tea was not hot; it was great to have something other than water to drink. She finished every morsel of the food and every drop of the tea. Feeling satisfied for the first time in a couple of weeks, she sat back and looked at the cot. Did she have time for a quick nap before the afternoon session began? It was very tempting to lie down for a bit of a rest. They had woken her very early this morning at Millbank so she would be at the courthouse by nine o'clock. Yes, a quick nap would be lovely. The mattress looked clean enough, so she covered her head with the shawl she had left in the waiting area before entering the courtroom and lay down. Soon her eyes were drifting closed, but before she knew it the warder was back and opening her cell. It was time to carry on.

***

Another two men were not far away having lunch in the corner of a pub, while Bethany had been eating and resting. Howard and Frank were reviewing the morning's court session and wondering how to refute Mr. Damon's innuendos about Howard's potential involvement in Bethany's arrest. They both agreed he had cast doubt on how the scenario had played out, by suggesting Howard had set it all up to frame Bethany and gain control of the estate, which, of course, he had. But they did not want the judge to start thinking in that direction. So they needed a plan to divert his attention back to the suspect, Bethany Stillwater. Neither of them could think of anything at that moment, but Frank was sure they would have at least another day in court, so perhaps something would come to them before tomorrow. Right now, they needed to stay with their present stories, and that meant Cassandra needed a forceful reminder of her duty to Howard.

Howard told Frank he needed a place to stow the boys for the night, someplace safe, but somewhere Cassandra could not find them. Frank suggested his home. He had a housekeeper who would look after the boys, and Cassandra did not know where he lived.

Howard agreed that would be a good place for them; he said he would take Cassandra out for a bite of dinner before taking her home that evening, which would give Frank ample time to collect the boys before he and Cassandra got home. Having made that plan, Howard looked at his pocket watch and exclaimed, "It is almost one o'clock. We need to hurry back to the courtroom." They threw payment for the meal on the table and rushed out of the pub. It would never do to be late for court.

***

The court resumed promptly at one o'clock, with Frank and Howard barely making it in the doors before the guards shut them. They were just about to take their seats when the door to the judge's chamber opened. The bailiff called, "All rise!" Resuming their seats after the judge sat down, they heard the bailiff say, "Court is now in session. Judge Owen Henley presiding."

"Mr. Walden and Mr. Damon. Are you ready to proceed?" asked the judge.

"I am, Your Honour," said Frank.

"I am as well, Your Honour," replied Steven.

"Very well. Let us begin. Mr. Walden, you may call your next witness."

"I have no further witnesses, Your Honour. I defer now to my colleague, Mr. Damon."

"Are you prepared, Mr. Damon?"

"Yes, Your Honour. I call to the witness stand Mr. Albert Kingsley."

Kingsley stood up and made his way over to the witness stand. After taking the oath of truth, the bailiff asked him his name, and then Steven was asked to proceed.

"Thank you, Your Honour," said Steven as he strolled over to the witness stand.

"Good afternoon, Mr. Kingsley. How are you?"

"Fine, thank you, sir. And you?"

"Very well, thank you. Now that we have the pleasantries out of the way, will you tell me your occupation and your relationship to the defendant, Miss Bethany Stillwater?"

"Certainly. I am employed at the Stillwater Estate and have been the butler there for the past twenty years."

"So you and Miss Stillwater are well acquainted."

"Very well acquainted, sir. I have known her since she was born."

"And do you also know Mr. Howard Stillwater?"

"I do. He joined our household as a young man of eighteen years, about sixteen years ago. His mother was Miss Stillwater's nanny before she married Bethany's father."

"Tell me, Mr. Kingsley, prior to this event, have you ever known Miss Stillwater to commit a crime of any sort?"

"Other than snatching fresh cookies off my wife's cooling rack, no, Mr. Damon. Bethany was always an obedient child."

"Well, I suppose we have all been guilty of stealing a cookie or two from our cooks, Mr. Kingsley," laughed Steven. "I don't believe that leads us to a life of crime, though, does it?"

"No, indeed, Mr. Damon. And no one can resist my wife's freshly baked cookies."

"I hope I have a chance to sample them one day, Mr. Kingsley, to see if they are worth stealing. Now, how would you describe Mr. Howard Stillwater's behaviour?"

"Objection, Your Honour," cried Frank. "Mr. Damon is proceeding down the same path he was pursuing this morning, taking the focus off the defendant and placing it on Mr. Stillwater."

"Sustained. Mr. Damon, I warned you this morning about your line of questioning. Is this going somewhere?"

"Yes, Your Honour, it is. In a few minutes, I will refute Mr. Howard Stillwater's assertion that he is a man of peace. Mr. Kingsley will help me establish that fact."

"Very well, but stick to questions pertaining to the case, Mr. Damon, and not just aspersions on Mr. Stillwater's character. You understand?"

"I do, Your Honour, and thank you for allowing me to proceed. Mr. Kingsley, let me rephrase my question. Have you ever seen Mr. Howard Stillwater become angry with his stepsister, Bethany?"

"I have, sir, and quite recently, in fact."

"Please tell the court what you saw and heard."

"Well, I was at my station in the front hall of Stillwater Estate when Mr. Stillwater came calling on Miss Bethany. He came often, but more frequently in the past few months."

"Why was he calling?"

"He came to get money from her."

"Money? I understood they paid him a good wage to be the manager of the estate. What other money was he asking for?"

"Money to look after his household expenses; to look after the missus and the children properly."

"And did Miss Stillwater give him what he asked for?"

"Prior to this last occasion, yes. She was always looking out for her sister-in-law and nephews. She did not want them suffering, so she would give Howard the money he requested."

"That was very generous of her, considering he had no stake in the estate."

"Yes, and she felt badly about that as well."

"But not enough to give him a share of the estate."

"No, she felt that the estate was better handled as a whole, and she wanted to keep it running smoothly as a legacy to her parents."

"Any other reason?"

"Well, uh, she was starting to hear rumours, whenever she came to the city, that Howard was running up some very extensive gambling debts with some unsavoury characters. She wondered if the money she was giving him was going to pay off his debts rather than pay living expenses for the family. That she would not condone. So, the next time, the last time he came to the estate looking for money, she confirmed her suspicions and refused him any more cash handouts."

"That must have made him angry."

"More than angry, Mr. Damon. He was furious. I thought he was going to strike her, but instead he came up, nose-to-nose with her and said, 'You will regret this action, Bethany. I guarantee it. When I have full control of your late mother's land, I will sell it from underneath you and use the profits for my own gain and happiness.

You have crossed me to your detriment, dear sister, and nothing can save you now. I will leave now, but soon you will pay the price for what you have done.' Those were his exact words, Mr. Damon."

"That sounds rather like a threat, Mr. Kingsley. Then what happened?"

"Miss Bethany showed him the door, and I shoved him through it, making sure it hit him on the backside when he left." Kingsley chuckled at the memory.

Keeping a straight face when he would rather have laughed at the image, Steven said, "Did you have further encounters with him after that day?"

"No, not until I saw him come in here this morning, dressed like a peacock. He sure suits his middle name, doesn't he?"

The crowd laughed until the judge slammed down his gavel and said, "Order, order, in the courtroom."

"Mr. Kingsley, as a trusted long-time employee of Stillwater Estate, did you ever hear Mr. Stillwater, Bethany's father, talk about willing the estate to Howard?"

"No, sir, I did not, and I was privy to many conversations in that household. They knew me and my missus were devoted to them and that we would never gossip about what we heard. No, Mr. Stillwater, even though he remarried soon after his wife's passing, was only interested in getting a mother for Miss Bethany, not another wife. And he had no intention of passing the estate over to Mr. Howard. It was Miss Bethany's legacy, and her father kept it for her."

"Thank you for your time, Mr. Kingsley, and perhaps someday soon I will make it out to Stillwater Estate to sample your wife's cookies."

"Anytime, Mr. Damon, you can come any time you wish to. You will always be welcome."

"Thank you." Turning towards the judge, Steven said, "I have no further questions for this witness, Your Honour."

"Very well. Mr. Walden?"

"Not at this time, Your Honour."

"Very well. You may step down, Mr. Kingsley."

"Thank you, Your Honour," he said, before leaving the witness stand and going back to his seat beside his wife.

"Your next witness, Mr. Damon, please?"

"Thank you, Your Honour. I would like to call Mrs. Harriet Hayward to the stand at this time."

Harriet got up from her seat and walked over to the witness stand, while the crowd whispered amongst themselves. "Isn't that the vicar's wife? Why is she a witness at the trial?" The questions buzzed around the courtroom until Harriet walked into the witness stand and was sworn in by the bailiff.

He asked for her full name, and she said, "Mrs. Harriet Ann Hayward."

The bailiff stepped away from the witness stand and Steven came forward. "Good afternoon, Mrs. Hayward. How are you today?"

"Fine, thank you, sir. And you?"

"Very well. Thank you for coming to testify on Miss Stillwater's behalf."

"Thank you for asking it of me, Mr. Damon. It is my Christian duty and my care for a dear friend that brings me here today."

"I only wish there were more Christian women like you in our society, who would put themselves out for others," said Steven, digging at the consciences of the women in the room who had refused to testify for Bethany.

"Now, Mrs. Hayward, would you state your occupation for the court's records?"

"Certainly. I am the wife of a local vicar, and a homemaker."

"And you said you are a dear friend of the defendant, Bethany Stillwater. How do you know her?"

"Bethany attends our church, and we are also involved together on many charitable committees."

"I see. Have you known her long, Mrs. Hayward?"

"As a young woman involved in the community, no, only for the last year or so. But before that she attended church with her father and stepmother. I did not know her mother; she died before my husband took over this parish."

"How would you describe Miss Stillwater?"

"A beautiful young woman with a heart of gold, Mr. Damon."

"That is quite a commendation. Has she no flaws?"

"As Mr. Kingsley previously alluded to, a taste for fresh-baked cookies. At our meetings, I have seen her take more than one or two for tea." Harriet laughed.

Damon smiled. "I also tend to overindulge when the temptation is in front of me, Mrs. Hayward. But . . . have you ever seen Miss Stillwater commit a crime, or in the words of the Bible, sin?"

"She is only human, Mr. Damon, as we all are. None of us are perfect. So, occasionally, I have seen Bethany lose her temper, but it is usually at the injustices we see around us."

"In relation to what they charge her with, Mrs. Hayward, could you ever see her doing such a thing?"

"Objection, Your Honour," called Frank. "Mr. Damon is leading the witness."

"Sustained. Mr. Damon, you will rephrase your question."

"Yes, Your Honour. Mrs. Hayward, let me put it to you in another way. Would Miss Stillwater have the means to purchase her own sapphire necklace, if she wanted one for an event, rather than steal one from her sister-in-law?"

"Yes, Mr. Damon. Her father left her well-off, and she also has the profits from the estate. She would never have to steal a necklace from anyone. Bethany, unlike most young ladies in society, seldom buys anything new for herself. Why, the blue gown she was wearing on the night of the gala has served that purpose for the past few years, ever since she was a debutante. For that ball, she had to wear a white gown, but since then she only wears her old blue one. She sees no reason to buy another while one is still serviceable. I expect now she will though, after where she has been in the past few weeks, poor dear. No, Bethany would rather give her money away to those who need it than to spend it on fripperies such as gowns and jewellery. I know for a fact, being the treasurer on many committees with her, she will top up funds with her own money to meet the needs of those we are working for, just to make sure we meet our goal for that project. Is that the action of a young woman who would steal another's necklace? I think not."

"Thank you, Mrs. Hayward. I have no further questions for you at this time."

"Your witness, Mr. Walden."

"Thank you, Your Honour," said Frank, passing Steven on his way to the witness stand. "Made her out to be a paragon of virtue, Damon. Nice work," he sneered.

Upon reaching the witness stand, Frank dived right in with no pleasantries. "Mrs. Hayward, you have painted quite a pretty picture of Miss Stillwater, almost saintly. I commend the artistry of your words. But you mentioned that Miss Stillwater had quite a temper, which Mr. Damon passed by on. I would like to explore that not so virtuous trait of Miss Stillwater's with you. Please tell the court of her temper tantrums and who were the unlucky victims of her wrath."

"I did not say—"

"Ah, but you did, Mrs. Hayward. Clerk, please read back Mrs. Hayward's comment about Miss Stillwater's temper."

The clerk read, "'So, occasionally, I have seen Bethany lose her temper . . .'"

"Thank you, that will be all, clerk. Those were your own words, Mrs. Hayward, were they not?"

"Yes, but—"

"Please answer the question only, Mrs. Hayward."

"Yes."

"So we have established that Miss Stillwater has a temper and lashes out at people. Am I correct?"

"Occasionally."

"And perhaps on this recent occasion, instead of berating poor Mrs. Stillwater for spending money on—what did you call it, fripperies such as jewellery, instead of buying food and clothing for her sons, Miss Stillwater stole the necklace so she could pawn it and purchase household necessities for the family. Would she rather see food on their table than a valuable necklace around Mrs. Stillwater's neck?"

"Of course she would, but—"

"And perhaps at the gala she was flaunting the necklace in front of everyone to disgrace her poor sister-in-law and brother, with whom she has a poor relationship."

"No, Bethany would never—"

"And did her butler not testify she humiliated her stepbrother by having him kicked out of the house just for asking for money to feed his family?"

"Objection, Your Honour," called Steven. "Mr. Walden is making a supposition."

"Sustained. Mr. Walden, please refrain from using such speculations. Stick to the facts."

"Yes, Your Honour. Mrs. Hayward, did Mr. Kingsley not say that he pushed Mr. Stillwater out of the manor after Miss Stillwater became angry and told him to leave."

"Yes."

"Then the picture you paint of a lovely young woman with no flaws is incorrect, is it not, Mrs. Hayward?"

"I did not say—"

"Please answer the question, Mrs. Hayward."

"Yes."

"No further questions, Your Honour."

"Mr. Damon, do you wish to re-examine the witness?"

"Not at this time, Your Honour."

"Mrs. Hayward, you may step down. Your next witness, Mr. Damon?"

"I have no one, Your Honour."

"Mr. Walden?"

"None, Your Honour."

"Very well. This court will recess until nine o'clock tomorrow, at which time Mr. Walden and Mr. Damon may call their last witnesses or re-examine those who have testified today. If there are no further testimonies, I will retire to my chambers and bring back a verdict. Court dismissed." The judge rose, as did the audience, and after he had left the room, the courtroom started to clear of spectators.

Hearing Mrs. Hayward softly weeping behind him, Steven turned and said, "You did well, Mrs. Hayward. Don't worry about what you said. Mr. Walden just manipulated your testimony into something it was not. That is what he does. It is not your fault."

"But what if I ruined Bethany's chances for freedom, Mr. Damon? What then? I feel terrible about what just happened."

"If we do not get the result we are looking for, Mrs. Hayward, I will immediately appeal the verdict. But we still have a chance of turning things around. Mr. Brown and I need to confer for the rest of the day on how to proceed now. Please keep up hope and keep praying. That is my request for all of you," he said, looking at both the Haywards and the Kingsleys. "God is on our side. I know He is."

After thanking Mr. Damon for all his hard work to date, the couples got up and left the courtroom. Steven and Mr. Brown started gathering up their notes when a voice from across the aisle said, "Good day, wasn't it, gentlemen? Pity your last witness fell apart under my cross-examination, Damon. Perhaps you should have prepared her better as to what to expect today. But therein lies the problem, does it not? You are relying on the truth being told and the judge buying into your fairy tales, while I dig below the surface for the facts. And the fact is, Damon, your client is going down.

Hope you bring a large handkerchief tomorrow to contain your tears of defeat. You are going to need it." Walden laughed.

"Your version of the facts is altered, Walden. Even if I lose the case tomorrow, I will never stoop to your level of twisting the truth. Never. I don't know how you can sleep at night after doing what I just saw. I pity you, sir, and we will see who comes out on top tomorrow. Good day to you."

"Ah, such piety. No wonder you enlisted the aid of a vicar and his wife. Too bad your strategy did not work, Damon. I look forward to seeing your face when the judge pronounces your client guilty tomorrow and ships her off to prison. Until then, have a good night." He and Howard walked out of the courtroom.

Steven sank back in his chair. "What did I do wrong, Mr. Brown? I thought the witness of Mr. Kingsley and Mrs. Hayward would turn the tide, but now I am not so sure. We are facing an uphill battle tomorrow to win Miss Stillwater's freedom. So, let's get at it. At my office or a coffeehouse?"

"A coffeehouse, Mr. Damon. You look like you need a cup. Remember, all is not lost. God is still on our side. Right?"

"Right. Thank you for reminding me. Let's go get that coffee and strategize."

The men gathered up the remaining papers and left the building.

***

After the judge left the courtroom, Bethany left as well and went back to Millbank for the night. After a meagre supper of watery soup and a slice of dry bread, she curled up on her cot and began to review the day's proceedings. Earlier she had thought the judge would choose in her favour after Mr. Kingsley and Mrs. Hayward's testimonies. But now, after Mr. Walden twisted Mrs. Hayward's testimony around, Bethany did not know what to think. She had glanced over at Mr. Damon while Mrs. Hayward was being cross-examined, but she could not tell from his face whether he was worried about her cross-examination. He maintained a slight smile throughout the day's proceedings, even when Mr. Walden was questioning Mrs. Hayward. Would Mr. Damon put her on the stand tomorrow so she could tell the court the truth about Cassandra's necklace? If so, she was sure Mr. Walden would cross-examine her and twist her words, just as he had Mrs. Hayward's today. Was she strong enough to bear through such an ordeal? She did not know. She only knew she had the best barrister defending her and that God was on her side. Wasn't He? She was beginning to wonder about His faithfulness to her . . .

***

The next morning, they packed the courtroom to capacity and beyond. People were almost sitting on top of each other on the benches, while they filled the side aisles of the lower room with standing bodies. The gallery also was overcrowded; they filled every inch of space with a human body. Obviously, the word had gone out after yesterday's spectacle, and everyone who was anybody in the city wanted to see what was going to happen next. Most of those who had come were secretly rooting for Bethany, but others, not because they were fans of Howard's, but because of his outrageous demeanour and dress, were rooting for the other Stillwaters. Whoever they came to support, it did not matter. They were there for the event, and there was a party atmosphere about it.

Even the chairs for the prosecutors and the defence team were not off limits. The bailiff caught one man trying to carry away a chair from the prosecutor's table; he forced him to put it back. Steven and Mr. Brown arrived early enough to secure their chairs, but the bench behind them started filling up with spectators as well, until the bailiff cleared them away, too. Soon, there was no room left in the courtroom, neither upstairs nor down, so the guards at the door started refusing entry to anyone they recognised neither as a witness nor a member of the prosecutor's team. Frank, Howard, and Cassandra had to fight their way through the crowds to gain entrance to the courtroom, as did the Haywards and the Kingsleys. As they slid into their assigned seats, leaving space available at the other end of the bench, spectators tried to squeeze their way into those spots. After discussing the situation with both Mr. Damon and Mr. Walden, who both said they had no more witnesses arriving to testify, some spectators were allowed to sit down on the benches. Cassandra clung to her side of the bench. After what she had experienced when she left the courtroom yesterday, she did not want anyone near her.

At the end of yesterday's session, she had waited for Howard and Frank in the courthouse's hallway. When they appeared, Howard had surprised her by asking if she would like to dine out with him before they went home. Suspicious of his motives, but not having any reason to say no, she had agreed, and they had a spent a surprisingly pleasant time together. But when she arrived home, she found the reason for Howard's invitation. The boys were gone. She found out that Frank had taken the boys to his home for the night, even though they had not wanted to go. The cook was crying and wringing her hands when Howard and Cassandra got home. She told them she had tried to stop Mr. Walden, but to no avail. He had picked up the two youngest boys, Arthur and Calvin, under his arms and carried them out to his carriage. The older boys had gone with him to protect their younger brothers from danger. Frank told the cook his staff would look after the boys well, and as Mr. and Mrs. Stillwater were dining out, she now had the evening off. Then he had jumped into the carriage and left with the boys.

Cassandra would have been frantic too, except for a soft word from Howard. He told her this was her punishment for failing to do her duty at the courtroom that day, and a taste of what would happen if she was not more obedient the next day in court. The delicious food almost came back up in Cassandra's throat, and she ran upstairs to her bedroom, shutting and locking the door behind her, before throwing herself on her bed in despair. There was nothing she could do that night for her sons, but tomorrow she would obey Howard and Frank to the nth degree. She would do it for her sons; they were what she lived for, nothing more.

So, here she was again, huddled into a corner of the witness bench, looking down at the floor and wishing she had never even heard of Howard Peabody Stillwater, much less married him. But then she would not have her wonderful boys, whom she adored. Life was so confusing. She hoped today's session would be quickly over so she could go home to her sons and never venture out again. She prayed she would not be called back to the witness stand, but if she was, she would follow the exact guidance of the men seated in front of her. It was her only hope to keep her boys.

***

Mr. Damon and Mr. Brown, after deliberations that went far into the night, decided not to recall either of their witnesses to the stand. They discussed putting Bethany on the stand in her own defence but decided against that as well. If Frank called her to the stand, they would certainly cross-examine her, but Steven doubted he would. Frank was looking very smug as he sat behind the prosecutor's table, as if he had already won the case. Howard was also looking smug in his bright costume of the day, a silky white shirt, accompanied by a bright blue vest and covered by a scarlet coat. It almost hurt Steven's eyes to look at him.

The judge's door opened, and the bailiff called out, "All rise, Judge Owen Henley presiding."

When he had gained his high seat, the judge sat down, and everyone in the room followed suit. He said, "Before we get started this morning, I want to warn both Mr. Walden and Mr. Damon that I am not in the mood for any theatrics this morning. Please keep to the facts and do not harass the witnesses. Do you understand me? Mr. Walden?"

"Yes, Your Honour."

"Mr. Damon?"

"Yes, Your Honour."

"Very good. If either of you deviates from this manner, you may be removed, and I will adjourn this trial until we can replace you. Now, let us begin. Mr. Walden, do you wish to call any further witnesses to the stand?"

"No, Your Honour, I do not."

"Very well. And Mr. Damon?"

"No, Your Honour."

"If no more witnesses are to be called, this should shorten our day considerably. Guard, please take Miss Stillwater back to her holding cell and I will retire to my chambers to consider this case. I will return later with a verdict." He got up and left the courtroom.

Bethany, who had just barely sat down, arose and, after they released the chain to the chair, walked back with her guard to the cell in the holding area. There, she was secured to contemplate her uncertain future. Her hands shaking, Bethany wondered if this was a good sign or a bad one, that neither the prosecutor nor the defence team were calling more witnesses? She did not know. When Mr. Damon did not come into the holding area to speak with her, she knew her answers would only come when the judge returned his verdict. Again, she wondered . . . if the judge took a long time deliberating over his verdict, was that a good sign or a bad one, but if he came back into the courtroom quickly . . .? She did not have to wait long for her answer. She heard the bailiff cry, "All rise. Judge Owen Henley presiding." The warder came over and unlocked the cell door. "It's time, Miss. Time to learn your fate." Then she motioned Bethany to precede her through the door and back into the prisoner's box, where she immediately resumed her seat.

"Will the prisoner please rise?" asked the bailiff.

Bethany did so, but she could barely stand with the sudden weakness in her legs.

The room was quiet as the judge turned to her.

Chapter 4

"Guilty! Bethany Anne Stillwater, you have been found guilty of the charge of theft over £100 sterling. I hereby sentence you to be transported to the colony of Western Australia to serve seven years of prison time in the Fremantle Gaol. You will be held in the custody of the British people and their beloved Queen Victoria until such a time as a ship transports you there. You are also immediately relieved of any properties that you own in England; they will forthwith be under the custodianship of your brother, Howard Stillwater, while you are serving your sentence. When you return to England upon the completion of your sentence, the court will decide at that time if the properties should be returned to you or permanently be given over to Mr. Stillwater. Do you have anything further you wish to say to this court before we take you back to your cell?"

Bethany shook her head, but she was not aware of doing so. The lights of the courtroom faded to pinpricks; the noise became a distant hum. Until . . .

The judge slammed his gavel down on his desk and declared the court dismissed.

Bethany jumped, then looked up and over at the courtroom spectators. She tried to catch the eye of her sister-in-law, but Cassandra turned away. Instead, Bethany saw Howard approaching her box. He got close enough to say in a low voice, "I told you things were going to happen to you if you did not give me money when I asked for it, dear sister. Now I am in control of the estate, and you will never see your dear home again. Enjoy your incarceration, Bethany. It may be the last home you ever have."

"Haven't you done enough, Howard?" she asked, glaring at him. "You and I both know I am innocent of this crime. I don't know what you said to Cassandra to make her lie on the witness stand, but it must have been something dreadful. Rest assured, Howard, I will survive this incarceration, and I will be back to recompense you for what you have done. In the meantime, dear brother, you might want to confess your sins to God and repent of them. Otherwise you are destined for an eternity of paying for them."

"Tsk, tsk . . . your temper is showing, Bethany," mocked Howard. "Heaven and hell are just myths. There is no reality but the life we live on earth. And after that . . . poof, we're gone. Now, I intend to enjoy my life, and the money from the estate once I have sold it. There is nothing you can do to stop me. So, until, or if, we ever meet again, dear sister, have a wonderful life." He turned and walked away.

Then a hand came down on her shoulder, and she looked up into the face of her guard. "Get up, girlie," she said, not unkindly. "It's time for you to go back to your cell."

Bethany rose, the chains around her ankles clanging as she started shuffling towards the door that led back to her prison cell. Her trial was over, and her nightmare was only beginning.

***

When the judge pronounced his verdict, Steven could not believe his ears. Guilty, and to be transported to a colony prison for seven years? He had mentally braced himself for bad news, but this was worse than he could ever have imagined. He had failed her and failed her badly. What must she be thinking of him right now? He looked up at the prisoner's box and saw her sitting there with her head hung low, her eyes on the floor. He needed to reassure her in some way that this was not over; the sentence would be appealed, and she would be free before the ship left for Australia. Yes, that is what he would tell her. He just needed to compose himself before going round to speak with her.

Steven looked over at Mr. Brown. The poor man was shaking. He had his elbows on the table and his head down in his hands. Was he weeping? Steven wanted to, but he was not going to satisfy Frank with such a display of emotion. Instead, he put his hand onto Mr. Brown's back and said, "I'm sorry, Mr. Brown. You were counting on me to free her, and I've let both of you down. I will start the appeal process immediately."

Mr. Brown looked up at Steven. "It is not your fault, young man. You did your best. No, God has a plan in all of this, and even though we do not know what it is, He is still in control. I believe that."

"I hope Miss Stillwater feels the same way. If I were in her shoes right now, I am afraid I would have trouble trusting in God's goodness to me."

"She may not see His goodness right now, but knowing Bethany as I do, she will come around to it eventually. She is a faithful follower of Christ and has been all her life."

"I hope you are right, because she has just received the worst news of her young life."

"Yes, but you, too, can give her hope. Just as you said, you can start the appeal process right away, so she never leaves these shores as a prisoner."

"Perhaps we should give her a few minutes before we go and see her, Mr. Brown."

"Not too long. I see Howard heading over there now. I am sure he is gloating over his victory. She will need support from us soon."

"You are right. Let's go around back into the holding cell area to await her arrival."

"Good idea," said the older man, gathering up the papers to prepare for leaving the table.

"Leaving without saying congratulations and good day, Mr. Damon?" said a familiar voice from beside them. "Rather uncivil of you, is it not?"

"Congratulations, and good day to you, sir. There, that is all I have to say to you. Now, if you will excuse me," said Steven, trying to get past him.

"What is your hurry? She is not going anywhere, at least not for a while. And then it will be *bon voyage, Miss Stillwater.*"

"She will be back, Walden. Eventually, she will return. And if you are still in the land of the living, both you and Howard will get your comeuppance. I guarantee it."

"Well, I will have almost a decade before that occurs. A lot can happen in those years. So, I won't lose any sleep worrying about it."

"You may not worry about her, but you should worry about me. I am going to keep a close eye on you and your law practice. The law society has been hearing rumours about your questionable activities, both within your practice and outside of it. You know they do not condone any illicit activities by their members. Once they find you out, and they will soon, you will be disbarred, and I will gladly watch the society do it. So, be aware, you are under my surveillance from this day forward."

Frank's hands shook a bit at this pronouncement, so he stuck them behind him. He knew just what Damon was alluding to and it worried him that the law society was watching him. Without his practice, he would have nothing, nothing to live on, and nothing to gamble with. He needed to watch his step. But today was his day, not Damon's, so he said, "I'll look forward to seeing you about town then, Damon. But ten years from now, I will still be practicing law. I wonder where you will be after this fiasco of a performance. Good day, sir, and best of luck in the future. You'll be needing it." He turned away and allowed Steven and Mr. Brown to brush past him on their way to the doors of the courtroom.

***

Steven and Mr. Brown made their way through the back hallways of the courthouse until they came to the door of the holding area. The guard recognized them as Miss Stillwater's defence team and let them into the room. Bethany was back in her cell, waiting for transportation back to Millbank. Upon seeing them enter, she stood up and came forward to the bars of the cell.

"Miss Stillwater," said Steven, rushing forward to grasp her hands through the bars. "I am so, so sorry. I do not know what else to say."

"What happened, Mr. Damon?" cried Bethany. "What went wrong? Please tell me why I am going to prison when I thought I would be going home today. Why? Why? Why?"

"I erred, Miss Stillwater. I should have prepared a better defence for you. And I should have re-examined Mrs. Hayward to refute how Mr. Walden misled the judge. It is all my fault. Please forgive me."

"I am frankly not in a very forgiving mood right now. Perhaps later, but not now. Mr. Brown assured me you were the best and I counted on you. Now I wonder if I made a good decision when hiring you. Perhaps you were just too young and inexperienced to handle my case. I don't know. I can't think straight. Maybe later, when I am back in my cell awaiting my lovely dinner of soup and bread, I will have kinder thoughts of you. But as of this moment—"

"Bethany," interjected Edwin Brown. "This was not Mr. Damon's fault. We did not have enough time to prepare properly for your defence. Mr. Walden manipulated the court clerk into scheduling your trial before we were ready. If anyone is to blame, it is him, not us."

"Regardless of who is to blame, the judgment has been made and I am now a convicted felon. My reputation in this city is in tatters and my work with all the destitute women will fall by the wayside. Everything I have ever done for good is gone. I am no longer a citizen of London, only a prisoner of the glorious empire."

"Miss Stillwater," said Steven, "that is not true."

"Is it not? After this, will the women of society still meet with me to further good works in the city? I think not. Instead, I will be shunned, if I ever return home, and my place in society will be no more."

"I will start an appeal—"

"For what purpose? No, let me be. Do no further work on my behalf, Mr. Damon. I am done."

"You would rather they send you away than have me file an appeal?"

"I don't know. In fact, I am so weary that I am not sure of anything right now, except for this one thing. Mr. Brown," she said, turning to him. "I am afraid of what Howard will do now that he has control of the estate. Is there anything we can do to stop him from selling it?"

"Yes, he is only the custodian until you return, dear lady. He has certain privileges, but he cannot dispose of the estate."

"That is good news. Will you be staying on as solicitor for the estate?"

"Only if Mr. Howard retains me, Miss Bethany. He may look for another solicitor, knowing how close I am to you."

"I hope not. You are the only one standing now between the estate and disaster."

"I will do my best to convince him to continue retaining me. But it is his right to have a solicitor of his choice."

"What about my staff? The Kingsleys, for example. Can he discharge them?"

"They are safe, Miss, but maybe not some of the other staff. The Kingsleys are part of the estate, and as such cannot be let go. Howard will probably keep the other staff as well, as he has no quarrel with any of them. I am sure he does not plan to live a country life, so he needs good staff out there to continue bringing in a good income for him."

"I just hope he does not make life miserable for them now, after Kingsley testified against him in court."

"Don't worry. They can take care of themselves."

"I am sure they can, but this whole unfortunate situation falls heavily on my shoulders."

"Now, none of that, Miss Stillwater. You are not to blame for any of this. It is all the Stillwaters' fault, and we need to keep that in mind, no matter what the court has said."

"I'll try, Mr. Damon. And you, my dear friend, Mr. Brown. I do not know what I would have done without you these past few weeks. Now I see by the guard's motions that my carriage has arrived." She laughed at the thought; the prison wagon was not a well sprung carriage, but it was something she would have to get used to. "So, gentlemen, good day for now. You know my address." She laughed again. "You must take your leave of me so I can go back to Millbank."

With sad faces they tipped their hats to her, promising to visit soon, and then left. The guard opened the cell door, and after securing Bethany's wrist and ankle shackles, she led her out to the waiting prison wagon. Once Bethany was inside the wagon, she sat down on the hard wooden bench and braced herself for the horses to start moving. They did with a sudden jerk, and then the ride was smoother, although she felt every rough track and pothole in the streets they passed through. After a long ride, they arrived back at Millbank. To her surprise, the warder led her to a different cell than her previous one. She was told this was because she was now a convicted criminal awaiting transport to the colonies. As before, they gave her a gown with a number on it, by which she would now be identified. She moved into the cell and the warder locked the door behind her. Bethany collapsed on her cot, the tears flowing freely down her face. She muffled her sobs in the blanket and cried herself to sleep.

***

During the next days of her stay at Millbank Penitentiary, Bethany became acquainted with the women in her cell block, all of whom would be transported with her to Fremantle Gaol, in the Territory of Western Australia. Her face paled as she learned the age variation of her fellow inmates; they ranged in age from Susie, who was only fourteen years of age, to Clara, seventy years old. But many of their stories were the same. They had been arrested, like Bethany, on charges of theft, but their only crimes were that they, or their families, were starving, and they had taken a loaf of bread, or an apple, to feed them. Susie said she had been looking for food for her younger brother when the bobby had arrested her. She had seen a loaf of bread drop off the baker's cart onto the street and she had picked it up, knowing if she did not take it, the rats would come out of their hiding spots and snatch it. But the baker did not believe her story and called for a bobby. He had taken her immediately to the station, and she had been tried and convicted soon after that. Her biggest worry was for her brother; how would he survive without her? Other stories were very similar to Susie's, so the women shuddered at Bethany's tale. But they all had one thing in common: they were going to Australia.

***

Steven had tried, without success, to launch an appeal for Bethany's freedom. But bad luck, or Frank Walden, was always a step ahead of him. He could not find a judge in the entirety of London who would hear Bethany's appeal. Steven vowed to never give up, even if Bethany left for Australia. Someday he would free her. On his frequent visits to Millbank, he always reminded her of his promise. Although she had forgiven him for not being able to secure her freedom, she doubted his word. She would not trust him fully again.

And then it came. The news they had all been dreading. Their transportation would begin the next day with a wagon trip to Portsmouth, where they would board a ship for their final destination, the Colony of Australia. The journey would begin at dawn and end at dusk. There would only be a couple of stops along the way to change horses and allow the prisoners to take care of their personal needs. They would eat their meals as they travelled, so as not to lose any time with breaking for meals. The women heard the news with both fear and some excitement. The law had confined them in Millbank for the past few months and now they would have fresh air for more than just an hour a day, or so they thought. Little did they know what life about the convict ship would contain for them. That last night, the warders gave them pieces of parchment and quills with ink to write their last notes to their loved ones. Bethany sat down and penned notes to both the Kingsleys and the Haywards, thanking them again for their support at her trial, while letting them know she would keep them forever in her heart. She also sent quick notes to both Mr. Damon and Mr. Brown to let them know of her imminent departure. Once her notes were done and given to the warder, she helped other women—many who could neither read nor write—compose their own notes to family and friends. After they sent the notes off, the women washed each other's hair with a bit of lye soap and water. While the hair was still wet, it was cut again. Bethany cringed to see how much fell to the floor at her feet. Her hair had grown long enough that she could braid it once more, but now it was back to chin length. Just another painful reminder that she was no longer in control of her life. And then they registered for the journey. Bethany received another shock. Her name had been changed. She was now Mary Worthless, no longer Bethany Stillwater.

She questioned the warder about the change, who said she did not know anything about it. All she knew was that Bethany was now Mary, and that was how she would be registered on the ship's log. None of the other women had had their names changed, so Bethany knew it had to have been Howard who'd instituted the change and given her such a ridiculous name. When she got to Fremantle, she would see if she could not get her real name back, but until then she would go along with it. Finally, each woman was given an old, but clean, shawl. They would need to use it as their blanket on board the ship and any other time they were feeling cold. Bethany's shawl matched her gown; it was a muddy brown colour and showed signs of wear among the weaves. But it was a shawl and would serve its purpose for the voyage. Her days of clean dresses and new shawls were behind her. For the next seven years her scant wardrobe would consist of a prison uniform.

The next morning, the women were shackled and chained to each other before being loaded into a prison wagon that would take them to Portsmouth. Susie was just behind Bethany in the line-up. Bethany was thankful for that. She had taken a liking to young Susie and almost felt like her mother, even though their ages were not far apart. Susie, too, seemed to appreciate Bethany, and often sought her out in the prison yard while they were there for their daily exercise. It was nice to have company, even in such surroundings. Once the women were all loaded into the wagon and seated, the driver flicked the reins and their long day began.

**

It was a horrible day of travel. The road was rough and full of pot-holes, so the women were constantly bouncing up and down on the benches. They tried to pad their seats with their folded shawls, but that only provided minimal relief. Some of them sat down on the floor to see if that would relieve the jarring of their backs, but they had little success. Each time they stopped for a break, the women piled out of the wagon, not only to relieve themselves but also to stretch their weary backs. And then it was back into the wagon for several more hours of agony before they reached their next stop. Finally, as daylight faded, they started smelling salty air; their destination was close at hand. Whatever lay ahead could not be any worse than the day they had just experienced. Could it?

They arrived at Portsmouth harbour and were unloaded onto the pier, along with a wagon filled with male convicts. The women were told to wait until the men entered the hold of the ship. Any other passengers, who were not convicts, had cabins on the deck near the captain's cabin. It was very unusual for passengers to book themselves on a convict ship. Some did, either because it was cheaper than a passenger ship, or they needed to head to the Colony now and there were no passenger ships available. When it was time for the women to board, Bethany glanced up and saw the profile of a man in gentleman's attire. He almost looked like . . . but no, it could not be. He would not be travelling all the way to Australia on a prison ship. No, she must be mistaken. The man could not have been Samuel Yardley, the second son of the Duke of Yardley. It could not be him. Then she and the other women headed down the stairs towards the steerage compartment, and he was lost to sight.

***

Samuel Edward Yardley was indeed standing in the cockpit when Bethany boarded the ship. He was heading south to Australia on business reasons. The male members of the Yardley family had returned from Scotland a short time ago, but Sam was eager to find some Australian wool to ship back to his family's mills. This wool, combined with Scotland's finest, would create beautiful fibres for weaving into blankets and garments. He'd had a swift turnaround before boarding this ship, the only one leaving for Australia for months to come. So, forgoing the comforts of a real passenger ship, he booked a berth on this ship. Having arrived earlier that day by train, he had already stowed his gear and now stood with the captain in the cockpit to view the convicts being loaded on board. He wondered how many of them would survive the trip. The captain said the men would go down into the hold for the journey and the women would live in steerage. Sam had explored ships in the past and knew both areas of a ship. Neither one was suitable for an ocean voyage, especially the hold, but these were convicts, and to some they were now considered less than human beings. Sam did not hold that view, but he stood in silence as they herded them on board like cattle. One woman caught his eye. Her prison gown, hanging loosely on her frail body, was drab brown. Her raggedly cut hair lay limp against her scalp. She looked just like the rest of the women, wrapped in an old woollen shawl, her feet clad in a pair of loose, floppy, brown shoes, except for one thing. She did not walk like them. Holding her head high, she looked straight ahead instead of down at her feet. At one point, when Sam turned to speak to the captain, he saw her glance up, but when he looked back down at her again, she had averted her gaze again. He wondered who she was, and if he had seen her before this day. Perhaps he would get a chance to find out during the long voyage, but even if he did not, it would help to pass his days. There was plenty of time to search out the mystery to this woman. Now it was time to go to his cabin and prepare to be away from home for many months to come.

**

Sam's mother was dealing with her conscience while Bethany and Sam were settling into their respective bunks on the ship. The duchess was reminded of Bethany Stillwater's trial a few months prior, knowing that Sam was sailing on a convict ship. Would she be on the same ship as Samuel? If she was, would there be a chance that they would meet and Sam would find out why she was a prisoner of the Crown? How would he feel if he found out that she, his mother, had been at the event when Bethany was arrested and had done nothing to change Bethany's fate? The duchess feared her son would be very disappointed in her. He was a champion of the lowly and oppressed and never failed to step in to right a wrong if he could. But what could she do now? The verdict was in, and Bethany, if she was not already on her way to the colonies, was sure to leave soon. Her hands were tied, were they not? Perhaps she had been remiss in not informing her husband about the trial, and the resulting conviction of Miss Stillwater, when he and his sons had returned from Scotland. If there was anyone in London who could wield influence and make sure that justice had been served, it was the Duke of Yardley. Yes, she would speak with him this evening, confess her sin of omitting to aid Miss Stillwater in her time of trouble, and then discuss what steps they could now take on her behalf. But in the meantime, she would also do something she rarely did: she would get personally involved in the charities that Bethany had left behind. Sometimes one had to get their hands dirty, and not just fund projects for the poor and needy. That was what Bethany was best known for: meeting, and helping, the impoverished women of London. Without her at the helm of her committee, things might flounder, and the women would miss out on the necessities of life. But who to contact? Then the duchess remembered the vicar's wife, Harriet Hayward. She knew Mrs. Hayward had worked closely with Bethany and her charities. She would know how the duchess could get involved with their causes. Having that thought, the duchess went to her desk and penned a note of invitation to Mrs. Hayward, to come for tea at her townhouse the very next afternoon.

Within a few hours of sending the invitation, the duchess received a reply. It stated that Harriet Hayward would be pleased to come for tea the next day, and that she looked forward to her visit with the duchess. With that project now underway, the duchess geared up to speak with her husband that evening about Bethany's trial. Having sought God's forgiveness as well for her omission, she was ready to move on and serve Him and His people in a more satisfactory way.

The next day, at precisely three o'clock, Harriet Hayward arrived at the townhouse. Although a bit unsettled by the invitation, having only known the duchess from church services, it pleased her that the duchess was looking for a way to assist the committee with their work. Since Bethany's trial and conviction, they had done nothing for the destitute women of the city. The other women who served on the committee had come up with various excuses why they could not continue to work with Mrs. Hayward. Harriet knew it was just a matter of pride. They did not want to continue being associated with a cause that a convicted criminal, even in her absence, had championed. The duchess had always been generous in her monetary contributions to the charity, but never served on the committee. Was she having a change of heart or was she only going to hand over a check to Harriet today? Harriet knew she would not find the answer standing on the doorstep, so she reached up and tapped three times with the ornate door knocker.

Almost instantly, a man in black and white livery opened the door. "Yes?" he said.

"Good afternoon. I am Mrs. Harriet Hayward. I am here to see the duchess."

"Oh, yes, Mrs. Hayward. The duchess is expecting you. Please come in." The man then stepped aside so Harriet could pass through the doorway and into the foyer.

"If you would like to take a seat." He gestured to a chair just off to Harriet's right. "I will tell the duchess you have arrived."

Thanking him, Harriet sat down and gazed around at the paintings on the walls. Some were from the great masters, but others appeared to be portraits from years ago, probably of former Dukes and Duchesses of Yardley. Although the title was relatively new, only a century or so, they could trace the family name back for hundreds of years. It was an old and distinguished family.

Soon the gentleman was back and escorted her to a cosy room filled with sunlight. The duchess was already seated in a chair beside a small table loaded with delicacies and a pot of steaming tea. When she saw Harriet, she got up and came across the room. "Thank you for coming, Mrs. Hayward. I am delighted you could make it on such short notice. Please, come in and have a seat," she said, indicating a chair on the other side of the table.

"Thank you, Your Grace. It is a great pleasure for me as well," said Harriet, dipping a small curtsey before seating herself at the table.

"It is long overdue. I apologise for my tardiness in not having you over for tea before today. Jasper," she said, turning to the gentleman who hovered in the doorway. "That will be all for now. We will serve ourselves, thank you."

"Very good, ma'am." The liveried gentleman turned around and left the two ladies alone.

"Now we can be private," said the duchess. "Not that I worry about my staff spreading gossip, but they do not need to hear our conversation. Now, please, help yourself to some goodies while I pour your tea. Cream? Sugar?"

"A dash of cream and two lumps of sugar, Your Grace. Thank you."

The duchess handed the cup to her, and after fixing one for herself and reaching for a biscuit off the tray, she settled back in her chair. "There, we have what we need for the moment. Please don't hesitate to ask for more tea if you wish some. I would like you to enjoy our time together this afternoon."

"I am sure I will, Your Grace. Everything looks lovely and the tea smells divine. Do you have your own blend?"

"Yes, I must admit I am a bit of a snob when it comes to my tea. Nothing else tastes quite the same to me, so I do spoil myself in this one thing."

Taking a sip, Harriet smiled and said, "It is delicious. I can see why you love it and only drink this blend."

"I will have the cook put some in a small tin for you to take home as a memento of our afternoon together. Would you like that?"

"Very much, Your Grace. Thank you for your kindness."

"It is no problem. Just remind me before you leave."

Harriet knew she would not do that, but she smiled and nodded her head in agreement. How did one politely remind a duchess of her forgetfulness? She had no idea. She would rather leave empty-handed than remind the duchess of her need for the gift.

"Now," said the duchess, "you are probably wondering why I asked you over here this afternoon, are you not?"

"I am, Your Grace. The invitation came as a great surprise to me."

"Well, I have been doing some soul-searching in the past few days, and I have not liked what I have found."

"Uh, my husband is the vicar, not me. Perhaps it would be better to speak with him if you need spiritual counselling."

"No, I am not in need of his services," laughed the duchess. "God and I have spent time together, and He was the one who brought to mind my sin of omission."

"Sin of omission?"

"Yes, I am sure you are aware of the verse in the book of James where it says, *therefore to him that knoweth to do good and doeth it not, to him it is sin.*[1] Well, I have realised that verse applies to me. I had an opportunity to do good, and I ignored it. Now, after confessing my sin to God, I wish to do something about it."

"And what is that?"

"I wish to become an active part of your charity committee, and in doing so, rectify my sin of not supporting Miss Stillwater in her trials."

"That is very kind of you, Your Grace, but Miss Stillwater is, at this moment, sailing to the Colony of Australia. You can no longer help her."

"Yes, I was afraid of that. My son is also sailing on that ship. Not as a prisoner, but as a passenger to do business in the Colony. No, I realise my time to help Miss Stillwater has passed, but I was hoping I could assist with her mission to help destitute women while she is away."

"We could use your help. Thank you for volunteering. Many of the women on our committee have left us, for various reasons, but I think the main reason is they do not want to be associated with a charity that Bethany headed up, now that she is a convicted criminal."

"I know many of those women, Mrs. Hayward, and I agree with you. Their status in society is the most important thing to them, and they will do anything to keep themselves from being besmirched in any way. I, on the other hand, have no such qualms. My reputation does not stand on such foolish notions. Therefore, I wish to assist you in any way I can, to help those less fortunate in our city."

"We will greatly appreciate your aid, Your Grace. Our next committee meeting is at the manse, a week from Tuesday. Would you be able to attend our meeting so those who remain on the committee may meet you?"

"A week Tuesday? At this moment, I do not think I have any other commitments that day. It would please me to attend your meeting. What time is it?"

"Two o'clock."

"Excellent. I will put it on my calendar. Now, would you like some more tea?"

"Yes, that would be lovely, thank you . . ."

The ladies enjoyed another hour of tea and conversation before Harriet said it was time for her to leave. The duchess remembered her promise of a tin of tea for her guest, and sent the butler, Jasper, to retrieve one from the kitchen. Tea in hand, Harriet thanked her hostess for a wonderful afternoon and left with joy in her heart. Perhaps Bethany was not there to continue her work, but God had provided an able substitute for her. He was continuing to look out for the needy women and children of London.

The duchess was also feeling good. This was a way she could recompense Bethany. And she knew of other women who would be glad to help in the cause. Now, if only her husband could find out what happened with Bethany's trial, and if there was any way to help free her from her sentence. That would be a much harder task, but surely something could be done.

Chapter 5

The steerage compartment of the ship was small and had only basic amenities. Slabs of rough wood comprised the beds; there were no mattresses atop the wood. There were only ten beds in the room, meaning that most of the women would have to double up on each one. The women moved quickly to claim a bed once their chains were removed. Bethany and Susie chose one nearest the door. Perhaps that would give them fresher air than a bed farther back in the compartment. There were a couple of metal washbasins set in a stand near the back of the room, along with two small, covered pails that Bethany assumed were for their necessities. There was nothing else in the room. The air now was fresh, but how long that would last was questionable. They would only open the door to steerage once a day to allow the women to walk on deck for an hour before descending back downstairs. If the weather was bad, there would be no time on deck. Upon hearing this news from the first mate, the women groaned and prayed that there would be few storms on their journey. A bucket of fresh water along with a communal ladle, would come down each morning along with breakfast. This water was to be used for consumption only, and it was the only water they would get each day. Wash water from collected rainwater was supplied each day as well. They would each receive a bowl and spoon for their own use, and they were to use that for each meal. One of the prison warders would be always situated outside the door. The women were to pass any urgent messages to either himself or the captain through the warder. The door to the compartment would be kept locked to provide the women with protection from the sailors. They were forbidden to fraternise with the sailors and officers. However, they recognized it might happen occasionally. Any concerns about the crew should be relayed through the warder to the first mate, and he would deal with it. After giving the rules and regulations to the women, he left, the door was closed, and the women heard the click of a lock. At first it was pitch black in the room, then as their eyes adjusted to the darkness, the cracks around the doorframe and in the ceiling above them let a little light shine through, just enough to allow them to see each other and the things in the room. Bethany and Susie looked at each other as they sat together on their bed. This was to be their home for the next several months, and they would survive it together. They made that silent promise to each other. With each other's help, they would live to come back home someday in the distant future.

***

Things in Sam's cabin, located on the forward deck, were much more comfortable. He had a narrow bed, but it included not only a mattress but also rough cotton sheets, a blanket, and a pillow for his comfort. His cabin measured about ten feet by ten feet; not large for a duke's son, but certainly adequate for his needs. His steward, who would serve the few paying passengers aboard the ship, would provide him with hot water each morning for washing and shaving. He would also do Sam's laundry. Sam's meals, unless he preferred otherwise, would be taken with the captain and his officers in their dining hall. Sam was welcome to wander around the deck at his leisure, except during the two hours that the prisoners were out for their fresh air. They would prefer, but not restrict, Sam from being on deck at those times, for his own security. Otherwise, he was free to roam at will. The only other time they would ask him to stay in his cabin would be during a storm. This, again, was for his own safety and the safety of the crew as they worked to keep the ship afloat. Having told him what to expect on the voyage, the steward asked if he had any further questions. Knowing the steward would have no idea who the mystery woman was, Sam said, "No," and thanked him for his detailed instructions. The steward then left the room, closed the door, and left Sam to his own devices. Sam had declined the steward's services, which included hanging up his clothes, so as he had nothing else to do at this moment, he opened his bag and took out his belongings, arranging them where they would be most handy to retrieve. It took only a few minutes to stow his belongings and then he sat down on the bed. Looking out his porthole, he watched the seagulls flying around the ship. Then he heard the anchor being pulled up and the captain's commands to untie the ropes that secured them to the pier. Soon the ship was bobbing and swaying, and the sailors unfurled the sails. The ship moved away from the pier, then turned into the currents. The voyage had begun.

***

Calm waves gave way to whitecaps as they left the port and the winds picked up. The convicts soon learned what their life would be like for the next several months. They needed to move cautiously, as a wave could whisk them off their feet and land them on their backs on the hard wood floor. Water also seeped through the cracks in the floor before draining again into the bilge. So, to stay dry, the women spent most of their time either sitting, or lying, on their beds.

As they travelled down the coast of Europe, they saw little of it. Only when they were up on deck could they see the rugged coastline.

They also did not see many sea creatures, but sometimes overheard the sailors talking about they had seen on their watch. It was early January when they left London, so the large whales were not migrating; they had reached their southern waters and would only migrate back north in the spring. They saw the fins of various types of sharks, and it was common to hear a sailor say to someone, "Be careful, or I will feed you to the sharks." Thankfully, that never happened.

As the ship moved farther south, the temperature in steerage changed. Instead of having to huddle together for warmth, the women found the temperatures more bearable. It was still chilly on the deck, so they wrapped their shawls around themselves to ward off the cold, but they could discard them when they went below. By the time they dropped anchor in the port city of Cadiz, Spain, the women, mostly, were enjoying the weather. In Cadiz, they only stayed long enough to purchase supplies that would last them until they got to Cape Town, South Africa. Then the ship set sail again. Passing the entrance to the Mediterranean Sea, they came to Africa. Many of the women had heard stories about Dark Africa, from missionaries who had ventured there to spread the gospel. Frightening but fascinating, there were tales of head-hunters and cannibals. But perhaps the saddest stories were of the slaves, who had been stolen from their homes and marched to the west coast to be sent overseas to the Americas. Although it was said this practice was now outlawed, it still occurred. Bethany, having heard of their plight, was outraged at the thought of such atrocities. She had heard of the work of John Newton, who had been a slave trader before seeing the trade in human flesh for what it was, and then preaching against it. She also knew of William Wilberforce, who worked tirelessly in Parliament to abolish the purchase and shipment of slaves to Britain. Bethany prayed that the buying, selling, and breeding of slaves would soon be a thing of the past.

As the ship sailed down the coast of Africa, the weather warmed up. Now the women melted in the heat. This, combined with the

smell of the bilge water below them, and the stench of their necessity pails, forced the women to tear off parts of their tattered gowns
and use them to cover their noses to help them breathe better. Not
only were they confronted with the smell from the pails, but illness
had struck. Close quarters and a poor diet caused several of the
women to suffer from gastric disorders. This led to vomiting and
diarrhoea. The sailors agreed to empty the pails as soon as they were
full, but the stench continued. They gave them vinegar to swab the
wooden planks, which helped somewhat, but it was not enough.
Some women could not fight the disorder. Bethany cried the first
time she helped wrap a body in sailcloth. Sara had only been ill for
a couple of days. But that was all it took. Because the women were
already malnourished, it did not take long for gastric disorders to
end their lives. Bethany had nursed Sara as best she could over those
two days, but to no avail. Her frail body just could not cope with the
onslaught of diarrhoea and vomiting. That, along with an attitude of
despair rather than hope, was enough to end her life. After wrapping
her in a shroud, two crewmen came down and carried her body on
deck. Then the captain commended her to God and she slid into the
ocean depths. Bethany wondered how many of the bodies reached
the ocean floor to decay there—or did they become food for the
creatures of the sea? She tried not to think about it, but it was always
there in the back of her mind, every time she heard the splash of a
body hitting the waves.

This way of life continued for Bethany for the next couple of
months. When up on deck, she avoided any advances from crew
members, even for the promise of a bite of fish for an innocent kiss.
Bethany knew what that innocent kiss might lead to, and she was
not going down that path.

Finally, they reached the South African port of Cape Town. Here,
they anchored for more than just a day. It was a time for the officers and sailors to take a break before heading around the Cape of
Good Hope. They would also replenish their supply of fresh water

and food for the next part of the voyage. Having no place to secure the convicts on shore, they confined them onboard. They were still allowed their hour on deck each day but spent the rest of the time in their designated spaces. Bethany, if she had been a free woman, would have loved to explore the beautiful surroundings, but as a convict, that was of course out of the question, so whenever she was on the deck, she drank in the sights and sounds as delightful memories for the future. Susie had not fully recovered from her illness, so spent most of her time below, not joining Bethany for their breaks.

***

In contrast to the prisoners, Sam took full advantage of the time off the ship to explore the town and surrounding area. He was enjoying good health. He spent most of his days on deck enjoying the sights and sounds around him, having found his sea legs early in the voyage. To his dismay, he had not seen the mystery woman again. He wondered if she had been in one of the wrapped sailcloths he had witnessed the captain commend to God and then dump in the ocean. It saddened Sam each time this happened, even though he knew it was a regular hazard of sailing. He also knew those who lived below deck were not eating the same good foods as he was. They had to make do with watery soups and stale bread most days. Not a diet to sustain a body for very long. He only hoped that when they anchored in Fremantle, the mystery woman would walk out of steerage, again with her head held high. That would be a satisfactory end to her story.

***

Soon the break was over, the anchor lifted, and the ship set sail once again. The first mate warned the women the next part of the journey might be the most hazardous. Although they would continue sailing south before turning east at the point where the icy waters of the

Atlantic Ocean and the warm waters of the Indian Ocean met, there were often enormous waves and stormy conditions. If that happened, the women would be confined to their area, with no breaks above deck. He said he would also bring some ropes the women could use to secure themselves to the bedframes. There would be no hot soup, only hardtack, if the seas were too rough. Hopefully this would not last for more than a few days, but he wanted to prepare them, he said, before leaving them to plan for the next while.

Bethany was not afraid of what was coming; she knew her fate lay in God's hands. Even though she did not sense His presence, she knew that her soul was secure with Him and that brought her peace. Some of the other women were not as comfortable leaving their futures with God. So Bethany gave them solace and helped them to prepare for what lay ahead.

Sam, on the other hand, was quite looking forward to the next few days. He, too, put his trust in God's faithfulness and refused to worry about what lay ahead. His family, although concerned about such a voyage, knew that God's hand was upon him and whatever happened was in God's plan. Remembering the words of warning when he had first boarded in London, Sam secured his belongings once again and waited for the worst while hoping for the best.

***

Two days out of Cape Town, the worst hit. The waters began churning around the ship, and the waves were ten to fifteen feet high, splashing over the deck and down the stairs towards steerage. The ocean water continually seeped under the door, making the wooden planks wet and slippery. It was useless to mop up the water; as soon as it was dry, more water would come in, so the women finally gave up and instead took off their shoes and stockings and walked around barefoot—that is, when they could get up. Most of the time they tied themselves to the beds and held on tight, so as not to fall off the bed into the water. The warder checked on them from time to time, but as the ship increasingly rolled from one wave to another, she unlocked the door and left the women alone. She said she was going to find a berth on the next level and that they were on their own until either the storm subsided or the ship sank. After those comforting words, she left and headed up the stairs. The women quickly forgot about her; they only had one thing in mind, and that was to survive the storm.

***

Sam spent the time also tied to his bedframe. Occasionally, when the waves were high enough, he would get water leaking around the edges of his porthole, but other than that, his cabin stayed dry. His steward, prior to the storm, had supplied him with fruit, bread, and cheese, plus an ample flask of fresh water. He said he would come back as soon as the storm abated. Sam thanked him for the supplies and wished him well during the storm. Then he settled in his bed and tried to read a book he had brought with him on the voyage but had not opened yet. But it was useless. The room tossed and turned, and reading churned his stomach, so Sam gave up, put the book under his pillow, and lay back to rest. He wondered how his mystery woman was faring. He sent up a brief prayer for her and all the other unfortunate convicts. Then he went to sleep.

Sam woke up hours later. Opening his eyes, he watched the room continue to pitch and roll, but it did not seem as severe as when he had gone to sleep. He got up, made his way over to the water closet, and after relieving himself, picked up some fruit and cheese before heading over to the table below the porthole. Sitting down, he pulled back the covering over the porthole and looked out the window. Yes, the waves were still very large, but they were not as high as they had been when the storm first started. And was that—yes, he could see a bit of blue sky in the distance. If they were heading in that direction, they would soon be out of the storm. Smiling, he sent up a prayer of thankfulness to God before picking up his snack.

Bethany and the other women were not faring as well as Sam was. Many of them, including Susie, had spent the hours vomiting. Bethany was thankful she had a strong stomach, but that only meant she spent her time weaving around the beds, caring for the sick. She offered them sips of water and bites of hardtack. For some it helped, but for others, such as Susie, it only appeared to make the symptoms worse. Bethany kept a close eye on those most affected by the storm; after Sara died, she was well aware of the symptoms of dehydration. All of them were in poor health, but the storm was wreaking havoc on those who had no reserves left. Bethany hoped and prayed that when the storm abated there would be no more bodies to send to the ocean's depths. She was determined to do all she could, so she worked tirelessly throughout the storm.

And finally, it was over. Twenty-four hours after it began, the ship stopped rolling. The waves abated and water stopped running down into steerage from the deck. Bethany, now weary to the bone, picked up a blanket that had fallen to the floor and used it to mop up the remaining ocean water. The women who had been ill fell asleep after Bethany offered them one last drink of water. Then she collapsed onto the bed beside a sleeping Susie and succumbed to sleep herself, the first sleep she had had in the last twenty-four hours. It would take a lot to wake her up again.

***

Once the ocean calmed, the warder came back down to steerage. She came in and checked all the women for signs of life. Only one had died during the storm. She headed back up the stairs to get a sailcloth shroud before descending again to the room. She called as she entered the room, "Wake up, ladies. The storm is over. You will get something to eat soon. But first, I need you to help me prepare a body for burial. One of your own has passed away."

Bethany woke with a start when she heard the warder's words. Someone else had died? Everyone had been alive when she went to sleep. Who was it? Seeing the warder head to the back of the room, she sadly realised it was Clara. She was surprised Clara had made it this far in their journey. Sending a seventy-year-old woman to a foreign land for stealing a piece of bread was totally unjust. Now she was at peace and eating ambrosia in heaven with her family. God rest your soul, Clara.

Bethany got up and stumbled over to Clara's bed. She helped the warder wrap her in the shroud and secure it. Then she headed back to her own bed while the warder went to get sailors to carry the body up to the deck.

"Who was it, Bethany?" whispered Susie.

"It was Clara."

"Oh. I wish I could feel sorry for her, but I can't. She is now in a place where nothing but good will come her way, and she will never have to contend with evil. How I wish I could have gone with her today."

"Susie, she was old and frail. You are young and healthy. You need to think of living, not dying."

"I don't feel the way you speak of me, Bethany. I feel old and tired. All I want to do is lay down and go to sleep forever. Is that so wrong of me?"

"I understand you are unhappy. You have not been feeling well for the past several weeks. Once we are back on land, I am sure you will feel better. I can't lose you to death as well, Susie. I cannot."

"Then for your sake, I will try to get better. I will start with some water and hardtack."

"That's the spirit. I'll get you some." Bethany fetched some water and hardtack and brought them back to Susie. "Here you are. And if you want more, please let me know. I will get it for you."

"Thank you. I don't know what I would have done if you were not here with me."

"Well, I am here, and plan to be by your side for the coming months and years. We are going to make it through this. I know we are."

"I'll take your word for it. I think I would like to sleep again. Is that all right?"

"That is exactly what you need. Food, water, and rest. Those things will make you healthy in no time."

Susie mumbled a response and soon was asleep again. Bethany looked down at her and wondered if her words would come true, or if Susie would leave her before the voyage was over. She was so thin, and her face was so pale. Would she even survive to see the prison gates, let alone survive to go back home in several years? Bethany prayed she would. She too would need a good friend to help her survive the years ahead.

Within minutes of Susie falling asleep, two sailors came into the room with the warder. They picked up Clara's body and carried it out and up the stairs. Then the warder closed and locked the door. Bethany heard the captain speak the words over her body and then the splash as it hit the water. Soon afterwards, two more bodies splashed into the dark waters. It had been a dreadful night for all of them.

***

Sam had not yet ventured on deck since the storm abated. He heard the captain commending the souls of those who had died during the storm to the Lord. Then he heard three splashes as the bodies fell into the ocean. He supposed it was not surprising a few people had died. He presumed they were convicts, not sailors or officers. If so, hopefully each of them had gone to a better place than where they had been headed on earth. He asked the captain how many women had died during the storm, hoping his mystery woman was still alive.

Now that the water was calmer, dinner would again be served in the dining hall in a few hours. Sam needed to get out and take a stroll on deck to stretch his legs and work up a bit of an appetite for the meal. It was good to be able to walk around without falling into something. He would never take that benefit for granted again.

***

From then on, it was smooth sailing all the way to Australia. Bethany thanked God for the pleasant weather so she could resume her hour breaks on deck each day. She tried to get Susie to accompany her, but Susie was still feeling poorly and wanted just to sleep all day. It worried Bethany, and she hoped when they got to Australia there would be a physician who could examine Susie. She often lifted her concerns up to God, hoping He would hear her and answer her prayers for Susie, even if He was not answering her prayers for herself right now. That was all she could do for Susie, except encourage her to eat and drink as much as possible.

***

Sam kept an eye out for his mystery woman for the last month of their voyage, to no avail. He decided she might always remain a secret, one of those things to ponder over the coming months while he was in the colonies. He hoped when they anchored in Fremantle, he would see her again, at least one more time. Perhaps she would even look up at him and they could connect for a moment. If not, she might always remain his mystery lady.

Then one day, after sailing east across the Indian Ocean, the lad in the crow's nest called out, "Land ahoy! I see land, Captain."

Sam was standing with the captain in the cockpit, and he grabbed his telescope, directing it towards the spot the lad was pointing to.

Sure enough, they were approaching a large land mass. As there were no islands in this vicinity, it had to be Australia. They were nearing their destination after many months at sea.

Sam strained his eyes, trying to see the faintest outline of the coast without the periscope. It was still too far away. But he could start imagining what he might soon see. He hoped he would not be disappointed.

The word came down to steerage that land was near. Bethany was both excited and worried at the same time. Excited to see a new land but worried that now her days as a prisoner would begin. When she was imprisoned in London, there had always been the hope Cassandra would reconsider her testimony, come clean about the necklace, and they would free Bethany. But now that dream had faded. They were thousands of miles away from England. Even if Cassandra had second thoughts about what she had done, it would take months for the notice of acquittal to reach Australia.

Then, dependent on available ships, it could take months, or even a year or so, before Bethany could get home again. No, it was better not to think about home, to concentrate only on living each day, marking them until she had completed her sentence and could go home to England as a free woman.

She was glad, in another sense, to know they were approaching Fremantle. Susie was continuing to withdraw into herself. She was a shadow of the girl Bethany had known in London. She hardly ate and spent most of the day curled up on the bed, not sleeping but just staring at the wall. It was like she had given up on living and was just waiting to die. Bethany hoped the news of their imminent arrival in Fremantle might cheer Susie up, but she was wrong.

"Why should that news make me happy, Bethany? We are only exchanging one prison for another. It is not like we are going to be free once we disembark from this ship. No, I do not care that we are almost there. It is all the same to me."

"That is true, but at least we will be back on land. And I hope there is a physician who will examine you and help you get well again. I dislike seeing you this way."

"I do not want to see any physician. He cannot help me. I am sure of that."

"How can you be so certain? Perhaps it is nothing more than extended seasickness. If that is the case, even being on land should help to heal you. I am praying for that."

"No one can help me, Bethany. I think I am not long for this world. I am sorry I will not be here for you during the length of your prison term. Something tells me I will be in heaven soon."

"Please do not speak like that, Susie. I need you with me to survive. I do not know if I can do it alone."

"You will not be alone. God will always be there with you."

"I am not so sure. I have not felt His presence in a very long time. What if He has abandoned me like everyone else has?"

"I cannot answer that question. But I do know He promised never to leave His children alone. We can rest in that promise."

"I will try, but I will do better if you are there to remind me of His promise every day."

"I only know how I am feeling, Bethany, but I will stay with you as long as I can."

"Thank you. That is all I ask of you. Now, will you eat something for me?"

"I'll try," said Susie, sitting up on the bed.

Bethany passed her a chunk of hardtack and held a ladle of water so she could more easily swallow the dry bread. She ate half the hardtack and took a few swallows of water. "That's enough for now. I will try to eat more later. Now I would just like to go back to sleep if I may?"

"You may," said Bethany, tucking their two shawls tightly around Susie's emaciated frame. "Have a good sleep, and perhaps when you wake up, we will be ready to put our feet on dry land. That will be good, will it not?"

"It will," mumbled Susie as she closed her eyes. "I am tired of this journey. I only want to go home."

Fearful of what she meant, Bethany patted her shoulder and then moved away to sit on one of the empty beds. She bowed her head and prayed for Susie, asking God to heal her.

The land grew closer. Soon the rocks and trees along the shoreline were visible to everyone on deck. Before they got too close, however, the captain turned the ship and headed south along the coast. From port side, Sam watched the changing scenery with delight. He could scarcely contain his excitement. And then, there it was, standing as an ominous beacon on a high hill. Fremantle Gaol's towers and walls of grey concrete stood out against the bright sun. Their journey was over. They had arrived.

Chapter 6

Bethany walked onto the ship's deck and waited for her eyes to adjust to the bright sunlight. She looked up and saw a huge, grey structure atop a nearby hill. It had to be the jail. Her home for the next seven years. She gulped and turned away from the sight, preferring to look back out at the ocean instead. There were only tiny waves rippling over its surface; otherwise, it shone like glass. Gulls flitted over the waves, squawking loudly. Saltwater aromas filled the air. If she had come here as a visitor, these sights, sounds, and aromas would have thrilled her. But no, she could not get the image of the immense building on the hill out of her mind, even when she chose not to look at it. This was an illusion; that was reality, and she might as well face the truth. So she turned her head once again and looked up the hill.

Sam, too, was viewing the sights before him. But when the female convicts came up from steerage, his eyes quickly moved to focus on them. Yes, there she was, his mystery woman. She had survived the voyage. She looked gaunt but still had her head up, even as she stood among the other women. He watched her swivel her head from looking at the prison to the ocean and then back again. What was she thinking as she viewed the imposing structure? It saddened him she would soon be carted off to such a place for an indefinite number of years. Sam laughed at his thoughts. For all he knew, she had committed a horrendous crime and was deserving of such a punishment. Perhaps her stance was one of pride, and she was unremorseful for what she had done. He could only see her outward appearance; God was looking at her heart. Now that he had seen she was alive, it was time to get her out of his thoughts and concentrate on what he was here to do, establish a trade in wool. Sam was about to turn and go back to collect his things from his cabin when the woman turned her head again, this time looking up at him. It was only a glance before she cast her eyes away, but it was enough for Sam to see her face. It appeared familiar to him, as if he had seen that face before. But where could that have been? He associated mainly with his peers in society, and none of them would have been sent down here as a criminal. No, she must bear a resemblance to someone he knew. But who would that be? Sam puzzled over that thought for a moment. Not bringing any young women of his acquaintance to mind, he shrugged his shoulders, and after one last look at the woman on the deck, he turned and went back to his cabin.

It startled Bethany to see the young man standing in the cockpit. He looked exactly like Samuel Yardley, the duke's son. But it could not be him, could it? Her eyes must be deceiving her. He would have no reason to be here, standing on the same ship she had travelled on these many months. Surely she would have seen him before today, if indeed he had journeyed with them. True, she had only been on deck for short periods of time most days, and perhaps he had chosen not to be out when the prisoners were taking their exercise. But if it were him, why was he here, and was there any chance of her being able to get in contact with him and plead her case of innocence? It was not likely he would make trips to the jail, and she would not have the freedom to wander around the village. No, their paths would never cross again. That thought brought a tear to her eye.

Once more, her hope for freedom was crushed. God was still not answering her prayers. She was on her own.

Bethany left the ship with the other women, shackled and chained once more. Once on land, a man helped them into a cart, and once it was full, mules pulled the cart away from the dock and started up the steep hill towards the prison. As the cart moved away from the dock, Bethany looked back at the ship and saw the man standing on the deck. He nodded in acknowledgment of her, and then the cart rounded a corner and she saw him no more.

When the cart was out of sight, Sam bent down and collected his bag before departing down the gangplank to look for a place to stay while he was here. He tried to clear his mind of the woman and her plight, but her eyes haunted him. There had been a look of surprise when she saw him standing there on the deck, almost as if she recognized him. Still struggling with the thought of where he might previously have seen her, Sam walked down the gangplank and wobbled for a few steps before finding his land legs again. He looked for a hack to take him into town so he could find lodgings and food before getting down to the business of what had brought him here.

***

Once inside the prison walls, the iron gates clanged shut behind them, and an iron bar fell into place on the gate. *It's true*, thought Bethany. *My nightmare is turning into reality. I am here and will be for the next seven years. Oh God, why have You deserted me in such a way? What did I do to deserve such a punishment? Was my sin that great that You cannot forgive me? Please, talk to me, Lord. I need to know You are still here with me, otherwise I will wither and die.*

Waiting just inside the prison gates was a small woman carrying a long black stick that she kept slapping into her hand. When the cart stopped in the yard, the woman came over and said, "Welcome to your new home, ladies. I am Mrs. Stone, the superintendent of the female section of the prison. You will answer only to me. Obey me, and I will treat you well. Disobey any of my orders, and I will be your worst nightmare come true. Do you understand me?"

"Yes, ma'am," came a weak chorus from the cart.

"I'm sorry, I did not hear you," yelled the warden, tapping her long stick against the cart.

"Yes, ma'am," came a loud chorus from the cart.

"That is better. Now, let's get you out of the cart and into your new lodgings. Driver, unhook the latch on the cart bars, if you will, and help the ladies out."

Helping them out meant the driver stood at the back of the cart and yanked them out onto the ground, one by one. They could not move far from the cart, because they were still chained to each other, so each woman, including Bethany, felt the pain as another woman fell to the ground. Finally, the last woman was out of the cart, and the superintendent said, "Good. Now follow me to your cells. I will take the chains off when we get inside your cell block. Any questions?"

"No, ma'am," the women replied in unison.

"Good. Then come with me and keep up. No use standing around in this heat when you can be inside and enjoying it there." She laughed.

Then the woman took off at a brisk walk across the yard. The chain of women walked as quickly as they could, but after months at sea, poor nutrition, and lack of proper exercise, they had a hard time keeping up.

Seeing that they were lagging, Mrs. Stone turned and yelled, "I thought I told you to keep up with me! Do you need some more incentive?" She slapped the long stick from palm to palm in warning.

"No, ma'am," said one weak voice. "It's just that . . ."

"No excuses! Did I not tell you what would happen if you disobeyed me? Now, who spoke just now?"

There was silence.

"I heard a voice. Who spoke to me?"

"I did," said Bethany, even though she had not. Susie could hardly walk, let alone keep up with the rapid pace the superintendent was setting. She had only just survived the voyage, and if the woman started hitting her with that stick . . .

"You?" said the superintendent, coming close to Bethany, so near that Bethany could see all her rotten teeth and smell her foul breath.

"Yes, ma'am," said Bethany, asking God at the same time to forgive her lie. After all, it was for a good cause.

"Very well. May this be a lesson for all of you, not just this prisoner." She raised her stick and then brought it down hard upon Bethany's left shoulder. Then she raised the stick again and hit Bethany on her right shoulder, almost causing her to crumple to the ground.

"Now, are you ladies going to keep up with me, or do I need to give another lesson in obedience?"

"We'll keep up," chorused the women.

"Good, then let's try this again, with no excuses. March, ladies, march," said the superintendent as she turned and walked briskly away.

"We'll help you," whispered a woman chained close to Bethany.

In a sea of pain, but with the help of the other women, Bethany got her legs under her and started moving as fast as she could. She was so faint that she did not know if she would make it to the cells, but she determined not to let Mrs. Stone get the best of her, especially on her first day here. As Bethany started moving, a verse from the Bible came to her, strengthening her body. *They shall mount up with wings like eagles, they shall run and not be weary, they shall walk and not faint.*[2] As this verse came to Bethany's mind, she felt power pour into her back and legs. Maybe God was here and already helping her. Perhaps this was a sign He was still with her after all.

"Well, here it is, ladies, your new home. I hope you enjoy your stay!" laughed the superintendent as they came inside the doors of the cell block. "Before my two warders show you to your cells, you will need to pick up a gown, and a blanket and pillow. These will be the only ones that you receive this year, and if you are with us longer than that, you will receive new ones once a year after that. So do not ask for anything more. Do you understand me?"

"Yes, ma'am."

"Good, then I need to register each of you. The rest of you will remain standing here until I call you into my office. Smith and Jones will keep you company while you wait your turn to see me." She nodded her head towards her two warders. "Any questions?"

"No, ma'am."

"Very well, and to show what a very kind person I can be, I will see you first," she said, pointing to Bethany. "Jones, please unlock her chains and show her to my office."

Jones, a tall woman with large muscular arms, came over to Bethany and unlocked her shackles before saying, "Okay, you heard the superintendent. Come with me now." Then she grabbed Bethany's arm with so much force that Bethany just about fainted from the pain. Looking down at her, Jones said, "What's wrong with you, woman? I said let's move, now!"

"The superintendent hit her hard," said one woman. "She is in a lot of pain and can hardly walk."

"That isn't my problem. If I don't get her down to the superintendent's office right away, I will be in a lot of pain, too. So get your feet moving, lady."

Once more, Bethany called on God to give her the strength she needed to walk, and once more she felt His power surge through her muscles. Straightening her back and lifting her head, she said, "I'm ready now. We can go."

Jones nodded and directed Bethany to walk in front of her down the dim hallway. She did not touch Bethany again, only directed her with words. At last, they came to the end of the hall, where a door was open.

"She's here, Mrs. Stone," said Jones.

"Well, it's about time. Did she give you any trouble?"

"No, ma'am. No trouble at all."

"Good. Well, show her in, and then bring the next one down. We won't be long."

"Yes, ma'am," said Jones, before she left Bethany in the office and walked back down the hallway.

"So, Miss Troublemaker, did you learn your lesson this afternoon?"

"Yes, ma'am."

"And what was that lesson?"

"Never disobey you."

"Or?"

"Receive the consequences."

"Correct. And just be aware that today's lesson was only a sample of what I can deal out, Miss Troublemaker."

"Yes, ma'am."

"Good. Just wanted to make certain you understood my message."

"I did, ma'am. Loud and clear."

"All right then. Now, let's get to your file that came with you from England. You are Mary Worthless?"

Bethany thought for a moment and then decided to keep her new name until she returned to England. If she told the superintendent her real name and she did not believe her, she could get into trouble again. So instead, she said, "Yes, ma'am, that is my name."

The superintendent laughed. "Quite the name, Mary, but I think it suits you. You are now worthless, and will be until the day you leave us, either by ship or by coffin. I refer to all the women by their last name, so from now on you are just *Worthless,* and you will answer only to that name."

"Yes, ma'am," said Bethany, inwardly cringing.

"Your crime?"

"Theft, ma'am."

"What did you steal?"

"They thought I stole a valuable necklace, ma'am."

"They thought . . . who are they?"

"My accuser."

"Did you steal the necklace, Worthless? Not that it matters. I am just curious."

"No, ma'am, I did not. My accuser set me up. I am innocent of the crime."

"Yes, I hear cries of innocence in here all the time. Makes no difference to me. You are here, and you will serve your time before you are free again."

"Would you not help an innocent victim, ma'am?" ventured Bethany.

"If I helped everyone who claimed to be innocent, Worthless, half of this prison would be out on the streets, committing more crimes. So, no, I do not help anyone, only myself. Now, that is all the information I need from you. Jones will get your things and show you to your cell. But before you go, I have one more question. Where did you learn to speak in such a fancy way? Did your mistress teach you, before she hung you out to dry for your supposed crime? Hear little of that talk here in Fremantle, and it might be best if you learned to speak like everyone else. Otherwise the other women might take offence to your speech. Get my meaning?"

"Yes, ma'am, and thank you for the advice. I'll try to speak differently so as not to get into trouble."

"Good, for as you know, I don't like trouble, Worthless. Now, that's all for today. Jones," the superintendent yelled, "are you here with the next prisoner?"

"Yes, ma'am," she said, appearing in the doorway.

"Good, then take Worthless here, get her some things, and take her to her cell. Dismissed, Worthless."

"Yes, ma'am," said Bethany, before she got up and headed out the door to start her new life.

***

Meanwhile, Samuel was checking out his new lodgings at the boarding house run by Nick and Sally Tremblant. Introducing himself only as Samuel Yardley, he struck up a conversation with Nick.

"So, Nick, you been here long?"

"Yep, almost fifteen years now."

"Like it here?"

"Better than England, that's for sure. You can make a life for yourself here if you work hard at it. In England, everything is owned by the nobility, who walk around with their noses in the air and don't care a bit about the people who are working for them. As long as they get their money, they're happy. But if they don't . . ."

"What happens then?"

"You end up here, staying in the big house up on the hill, Fremantle Gaol."

"Sounds like that happened to you. Did it?"

"Yep. Me and Sally both. Sold down the creek by our landlord because we couldn't pay the rent one year. Next thing you know, we were loaded on a prison ship and sent here. Ten years for one year of not being able to pay our rent in full. Can you believe it? But that's just how they are, always looking out for themselves and not for anyone else."

"That's tough. Were you and Sally married at the time that you came here?"

"Yep. Had just celebrated being wed for two years, and then they separated us for ten. That was the hardest part, not being able to be with my wife for so many years."

"You could not even spend time together, even though you were in the same prison?"

"Nope. The rule was no contact between men and women. Occasionally, I would see her in the yard when I was going out for my hour of fresh air and she was coming in, but that was it, for ten whole years."

"That's a long time, and yet your marriage survived."

"Only because of our love for each other."

"Why did you stay after you got out of prison? Did you not want to go back to England and seek revenge on your landlord?"

"At first we thought about going back and paying him a visit. But what would be the point? We were still just working class, and he is a noble. Things had changed little in the years we were in prison, so why go back? Besides, we liked the warm weather, so we stayed. We worked for a man who owned this place until he died, and then found out that he had given it to us because of our good and faithful service to him. And these last five years have been good to us, so we don't plan on ever going back to England."

"I'm glad that God rewarded you for your faithfulness. Sounds like you made the right choice. Um, what did you say the name of your English landlord was again?"

"Master Howard Stillwater. Have you heard of him? When you go back to England, and if you meet him, run the other way fast. He is not a man that you want to know, either socially or in business."

"I may have seen him once or twice in London, but I have never made his acquaintance."

"Steer clear of him, sir. Why, I even heard he sent his sister to prison here on charges of theft so he could get control of her estate. Mind you, it's just village rumours, but I would not put it past him to do such a thing."

"His sister?"

"Yes, Bethany Stillwater. Of course, I have never met her, but I pity her being a sister to such a man."

"How long ago did this rumour start? About Miss Stillwater?"

"We get all the old newspapers from London whenever a ship comes in from Britain, so I think it was first written up about a year and a half ago. The trial, that is. If it is true, then she came here within the last year. Haven't heard that she is here, so maybe the rumours are wrong."

"Do you think they falsely accused her?"

"Wouldn't put it past her brother to do that. The estate is hers. It came with her mother to the marriage. The newspaper said so. Howard is only Bethany's stepbrother, so he has no legal right to any monies from the estate. But that doesn't stop him. He lords it over everyone, and wants only to have money and prestige so he can be a part of the noble class. No, sir, if he thought his sister stood in his way to gain a fortune, I would not put it past him to lie, even under oath.

"Now, I have been standing here gabbing away for much too long. Sally will be looking for me downstairs. Are you happy with our lodging arrangement, sir? Anything else I can get for you?"

"It all looks good, Nick. And thanks for the company. I'll look forward to spending more time with you and your wife over the coming weeks."

"Thank you, sir."

"There is one thing."

"Yes?"

"While I am here, I would like you to call me Samuel, or just Sam. When you keep calling me sir, it's like I'm your boss, and I would like to be your friend, on an equal footing. All right?"

"Yes, s—I mean, Sam. I'd like that too. It just comes natural to me to call you sir, because you have a certain, I don't know, a certain way about you."

"Hopefully not the way of the uppity nobles?"

"Oh no, nothing like that."

"Good, now that we have cleared that up, I will let you go, and I will unpack my bag."

"Fine. We will see you in about an hour for lunch?"

"That would be great. I'm looking forward to some good home cooking after my long voyage."

"My Sally is the best cook around here, so you will enjoy our meals, Sam. Well, if there is nothing else, I will let you get to your unpacking, and I will help Sally. Come down whenever you are ready to eat."

"I will. Thank you again for the conversation."

Sam sank down on the soft bed to contemplate what he had just learned. If the timing was right, then it was quite possible the woman he had seen on the ship was Bethany Stillwater. And she was now in prison up on the hill because her stepbrother Howard had sent her there to get rid of her. Howard was probably hoping something would happen to her while she was in prison so he could gain her entire estate for himself. Well, if Samuel, second son of the Duke of Yardley, had anything to say about it, that would not happen. But first he needed to confirm that Bethany was in Fremantle Gaol. But how to do that without using his title and influence? That was something he needed to think upon for a spell. Perhaps a nap, and then lunch, would help him think. Just a short nap, he thought, before closing his eyes and drifting off to sleep.

**

While Sam was settling into his nap on the soft bed of feathers, Bethany was being introduced to her new home by Jones. "Here you are, Worthless, your new home for the next several years," she said. "Ain't it a beauty?"

"Beautiful is not exactly how I would describe it," replied Bethany, looking around her in dismay. The room was about six feet wide and perhaps ten feet long, much the same size as her cell in Millbank. There was a tiny window located high on the outside wall that was letting in a few rays of light. In one corner of the room was a wooden board laid over a metal frame. In the other corner sat a large, covered pottery bowl. Seeing no bed frame with a mattress in the cell, Bethany assumed the board was her bed. She confirmed it with Jones.

Jones laughed. "Yep, you are right. That is your bed, and that is your necessity pot." She pointed to the pottery bowl. "Underneath the pot you will find a hole where you can empty your pot. I would not leave the hole uncovered; critters like to come up through it and into the cell, so it's best to keep it covered at all times."

"Critters?"

"Yeah, like snakes, rats, spiders . . ."

"Snakes, rats, and spiders can come into my cell?"

"Yep, and other things as well, so it's best to leave the heavy pot over the hole. If something nasty comes in here, deal with it yourself. Neither I nor Smith will come to help you."

"But-but-but . . . what if they are dangerous, even deadly? Won't you help me then?"

"Nope. I survived this place for many years, and if you are smart, you can too. If not, well, I guess you will die here."

"You were a prisoner here, before you became Mrs. Stone's warder?"

"I got this job while I was a prisoner. Cut my prison sentence in half."

"But how?"

"Oh, don't be thinking that you can take my job, Worthless. You are too scrawny to be a warder. You have to be big and strong, like I am."

"I would not want your job. I just wondered how you got it while you were still a prisoner."

"Mrs. Stone fixed it for me."

"Oh, I see."

"Anyway, enough about me. Any other questions before I leave?"

"Yes. First, is there a mattress for my bed? Did someone forget to bring one for me? And how do I wash, both myself and my gown, with no basin, soap, or towelling?"

"No mattress. You will get used to sleeping on the board. You'll get a basin with cold water in it each morning at five o'clock. That is all the water you will get for washing both yourself and your gown. No soap, just cold water."

"But how will I keep clean?"

"Clean?" laughed Jones. "You sure are stupid, Worthless. In a little while, you won't worry about being clean. All you will think about is surviving, day by day. If you want to *bathe*, you will have to do that with your cold water. When breakfast comes at six. you will give your basin back to us until the next day. You cannot keep any personal items in your cell."

"But—"

"Enough questions," she said, pushing Bethany farther into the cell before slamming the door shut and locking it. "Welcome to Fremantle, Miss Worthless. Enjoy your stay."

Bethany stood in the middle of the room, with her small bundle, wanting just to fall to the floor and die. *I cannot do this*, she thought. *I will not survive long enough to go back home and revenge myself on Howard. He has won, and I have lost.* Feeling like her legs might give way under her, Bethany moved over to the "bed" and, after wrapping herself in the blanket, curled up in a foetal position on the hard board, before crying out her soul to God. *God, I thought You were with me today, but maybe I was wrong. Maybe I am all alone here. God, if You are present, please, please let me know. I am so afraid, and I don't know what to do, Lord. I need Your help. Please, God, I need You now!*

Just then, a weak ray of sunlight washed over her face. From deep within her, Bethany heard a tiny voice reminding her that God was always present in every situation. Just as He had been with her in England and on the ship, He was here too. She had to have faith. He would see her through this trial. She just had to believe.

***

"Sam! Samuel! Lunch time!" came a call from downstairs. Unfortunately, Sam was so sound asleep, he did not hear the call. Next thing he knew, Nick was standing at his bedside, calling his name again. "Sam, wake up! It's lunch time."

This time, he struggled up from sleep and saw Nick standing by his bed.

"Yes?" he mumbled.

"You sure don't wake easily, do you?" laughed Nick. "I had to come all the way up here just to tell you it is time to eat."

"Eat? Oh, I must have fallen asleep. I'm sorry."

"That's okay, but you need to get up now and come down for lunch. Sally doesn't like the food to get cold."

"I'll be right there. Just give a minute to splash some water on my face and then I'll come down. All right?"

"All right. I'll let Sally know you need a few minutes to wake up before you join us for lunch. But don't go back to sleep."

"I won't. I'm up. See you soon."

True to his word, Sam joined Nick and Sally a few minutes later at the table. "I'm sorry, Sally," he said. "I was just going to close my eyes for a few minutes, and next thing I know Nick was yelling in my ear."

"I was not yelling," retorted Nick. "I was speaking loudly."

"Well, whether it was yelling or loud speech, I don't know. What I know is that it woke me up from a sound sleep. And now I am ready to dig into this delicious meal. It looks and smells wonderful."

"I hope you enjoy it, Sam. But first, Nick and I always thank God for the food before we eat. Will you join us?"

"Absolutely."

Nick said a brief prayer of thanksgiving for the food and for Sam's safe arrival in Fremantle. After the prayer, they all dug into their meals with gusto.

"You are a very lucky man, Nick Tremblant. A beautiful wife, and one that cooks like this. A very lucky man indeed."

"Oh stop, Mr. Samuel," said Sally, blushing. "I'm just glad that you liked your food."

"Liked it? I loved it! Why, if you weren't already married . . ."

"But she is, and to me," said Nick. "So, don't you try charming my wife with your fancy speech and manners. Otherwise, you may find yourself out on the street with no place to stay," he laughed. "Don't you have yourself a gal back in England?"

"No."

"That's too bad. The only single women here are up in the prison. If others arrive single, they don't stay that way for long. I'm afraid you are out of luck if you are looking for a bride while you are here."

"That wasn't in my plans, so I guess I will stick to business instead."

"What kind of business?"

"Trade in wool, mainly. Are there any sheep farms nearby?"

"No, not nearby. You have to go up the coast to Geraldton, or east to Mount Magnet, before you will find any large sheep farms, or stations, as they are called here."

"How long would it take me to get to one of those places?"

"I'd reckon about a week by boat to Geraldton. It's right on the coast. I'm not sure about the inland stations. It might be difficult to find transportation to them."

"Do ships regularly run between here and Geraldton?"

"They do. Mostly cargo ships, though. Not too many passenger ships."

"I'm not fussy. Just need a place to lay my head at night. Where would I find out what ships are travelling to Geraldton? I'd like to head up there as soon as possible."

Nick told him he should head down to the mercantile and talk to the proprietor, Joe, who not only handled merchandise for the locals, but also looked after booking passages for them. Nick was sure Joe would know when the next steamer was headed north.

Sam agreed with Nick's suggestion and said he would head back down the hill right after lunch. And that is what he did, only after

Sally gave him a broadbrimmed hat to wear, to protect his English skin from the blazing sun. Walking down to the village, Sam soon found out the wisdom in Sally's words. The sun's rays were like nothing he had ever experienced, not even on his grand tour of Europe as a young man. He would be a fool if he did not wear one every time he stepped outdoors. He hoped he could purchase one for himself at the mercantile. Fortunately, he was in luck. After meeting the owner, Joe Winter, Sam booked passage on the next ship going to Geraldton. And before he left the store, he had a hat of his own, compliments of Joe. Sam quickly realised that in order to survive in this country you needed to learn from the locals, and being no fool, that was exactly what he was going to do.

***

While Sam was walking in the heat, Bethany was suffocating in it. She did not know which was worse, walking around and fanning herself with her hand, or lying on the hard wooden board that was her bed. If it did not cool down at night, she would not need the blanket. Maybe she could tear part of it into strips and dip them in the cold water in the morning to help cool herself down throughout the day. How did one survive the heat in this place?

"Hey, incomer," she heard through the bars of her cell. Going over to the door, she paused and waited. Then she heard the voice again. "Hey, girl, do you hear me?"

Remembering she needed to speak in simpler words than she was used to, Bethany called out into the hallway, "Are you talking to me?"

"Aren't you the latest to come to our palace?"

"I think so. What's it to you?"

"Just being friendly, but if you are not going to be . . ."

"Sorry. Just feeling the heat. Not used to it yet."

"You'll never get used to it. You just survive it."

"How?"

"You'll find ways, just like the rest of us. Right, ladies?"

A chorus of agreement came from the other cells.

"Well, I'd appreciate any tips you could give me," said Bethany.

"Ladies, seems we have an educated newcomer," jeered the voice. "Where you come from, girl?"

"London."

"What part?"

"Highgate."

"Oooh, Highgate. What they send you down for, my lady?"

"I'm not a lady. I just live—lived, in Highgate."

"All right. Don't care if you are a lady or not. What you here for, and how long?"

"Theft. They thought I stole some jewellery. And seven years."

"They thought? You say you innocent, girl?"

"Yes."

"Just like the rest of us ladies here," the voice laughed. Laughter also erupted from within several other cells.

"I am."

"Yeah, sure. Don't matter. You're here now, and you're staying until your time is up or you die."

"How long have you been here?"

"Fifteen and counting . . ."

"Fifteen months?"

"No, fifteen years, stupid."

"Fifteen years! How do you survive?"

"By learning who is the boss and paying my dues."

"Boss? I thought Mrs. Stone was the boss."

"Stone? Nah, she just thinks she is, but the real boss is in here."

"Who is it?"

"Me."

"You? But how will I know you, except by your voice?"

"I saw you come in, and now I know your voice, so I'll find you and introduce myself."

"When will that be?" asked Bethany, although she was not sure she wanted to know the answer.

"Today, during yard break."

"Yard break?"

"Yeah. Hey, didn't they tell you anything?"

"Not much."

"Figures. They're not big on words here, just sticks."

"Yeah, I learned that one real fast."

"Oh yeah? What happened?"

"I stuck up for one of the other women and got smacked for it."

"Well, good for you for trying to help, but if you want to survive, look out for only one person. Yourself."

"Isn't that selfish?"

"What are you, some kind of do-gooder? If so, you won't last long in here. Only long-termers like me last because I only care about myself."

"I don't think I can be that way . . ."

"It's the only way, incomer. Now shush, I hear Jones coming back. Probably bringing another one to the block. See you soon in the yard." Then the voice ceased.

A minute later, Jones arrived in their cell block with another prisoner in tow. It was Susie. Head down and moving slowly, Susie followed Jones to the cell next to Bethany's. Jones then gave Susie the same speech as the one she'd given to Bethany before slamming the cell door and locking it. As the warder was about to leave, the previous voice called out again, "Hey, Jones, you leaving it to the rest of us to fill in the details about how everything runs here? Incomer number one is sure in the dark about certain things."

"Such as?"

"Rules, yard breaks, who bosses things around here. You know, all the usual stuff."

"Official rules or your rules, Canter?"

"They're both the same."

"Only in your eyes, Canter. The superintendent thinks somewhat differently than you do."

"That's her problem, not mine."

"Be careful. You don't want to visit Stone again, do you?"

"No . . . not really. But give the new girls a break and at least tell them about yard time."

"All right. At least there are two now, so I won't have to repeat myself. Yard break, or fresh air and exercise time, is thirty minutes from now. You get an hour out of your cell to walk around the yard to get to know your cell block mates. Then it is back to your cells until tomorrow at the same time. Is that enough, Canter?"

"It'll do for now, Jones."

"All right. I'll be back in thirty minutes to let you out for your break."

"Uh, you forgot something, Jones."

"What?"

"The chain . . ."

"Thought I would save that for a surprise, Canter, but you ruined it. When you come out for your break, you will be chained, one to another, so you don't do anything stupid, like try to escape. As if anyone ever succeeded at that. I will open each door and put the shackle on your ankle, before attaching the chain to it. Then we will move to the next cell, and the next . . . you get the picture. I will take the ankle shackles off until tomorrow if you behave. If not, you get to wear the shackles for the next twenty-four hours. You'll be happy to obey me if you wear it for a day. Right, Canter?"

"You should know, Jones. You wore it often enough."

"True, and so have you. Now, if you are done talking, Canter, I have more work to do before I come back. I'll see you all in about a half hour." She turned and headed out of the cell block.

All was silent then. Not even Canter spoke a word. Bethany went back and sat on the edge of her bed. *More chains and shackles, Lord? What's next? No, don't tell me. I don't want to know unless it is good news. Otherwise* . . . Bethany lay back on the board and fanned herself with her hand. Could things get any worse?

***

A short time later, Bethany found herself having her own chat with the boss, Joann Canter, in the prison yard. They were walking around the perimeter of the yard, and Bethany found herself only a few metres away from Joann. Bethany had recognized her voice as soon as Jones opened Joann's cell door after chaining Bethany and Susie together. Once she was shackled, the warder led her out and chained her to Susie. "Well, well, well," Joann said. "If it isn't the new ladies. Welcome to our chain gang." From then on, while they were moving around the cell block and then out in the yard, she never stopped talking. She was also pushy about getting what she wanted. When Bethany was led over to the water barrel and given a ladle of water to drink, she kept saying, "Hurry up, new girl. Don't take all day. You aren't the only one waiting for a drink." Then, when Susie had her turn, Joann shoved her forward so that the water from the ladle half spilled down the front of her gown. When Susie asked for more, she was told that she could only have one ladle now, and one ladle before they left the yard. Protesting the fact that half had spilled on her made no difference; Joann shoved her forward and took her place at the barrel.

"That was not very nice of you, Canter," said Bethany.

"Nice. I'm never nice, incomer. And I get what I want when I want it. That's the way it works around here." She sipped at the ladle. Then, to Bethany's surprise, Joann reached out the empty ladle, and a warder filled it again for her

"I thought it was only one ladle per person now. How come you got two?"

"Because I'm the boss, and no one wants to get on the bad side of the boss. Get that, newcomer?"

"My name is not *newcomer*, Canter, so stop calling me that."

"Well, as no one has properly introduced us, princess, I don't know what else to call you."

"I am Mary Worthless."

"Worthless! Now, ain't that a pretty name for a pretty lady."

"It's just a name."

"No, it fits you, especially here. You are no good to anyone here; you are worth nothing."

"Not to God. In His eyes, I am worthy of everything."

"Oh no, not one of those! Are you going to preach at me about heaven and hell, Worthless? If so, you can save your breath. I've heard it all before and I don't believe any of it. So save your breath for another poor soul."

"I'm not a preacher, just a follower of Christ. I try to live my life by His commandments and serve Him any way I can."

"Well, try serving Him here. It won't help you at all. This place is a living hell."

"Not what the Bible says. Hell will be a lot worse than any place on earth. So, think on that for a bit."

"You haven't seen anything yet, incomer. Just wait, and you will see what I mean."

"Cut the chatter and get moving, all of you!" interrupted Jones. "I've heard enough from both of you, so close your mouths and move your feet."

"Yes, ma'am," said Joann, before she shoved Susie forward into Bethany, causing them to stumble and fall to the ground. The rest of the ladies on the chain laughed as they saw them lying there in a heap.

"Okay, knock it off, Canter," said Jones.

"I was only trying to get them to move faster and look what happened. They all falled down . . ."

"Get up, you two," Jones yelled, without attempting to help them. "If you can't walk, then you can run around the yard. Now, go!"

Bethany started running as soon as she and Susie got up. The pain in Bethany's shoulders intensified every time that her feet hit the hard ground. But she reached out to her Father, and He gave the strength to continue running. After two laps around the yard, Jones said, "Okay, that's it for today. Go back to the barrel and get your final ladle of water. Then it's back to the cells for all of you."

The prisoners protested they had only been out for half the allotted time, but Jones would not budge. So they lined up, had their water, and then headed back inside. Once she was back in her cell, Bethany almost felt a sense of relief. At least in here Canter could not physically harm her; she could only hurt her with words but not actions. She was going to have a hard time loving Joann as Christ told her to do in the Bible verse that said to love your enemies and do good to those who hate you.[3] It was going to take some doing in this wretched place, but she would try.

***

As Bethany was trying to figure out how to love Joann, Sam was having a much easier time loving his friends. After he got back from the port office, they invited him to have tea and crumpets with them. Again, Sally outdid herself with the treats.

"Sally, I have never, and I repeat, never, had crumpets as good as these are. What is your secret?"

"Just lots of love, Sam, lots of love, and a bit of luck."

"Well, I have been to many fine bakeries in London, and they could take some lessons from you."

"Careful, Sally," teased Nick. "Sam may try to get your recipe so that he can sell it when he gets back home and become one of those snobbish nobles."

Sam cringed. He was living a lie when he didn't tell them who he was or where he came from. He had not thought it would matter if they thought he was only a commoner, but their pain ran deep, and he was deceiving his friends. Before he could say anything, there was a knock at the door. It was Joe from the port office.

"Joe, come on in," said Nick as he opened the door. "We were just having tea and crumpets. Can you join us?"

"I would love to, Nick, but today I cannot. Just stopped by to let Sam know that the captain of the barge will be glad of your company tomorrow. You need to be down at the wharf at six hundred hours; they will leave soon after that. You can pay the captain once you get on board. Any questions?"

"No. Thank you very much for all you have done for me today. I appreciate it. I'll be at the wharf by no later than six o'clock tomorrow morning."

"That's good then. Sally, I hate to pass up your crumpets, but I have to be going back to the office. Some other time?"

"Any time, Joe. You know you're always welcome here."

"I do. Well, I'll be seeing all of you again soon. Have a good evening."

Once Joe had left, Nick said to Sam, "I guess that means you'll be gone for a while. Like I said before, we will keep your room available for you, and you can leave things here as well."

"Thanks. I don't know how long I will be gone, but I don't want to take much with me on this trip. I will pay you before I leave tomorrow, for tonight's lodging, and for the room while I am gone."

"Don't worry about that right now. We can figure it out when you get back."

"If that is the case, and there are no more crumpets to be eaten," he teased, "I will head upstairs to sort through my bag, to plan what to take and what to leave. I will see you both later."

***

The next morning, Sam was true to his word. He arrived at the harbour just before the barge was about to leave. After introducing himself to the captain, he stowed his satchel on his designated bunk before helping to load the remaining supplies. Then, after they'd secured everything on board, the sailors pulled up the anchor, tossed off the ropes to the pier, and they were on their way north.

It was a much different voyage on the steam-powered barge than it had been on the ship from England. The barge moved at a steady, slow pace, not dependent on the strength of the wind to power it. The sailors kept an eye on the supplies that they were taking to Geraldton, but other than that, there were only normal chores, like swabbing the deck, stoking the engine, and making meals for the crew. Sam enjoyed working with the other men; he did not want to miss any experience he could have on the vessel. Seeing his eagerness to help, the captain and his crew readily welcomed him, making him an honorary sailor for the trip.

About a week later, the port town of Geraldton came into view, and within a short time, Sam was back on dry land. After finding lodgings for the night, he headed into the business area of the port to delve into what he came to do in Australia, that of merchandising wool. Making the acquaintance of one of the wool merchants, Sam found out he could visit a sheep station the very next day, because the merchant was heading out to one of the largest stations, or *downs*, as they were called, to check on his next batch of wool. Eager to learn the business from the merchant and the farmers, Sam agreed, and headed off to get a good night's rest before their trip the next day.

The merchant, Tom, provided a great deal of information on sheep farming: shearing, packing the bales of wool, and then shipping them down to Fremantle, where they were loaded onto ships bound for England. He had had a small sheep station of his own until recently, when he had sold it to the man they were going to visit. Tom said that to be viable as a farmer, you needed quite a bit of land and large flocks of sheep. He had made a living off his small flock, but only that, so he had sold his business to go into just marketing the fleece. Tom was interested in what Sam's plans were and said that he would be glad to give him any advice on the business. He said that there was still a tremendous opportunity in both farming and marketing, so he was not in the least bit worried about Sam cutting into his profits.

Sam was pleased to hear that there was a chance he could become both a farmer and a marketer. From the limited experience he had had so far in Australia, he was thinking he might like to settle here, maybe even have a station of his own someday. But that was in the future. Today he was going to enjoy the trip and learn as much as he could about marketing fleece from Tom and the farmer.

Two hours later, they arrived at the large station. The spread of buildings was enormous. There was the main house, which was a large bungalow with a covered porch extending the entire length of it. There were barns and shearing sheds, plus a great number of outdoor pens. In the distance, on the rolling hills, Sam could see a multitude of tiny white dots, which the farmer said were some of his flocks. It was quite the sight to see, coming from the small sheep farms his father oversaw in England. Sam asked a lot of questions of the owner while they walked around the buildings, impressed with the whole layout of the station.

But all too soon, the visit was over. Tom completed his business and they were on the road back to Geraldton.

"So, what did you think, Sam? Still interested in getting into the business?"

"More than ever, Tom. Thank you so much for bringing me out here today. I learned a lot."

"Would you be thinking of striking out on your own, or going into partnership with a seasoned merchant?"

"Why? Do you know of someone who might be looking for a partner?"

"Yes, me."

"You?"

"Yes. I am getting older and have been thinking about slowing down a bit. When you came to talk to me yesterday, I started wondering if we could think about a partnership, and if things work out, you might want to eventually buy me out so I can retire."

"I had not thought of a partnership, but that would be a great idea. I am very green, obviously, in my knowledge of this industry in Australia, so a seasoned partner would be wonderful. Are you sure you would want to take me on?"

"From what I have seen of you in the past day or so, yes, Sam. Let's talk some more and then perhaps before you leave Geraldton, we can strike some sort of deal."

"Sounds like a good plan to me. Where would we start?"

As the men travelled back to the coast, they came up with a partnership deal that would suit both of them. Once they arrived in town, Tom said he would write out an agreement and, if it satisfied Sam, they would seal the deal the next day. Having that plan in place, Sam left Tom to head back to his lodgings for the night, to dream of his next part of the plan, which was to not only sell bales of fleece to England, but also to provide employment to the women of Fremantle prison by carding and spinning wool before it even left Australia. That might give him the opportunity to meet the women incarcerated in the prison and see if indeed Bethany Stillwater was a prisoner there. If so, he would have to come up with a legal way to get her released and sent home to England as a free woman. With all these thoughts in mind, Sam soon drifted off into a satisfying slumber.

But while Sam was having pleasant dreams, Bethany was waking up to a nightmare.

Chapter 7

Just as dawn was about to break, soft moans from Susie's cell awakened Bethany. At first Bethany tried to ignore the moans, to get a few more minutes of sleep, but they became louder and more frequent. Finally, concerned about Susie, Bethany called out softly, so as not to wake the others, "Susie, are you all right?"

"Oh, Mary," moaned Susie. "It hurts. It hurts so bad!"

"What hurts, Susie? Did something bite you?"

"No, nothing bit me. It hurts where-where-where my woman parts are. It's never hurt like this before, and I don't know how to stop it."

A voice from the other side of Susie's cell yelled out, "Quit your crying, baby. We have all had terrible pain with our monthlies. It'll go away. If you don't stop moaning, I'll give you some actual pain this afternoon in the yard."

"Canter," said Bethany. "Be quiet. I need to figure out how to help Susie. Susie, is this the first time you have had your, uh, monthly bleed? You know what I mean?"

"Yes, I know. But I have had my monthlies for a couple of years now, and they never hurt like this. Please, Mary, help me!"

Deciding that someone needed to go in and see Susie, Bethany called out. "Jones, are you awake?"

"I am now. Who wouldn't be with all this noise?"

"I'm sorry, but I think you need to check on Susie. She's in a lot of pain, and we need to help her."

"Okay, but if it is only her monthly bleed, Worthless, you are going to be washing her rags in your daily water. You understand?"

"I do, and I will. But please, hurry and check on her. I'm worried about her."

"I'm coming, I'm coming," Jones groused as she pulled her oil lit lantern down from its hook and headed down the hall towards Susie's cell. Reaching the cell, she pulled out her pass key, unlocked the door, and then swung her lantern around so that she could see into the cell. The first thing that hit her, even before she spied Susie curled up on the bed, was the rank smell of blood. It filled the air. Then she noticed in the lantern light a large dark stain on Susie's blanket, and a puddle of something beside her on the floor. It was blood, and there was a lot of it! Jones could not stand the sight of blood, so she stepped back into the hallway to get some fresher air. When she did so, she noticed Bethany standing at her bars. "She's bleeding. I can't stand the sight of blood, so I can't help her. I need to get someone else," she said before she turned to go back out of the hallway.

"Wait! You can't leave her alone. She needs someone with her."

"Well, that someone won't be me."

"Then let me go to her. Please . . . you can lock me in her cell if you want to, just don't leave her alone like this."

"Okay, but I warn you, it isn't pretty, and the smell, well, it's awful. Are you sure?"

"Yes, I'm sure."

She came back and opened Bethany's cell door. "Bring your blanket to cover your nose. The smell is terrible!"

Bethany ran back, grabbed her blanket, and followed Jones to Susie's cell door. "I'm not going back in there with you. You're on your own until I get some help." Then she turned to leave again, but Bethany grabbed her sleeve.

"Can you leave the lantern? It's dark in here."

"I don't know what you want to see, Worthless, but if you need it, I'll leave it behind. I can find another one."

"Thank you."

"Don't thank me yet. You may regret offering to help her," Jones said before she turned, and after locking the cell door, ran down the hallway.

With the lantern now in one hand, and her blanket in the other, Bethany turned and moved towards Susie, who was writhing around on her bed. Rushing over to her, Bethany said, "Susie, it's me, Mary. I'll sit with you while Jones goes for help. Is the pain still terrible?"

Unable to speak because of the pain, Susie just nodded her head.

"Oh, you poor thing. What can I do to make you feel better?"

"I don't know. I've never had pain like this before."

"Is it the time for your monthly?"

Susie shook her head. "I don't think so, but I haven't had one for a few months, so I don't know. It just hurts . . ."

"Okay," said Bethany. "Let me look and then try to make you feel better." Moving the lantern lower on Susie's body, Bethany gulped at what she saw. The lower part of Susie's gown and her entire blanket were soaked with blood. This was not a normal monthly.

"Susie, I am going to remove your blanket and wrap you in my dry one. That should make you feel more comfortable."

"Don't ruin your blanket for me. You don't get another one for another year, remember?"

"I don't care. You need to get warm, and your blanket will not do that for you. Perhaps they will give me another one to replace this one, but I don't care even if they don't. You are more important than a blanket."

"Thank you, Mary. You're an angel," whispered Susie as Bethany exchanged her blanket for the one twisted around Susie.

"There, that should be better."

"It is, thank you."

"You are welcome. Now, I'll just move this ruined blanket away from here and see what else I can do for you until Jones gets back."

As Bethany picked up the blanket to move it towards the door, something fell out of it. Swinging her lantern down, Bethany gasped. Amid all the blood was a tiny human form. It was a baby! She looked closer. The baby was obviously a few months along. What was she going to tell Susie? Should she question her about her behaviour on the prison ship? And what did she, Bethany, know about any of this? She, who had led the sheltered life of an upper-class maiden before all of this had occurred. Bethany decided that Susie's needs came first right now, and that questions, if needed, could come later. So she reached down and picked up the little form before wrapping it securely in the blood-soaked blanket and moving it out of Susie's sight.

"Mary," whispered Susie. "What is it? What are you keeping from me?"

"Uh, nothing," Bethany lied. "I just wanted to get the soaked blanket out of our way. That's all."

"Mary . . . was there . . . a babe in that blanket? I thought I saw . . ."

"Yes, I am afraid so. The baby was not far enough along to live outside of your body. I'm so sorry you lost it."

"I'm not. What would have happened to the baby if it had been ready to be born? Who would have cared for it? Would they have allowed me to keep it, or would they have sent it away? This way the baby's soul has winged its way back to heaven and waits for me there. And I think I will join it soon."

"No, you must not think that way," said Bethany. "But Susie . . . I have to ask . . . how?"

"It wasn't my choice," Susie wept. "A sailor . . . on the ship . . . I didn't tell anyone . . . Mary, I'm so ashamed. When I realised I might be . . . I just wanted to die. And now I am."

Realising—from the amount of blood that was now soaking into her blanket—that Susie was telling the truth and they could do nothing about it, Bethany said, "Go to our Father then, Susie, and rest in Him. I will miss you, my friend, but I would not call you back from that divine place."

"Would you hold me, please? I'm so cold . . ."

"Of course," said Bethany, before she gathered the blanket-wrapped Susie into her arms and held her. "Is there anything else I can do for you?"

"Would you see my baby gets a Christian burial? I don't want her to just get thrown on the trash heap."

"I will see what I can do, and for you as well."

"Mary, do you know any words from the Bible that will help me on my way? My ma used to tell me words from the Psalms every night when I was a little girl. It always helped me sleep better. Perhaps it would help me go to sleep forever."

"Psalm 23 has beautiful words, and the meaning is just right for you. Close your eyes and listen. I will recite it to you," said Bethany, tears choking her voice. Before beginning, she prayed for strength to do this for Susie. "*The Lord is my Shepherd; I shall not want. He maketh me to lie down in green pastures; he leadeth me beside the still waters. He restoreth my soul; he leadeth me in the paths of righteousness for his name's sake.*" Bethany felt Susie's body relax more fully into hers; her breathing became shallower. Bethany continued. "*Yea, though I walk through the valley of the shadow of death, I will fear no evil: for thou art with me; thy rod and thy staff, they comfort me. Thou preparest a table before me in the presence of my enemies: thou anointest my head with oil; my cup runneth over. Surely goodness and mercy shall follow me all the days of my life: and I will dwell in the house of the Lord forever.*"[4]

Then, with one last breath, Susie went to dwell in her Father's house. Bethany tenderly placed her back on the board that served as her bed. *I bet you are floating on clouds now, dearest Susie. No more hard boards for your bed. Goodnight, sweet girl. Until we meet again.*

"That was nice, Worthless," came Joann's voice from the next cell. "My ma used to recite that to me when I was little. You did real good for Susie. Is she . . . has she . . .?"

"Yes, Canter," replied Bethany. "Susie has left us. She is in heaven now."

"I wish I believed that, Worthless, but too many things have happened to me since Ma told me those verses. It's too late for me now."

"It's never too late, Canter, as long as you have breath in your body. All you have to do is repent of your sins, believe in Jesus as God's son, and accept Him as your personal Saviour. It's as simple as that."

"Maybe for you, but not for me. God would never accept me after what I did."

"God accepts all, even the worst of sinners. That is why Jesus died on the cross, for all sinners."

"Yeah, I bet you sinned bad, especially to get sent down here. What'd you do again? Steal a loaf of bread?"

"No, they accused me of stealing my sister-in-law's jewellery."

"Oh yeah, I forgot. But you are innocent, right?"

"Yes."

"Well, I am not."

"What did you do, if you don't mind my asking?" said Bethany.

"I killed a man. My husband."

"Oh."

"Yeah, but they couldn't prove it, so instead of stringing me up, they sent me down here."

"When is your time up?"

"Probably never. Even though they can't find a reason to hang me, they keep coming up with reasons to keep me in jail. So I'll most likely be here until I die."

"I'm sorry."

"Well, hey, at least I am still alive. That's better than the other thing. I hear Jones coming back. I'm not turning soft on you, but I thought you deserved to know my story."

"Would you tell me more someday? I think there is a lot behind what you just told me, and I would like to hear it all."

"Perhaps . . . Hey, Jones, what took you so long?" yelled Joann.

Jones arrived back at the cell block, but she did not come alone. The superintendent, Mrs. Stone, was with her. Jones opened the cell door, looked inside, and then, paling, took a step back. Mrs. Stone, however, strode right in the cell and looked around.

"Rather a stinking mess you have here, Worthless," she said. "After Jones carries out the trash, you will scrub this place until there is no trace of blood left in it. Do you understand?"

"Yes, ma'am. But . . ."

"What? You have something more to say?"

"Yes, ma'am. Uh, Susie just passed away a few minutes ago. Will she get a proper burial, with words said over her grave?"

"Proper burial? Words said over her grave? Where do you think you are? A convent?"

"No, ma'am, but everyone deserves a proper burial, even the worst criminal, which Susie was not. She was a child, only fourteen years old, and they sent her here because she stole some bread to feed her brother. Can't you find any compassion in your heart for her, ma'am?"

"No, Worthless. In the eyes of the law, she was a criminal, and that is how her body will be treated. Jones will wrap her in her blanket, and then after the men have dug a hole in our cemetery this morning, she will dump her body in, the men will fill in the hole, and that will be it. No ceremony, no priest or minister to say words over her. That will be it. Any more questions?"

"No, ma'am," said Bethany, her voice quivering.

"Good. In a couple of hours, I will talk to the men's superintendent about digging a grave. You start cleaning up this mess," she said as she kicked the blanket on the floor that contained the baby before leaving the cell.

"You shouldn't have to clean up the cell, Worthless," called Joann. "That's not your job. You've done enough already."

"I don't mind. It will help to take my mind off what happened to Susie. But, Jones, can we not at least get a clean blanket, or sheet, to wrap Susie's body in? These are both bloodied."

"No, it would be a waste of good blankets to wrap her in a clean one. Besides, she don't know the difference now."

"No, but I do," said Bethany.

"Me too," said Joann.

And there was a chorus of agreement from all the other cells.

"I have to account for everything that I take out of the storeroom. How do I account for one for Susie's body?"

"We also need another gown. Worthless' is ruined now."

"What else would you like, Your Highness?" Jones said to Joann. "China and silverware for your meals?"

"That would be nice," said Joann, "but no, I can make do with what I have. But Worthless here sacrificed her own blanket and gown to care for Susie when you wouldn't even go near her. So, don't you think she deserves a bit of a reward from you?"

"I'll see what I can do, but I'm not promising anything. You hear me?"

"Good enough. And Worthless, because I have been here so long, I have an old gown and blanket that we can dress Susie in. It's old, but it's clean, and she is welcome to it."

"Thank you. Would that be all right, Jones?"

"I suppose so. Never heard of you ever being that kind before, Canter. What's up?"

"Nothing. Just showing a bit of human kindness today."

"You, human?"

"Yeah, believe it or not, I am. But just today. Tomorrow I'll be back to my normal self again."

"That's good to know. Don't know if I could stand much of your humanity."

"Like I said, don't get too used to it. Now, come and get my things and give them to Bethany so she can dress Susie. Unless you want to do it?"

"No, I do not."

"Didn't think so. Blood doesn't agree with you, does it?"

Not wanting to admit to her weakness, she stayed silent as she went to Joann's cell and took the gown and blanket from her. Once she had given them to Bethany, she headed off to get supplies to clean the cell.

"Thank you, Joann," said Bethany. "That was kind of you."

"Well, I had no proper use for them, and I agree with you, Mary Worthless. When you die, even here, they should treat you with a bit of dignity, not like trash."

"Even so, you did not have to help. You hardly knew Susie."

"I did it just as much for you as for Susie, Mary. But don't get the idea my kindness will last. It will most likely be gone tomorrow."

"We'll just see, Joann. We'll just see."

Jones was soon back with a brush and a bucket of water that Bethany could use to clean the cell. By this time, Bethany had changed Susie's gown, and after placing the baby on her breast, she had wrapped them both securely in the clean blanket. Before she had covered Susie's face, she'd dropped a kiss on her rapidly cooling forehead. "There, Susie, you and your baby are together, just as I know you are in heaven. And until the day that Jesus returns and raises up your body, your baby will stay wrapped in your protective arms. Goodbye, sweet one, and pleasant dreams."

"Here is your bucket and brush, Worthless. I'll take Susie now to her resting place. What is this lump on her chest? No, don't tell me. I don't want to know. Just start cleaning and I'll release you from here once your work is done," said Jones, before picking up the bundle from the bed and heading out the door.

"Carry her gently, please? Don't drop her."

"Of course I won't. Just like Canter, today I have a bit of humanity in me, but it won't last long, only for today. Now, get to scrubbing that floor."

"Yes, ma'am," said Bethany as she picked up the bucket and brush and started scrubbing away the blood stains on the floor.

***

After lunch, and a gruelling morning of cleaning Susie's cell, Bethany and the other prisoners were once again shackled and chained to each other before being marched out to the yard for their daily dose of sunlight. Because of Susie's death, Joann was now chained to Bethany. Although Joann had shown her softer self earlier this morning by donating her clothes and blankets to Bethany, she was not sure what to expect when they were together in the yard. However, when they lined up for their ladle of water, after Joann had taken one and was offered her second, she said, "No, give it to Worthless. She deserves it after what she had to endure this morning. So I will only have one ladle now and one later. I'm practising human kindness today." She laughed.

Bethany gratefully drank a second ladle of water, and after they had finished and moved forward, she said to Joann, "Thank you, Canter. That was kind of you. You are full of good deeds today. Watch out, or this may become a habit for you.".

"Not a chance, Worthless," replied Joann with a grin. "But it is nice to surprise people occasionally. Keeps them on their toes." As they moved forward again, they carried on the banter until each woman had had her drink of water, and then Jones offered a surprise of her own. "Today, while you are here in the yard, you will be unchained from your mates and able to walk around the yard on your own. Your shackles will remain in place, but if you behave yourselves, this may be our pattern from now on." She moved down the line and unchained each of the prisoners from each other. When she got to Joann and Bethany, she said, "I don't want any trouble out of either of you. Got it? Otherwise everyone goes back on the chain."

Bethany and Joann agreed, and then just stood there for a moment, not sure what to do with their *freedom*. Then Joann said, "Uh, I see a patch of shade in the corner I am going to head towards, Worthless. You are welcome to join me if you care to do so."

"Thanks. My joints are so stiff from scrubbing this morning that I should move around, but shade would be nice. How much will I owe you for this kindness?" Bethany moved with Joann across the yard.

"My favours are free today. Tomorrow I'm sure I'll be back to normal."

"Well, I'll take what I can get today and see what tomorrow brings. After last night, I don't think anything will surprise me ever again."

Sitting down on the hard, sun-baked earth, Bethany wondered if she could get up again without help. Her back, legs, and arms screamed with pain as she gingerly lowered herself to the ground. Joann watched her as she cringed a couple of times before she got settled. "Are you all right?"

"I am feeling the effects of scrubbing that floor this morning. I may need your help to get back to standing later, but we will see. Uh, because you are handing out favours today, I have one more to ask of you."

"What's that? You're pushing your luck now . . ."

"Could we call each other by our first names while we are here and no one can hear us talking? I feel like I am losing part of myself."

"That's fine, Mary, but only in the yard and when we are alone. Agreed?"

"Agreed. So, what shall we talk about?"

There was a moment of silence until Joann said, "I don't know. Nobody here has ever asked me that question. We only talk about how to survive and nothing more. Is there anything else to talk about?"

"You know a bit about me," said Bethany, "but I know almost nothing about you except that you have been here fifteen years for murdering your husband. Did you really kill him?"

"They said I did."

"But did you?"

"What difference does it make? I'm here and I probably will stay here until I die. Nothing I say is going to change that."

"I was sent here unrightfully, Joann, and I sense you were as well. How old were you when you arrived?"

"Fifteen."

"Fifteen? Almost the same age as Susie. When did you get married?"

"When I was fourteen."

"How old was he?"

"Eighty."

"You said *eighty*, not eighteen, right?"

"Right."

"Did you want to marry him?"

"Look, Mary, I don't want to answer all these questions. If I tell you my story, will you stop pestering me?"

"All right, I'll try to keep my mouth shut."

"Huh! I'll believe that when I see it. But just to satisfy your curiosity, I'll tell you how I came to be here. But I don't know where to start."

"Well, you said that you understood a bit of what happened to Susie, and how she came to be with child. Is your story the same?"

"Not exactly," said Joann, before she started to tell her life story. It started with a loving Christian mother who had married a man who was sweet and caring, until after their wedding vows. Then he started to drink and became abusive to her mother. After Joann was born and he found out she was a girl, and not a boy like he had been hoping for, he became even crueller to his wife. She died when Joann was fourteen, while trying to give him a son, but the baby died as well. Then her father turned on Joann. She tried to keep out of his way as much as possible to avoid getting hurt. One day, her father told her to put on her best dress and come with him to the village church. She asked him why, but he told her it was none of her business. Not wanting to anger him, she did as he requested, and had willingly gone with him. When they got into the church, they saw the vicar standing at the altar, and to his left was an old man dressed in a suit. The vicar's wife was also there, holding a posy of wildflowers. When Joann and her father reached the altar, Joann was handed the bouquet of flowers, and the old man took the hand that her father relinquished to him. Only then had Joann understood what was going on. She was being married . . . to a man older than her father. She had tried to pull away, but his grip was surprisingly strong. When it came to her agreeing to marrying him, no one listened to her complaints, and the service carried on. Finally, the old man slipped a ring on her finger, and she became Mrs. Joann Canter. When the vicar pronounced them man and wife, he leaned down and gave her a dry kiss on her mouth, her first kiss, and it made her want to throw up. It was over as soon as it started, and then he turned to her father, reached into his vest, pulled out a sack of coins, and handed them over. Her father thanked him, then without another word to Joann, he turned and left the church; she never saw him again. The old man gave the vicar another sack of coins before pulling Joann out of the church and up the hill to his manor. There was no wedding celebration that day, for which Joann had been thankful, but the worst was yet to come. That night the groom tried to consummate their vows, but he was unable to do so. He tried several times over the next months to no avail. Joann learned to endure his hands on her body, but she secretly thanked God every time her husband failed. Then one night, about a year later, after his feeble attempts were unsuccessful again, he collapsed on top of her. Pushing him off, she thought he had lost his breath, but soon she realised he had lost it forever. He was dead. She ran downstairs and informed the servants of his death. The butler ran back upstairs to confirm her story before going for the village constable. Because Joann had been with him in the bed when he died, a story was circulated that she had murdered him. The family insisted he had been in excellent health and the local physician agreed with them. This had led to her being arrested, put on trial, and convicted of his murder. But because there was no conclusive evidence to support the claims, her sentence had been commuted from death to transportation to the colony for the rest of her life. She was never getting out of here. Concluding her story, Joann said, "And that is the end of my sad tale."

"Just a minute, Joann. You said you had killed your husband. But if he died like that, how did that make you his killer?"

"The doctor said if he had not been exerting himself so much, his heart would not have given out, so it was my fault that he died."

"What? And the court believed him? That's ridiculous!"

"Why would they not? My husband had been an *upstanding* member of their community for many years, and me, I was nothing to them. They also thought I killed him for his money, which, of course, I did not. He made it very clear to me that I would receive nothing from his estate. I knew that from the start of our marriage. So why would I kill him? But no one believed me, and here I am."

"I'm so sorry, Joann. I can't imagine what you went through in your marriage, especially being that you were just a child bride, and then to be convicted of something you never did. That is a crime unto itself. Did you not have a barrister to help you?"

"Yes, but he was a distant cousin of my husband's and only wanted the money for defending me, so he never said much at the trial. Now you know why, if once I believed in God and His love for me, I don't anymore."

"I can see how you might feel that way. My faith was very weak after I was put on trial and convicted of theft. But now I am starting to believe God has a plan in all of this for me and I just need to trust Him and obey what He tells me to do."

"Well, good for you, Worthless, but I don't believe anymore, and I never will, so you are wasting your time preaching to me."

Surprised at Joann's abrupt change, Bethany looked up and saw Jones approaching them. Then she understood why Joann had spoken like she did; she did not want the warder to hear them.

"Time to go back, ladies. Good thing you two are the first in my chain. I'll get you two linked and then we will get the others. Break is over."

Struggling to get to her feet unaided, Bethany suddenly felt a hand under her upper arm, helping her to stand. It was Joann. "Thought you might need a helping hand, Worthless, otherwise we might be here for a very long time waiting for you to stand up. Just another good deed for today. Piling up points with God."

"Thank you, Canter. Much appreciated. But you don't need points, just Jesus."

"Whatever you say. Now, let's get out of this heat. Can't stand any more of it, or your company."

Bethany agreed, and they headed off with Jones to round up the rest of their chain gang.

***

While Bethany and Joann were discussing their pasts, far across land and sea, another conversation was taking place in a seedy little tavern on the Thames River in London. This conversation, had she known about it, would have caused Bethany a great deal of unease, as it concerned her future, or lack of one. The two men talking had one goal in common: to make sure Bethany never returned to England to retrieve her estate. And they would stop at nothing to achieve that goal, not even murder.

Chapter 8

"So," said Frank, "it wasn't good enough that you sent her away to a prison on the other side of the world, now you want to make sure she never comes back. Is that what you are telling me?"

"Yes," said Howard. "Unless I have definitive proof that Bethany Stillwater is no longer alive, the courts will not allow me to gain legal possession of the estate. I am hoping she did not survive the voyage to the prison, but I need proof of that. And if, perchance, she is still alive, we need to end her life."

"And what would be my role in all of this? I assisted you in framing her for theft. That would be enough to get me disbarred. But if I assist you with this new plan, they could hang me as a conspirator to murder."

"I am not asking you to commit the murder yourself. I know how you like to keep your hands clean, as do I. But I also know that you have frequent dealings with those who are not so squeamish about carrying out such a task. That is what I am asking of you today, to locate such a man and direct him to me for further instructions."

"How much are you willing to pay for such a task?" said Frank. "That is the first question they will ask me."

"Enough to make it worth his while," said Howard.

"That's not good enough. I need an amount."

"£5000 sterling; two on agreement, and three when I have proof the task has been completed."

"£5000? That is an enormous amount. Where are you going to get that much cash?"

"Let me worry about that. If needed, I will sell some of Cassandra's jewellery. She would never miss a piece or two. I suppose I could always put a lien on the estate, but that might be difficult as I am not yet the recognized owner."

"I don't know, Howard. Suppose my man decides that £2000 is enough, absconds with it, and never returns."

"Then I guess you, my friend, will owe me that money, or word of your under-the-table dealings will leak out and kill your business."

"All right, I hear you. But I will need time to set this up for you. But can I ask you one last thing?"

"I guess so. What is it?"

"Why are you going to such lengths to get rid of your stepsister? It can't all be for just money . . . is it?"

"No, it goes deeper than that. Back to our early days as brother and sister. Bethany stole everything from me. My mother's love, her father's affection . . . it all went to darling little Bethany. She left nothing for me. I was an outsider to their perfect little family. And I'm tired of getting all of Bethany's scraps. I want it all. And this way I can have it all for myself, without having to share anything with my beautiful little sister."

Frank mused on Howard's words. *He is a very angry man, much more than I realised. If I could do something to stop this madness, I would. But I can't, and if I don't go along with him, he will expose me to the whole of London. I can't afford to have that happen, so I guess there is nothing more to be done but find him an assassin.* "How soon do you need this man?"

"Being that he has a long trip ahead of him, and back again, I need this to be set up soon."

"I'll see what I can do in a hurry. Where would you like to meet him?"

"Here, in seven days."

"That's a tight schedule, but I will try to make it happen. If that does not work, I will send you a message."

"Fine. But remember to keep your mouth shut. Word of this leaks out, and we are both in big trouble. Do you understand me?"

"I do, and I will make sure we keep this to ourselves." Frank got up from his chair, and after swirling his black cape around him and donning his top hat, he bowed and left the tavern.

Howard sat there for another minute. Contrary to what he had told Frank, he was not without feelings for Bethany. Most of what had transpired had not been her fault, at least not until recently. He had loved having a little sister who adored him and hung on his every word. But . . . those days were over. If only she had listened to him . . . now this was the only way to get his hands on the estate money. There were men breathing down his neck about the money he owed them, and it was not just his neck on the line, it was his arms, his legs, his . . . If worst came to worst, he could go down and do the deed himself, but as he had told Frank, he hated getting his hands dirty. Better to get someone else to do it, and then he could reap the benefits.

A few days later, Howard got a message from Frank. He had found his man, and he would do the job. They would meet with Howard in three days at the same tavern on the docks. He was to bring cash with him to pay the first instalment of the man's fees, otherwise the deal was off.

Knowing he now had a deadline to meet, Howard scurried around to find the cash to pay for Bethany's murder. Not having enough money in his bank account, he assessed Cassandra's jewellery and determined that a diamond necklace and earring set he had given her for an anniversary a while ago would not be missed immediately.

To Howard's delight, the jewels brought him the cash he needed and more. He now had enough for Frank's man, and a little on the side for a night out on the town. Perhaps tonight luck would be with him and he would bring home a bundle. One of these nights he would have the upper hand and win a fortune that would last until the estate came into his hands. From that time forward, he would live a life of ease.

Three nights later, the three men met at the tavern by the dock.

"You got my money?" asked a tall, heavy-set man.

"I do."

"Put it on the table. I want to see it before I agree to this deal."

"Isn't that rather unwise in here?"

"I suppose so. But you better be playing it straight, mister. Otherwise I might come after you instead of the target."

"I am. I have the money and will give it to you after we leave, and after I get your agreement to my plan."

"What plan? I do things my own way. You tell me who you want done in and where, and I do it."

"Okay. Here's the gig. I want you to find out if my stepsister is still in the land of the living, and if she is, get rid of her. Her name is Mary Worthless, and they sent her down to Fremantle Prison in Western Australia. She is doing seven years for theft, so if she did not die on the prison ship, she should be there. I want you to make sure she never leaves the prison. You can choose the method. I don't care how you do it; I just want it done, and I need proof of her death."

"What kind of proof?"

"Something that is specific to her. Don't try to pass off anything else to me, like a lock of hair or a piece of clothing. She has a heart-shaped birthmark on the little finger of her right hand. That should identify her to you, and would serve as proof of her death, if you were to—"

"Howard!" interjected Frank with horror. "You want him to . . ."

"What? She won't feel a thing or miss it. She'll already be dead. Right?" Howard asked his assassin.

"Right-o. Quick as a wink, after she's gone. No fuss, no bother."

"See, he's not as squeamish as you are, Frank."

"I don't know. It just doesn't seem right, doing that."

"Is any of what we are planning *right*?"

"No, I guess not."

"Then get over it and shut your mouth."

"Yes, Howard."

"Now, once I've given you your cash, man, it's up to you to book your voyage and make your way south. I can't be involved in that. It's too risky for me."

"Got it. Now, when did you want me to go?"

"As soon as possible. I need this over with now so I can get on with my life."

"All right. Do you need to see me again before I leave?"

"No, only after you get back with the proof."

"May take a while, mister."

"I know. But try to move as quickly as possible. If you do, there may even be a bonus in it for you. Now, it's time to leave. I suggest we leave separately and meet at my hack."

The other men agreed and then, one by one, they paid their tabs and left the tavern to saunter down the street to where Howard's hack was waiting. Once they were all there, Howard paid his assassin the two thousand pounds, and then the three of them split up. Howard sat back in the hack as it left the dock area and thought, *it's over now except the waiting, and that will be the hardest part. Just waiting . . .*

Fortunately for Howard, the assassin found a clipper that was heading to Australia within the week. Although they were not taking on passengers, they were looking for sailors, even green ones, so he signed on with the crew for the voyage. Being a clipper, and if the winds were favourable, they could be in Australia within three months, rather than the six to eight months it took the larger sailing ships. He could be down and back within the year, enjoying the fat wad of money Howard had promised him. Life was looking up. But first he had a job to do.

***

Bethany was finding that the hours of the day stretched long. There was nothing to do but sit in her cell. She looked forward to the hour in the prison yard, but even then, it was to sit and visit with Joann or walk in endless circles around the yard. Bethany had never been one to sit by while others worked around her, so she found boredom to be her constant companion.

"Is there never anything to be done here?" she asked Joann one day. "I mean, they put the men to work while they are here, but we just sit idle all day long."

"You want to be breaking up rocks, Mary?"

"No, I don't think I would have the strength to do that, but there must be something we could do to pass the time. Has anyone ever asked the superintendent about it?"

"Not that I'm aware of, but you are welcome to try. Just don't count anyone else in, at least until we know what it is."

"This boredom is killing me. I need to be doing something, anything, or I will go crazy."

"Well, here comes your chance to break your boredom," said Joann, motioning with her head towards the entry to the yard.

Bethany looked and saw Mrs. Stone entering the yard. Dare she ask her about things to do? Or would it just earn her another punishment, either a beating or another chore, like scrubbing out a cell? Deciding that it was worth a possible punishment for speaking out, Bethany got to her feet and cautiously made her way across the yard, her shackles clanging as she walked. When she got within six feet of the superintendent, she stopped and waited for Mrs. Stone to acknowledge her.

"Yes, Worthless. What do you want?"

"I was wondering if I could have a word with you, ma'am?"

"A word about what?"

Bethany decided to plunge right in and ask for work. "I was wondering, uh, ma'am, if there was any work here that I could help do. I am not used to being idle, and so I would like to be productive here, if possible."

"You want to be busy, instead of just being a lady of leisure?" she laughed.

"I don't know that I am a lady of leisure, but yes, I would like to be busy doing something."

"Like the men on the chain gang? Smashing rocks?"

"I don't know if I would have the strength to do that. Is there anything else that needs to be done?"

"Well, today may be your lucky day. I just spoke with the director, and he has informed me there may be work, and some money, coming our way."

"Money for each of us?" asked Joann, coming up behind Bethany.

"Yes, I think that was his plan, Canter, although I don't know what you would do with money. You get everything you need from us, so what more could you want? And where would you spend it?"

"I could think of a few things that I would like, ma'am," said Joann. "Like a mattress for my bed, perhaps some utensils for eating, and maybe even curtains for my window. What would we have to do to earn this money?"

"A young man from England is here to buy wool for his mills. But rather than sending it all in bales, he is thinking perhaps they could card some of it, spin, and then knit it into garments for sale both here and in England. He needs women who know how to do those things, or at least are willing to learn, and he wondered if we could supply the workers."

"Would we be able to go out and work in his shop, ma'am?" asked Bethany.

"Of course not. What, so you can escape? No, the wool will be brought in here, as well as the necessary tools, and you will work here."

"We cannot work in our cells, ma'am. There is not enough light there for such a task."

"Then you will work in the yard every afternoon until the sun sets. Would that satisfy you, Worthless, or do you need more than that to relieve your boredom?"

"That would be fine, ma'am," said Bethany. She heard a chorus of agreement come from the women behind her in the yard. Obviously she was not the only one needing something to relieve the boredom.

"Very well. I will let the director know, and he can make the arrangements with Mr. Yardley," said Mrs. Stone before turning around and leaving.

A buzz started in the yard as soon as she left.

"I wonder how much money we will make."

"Is Stone going to keep a portion of our earnings for herself?"

"Does anyone here know how to do anything of those things she mentioned? If not, how will we learn the skills?

"I know," said Bethany, "and I can teach you."

"You, princess?" asked Joann. "Where did you learn such basic skills?"

"My mother taught me,"

"For what reason?"

"So that I would never be idle, and so I could teach others. I guess she was right."

"You won't get paid for teaching. We'll most likely get paid based on how much we produce."

"I don't mind. This sounds good to me because I need something to do with my time. This is another sign that God is looking after me."

"Oh, there you go again, Worthless, with your religious talk. I told you I didn't want to hear any more about God or Jesus."

"Sorry, Canter, I can't help myself."

"Well then, help yourself in silence and don't bother the rest of us with your words. Right, ladies?"

While a murmur of agreement came from some women in the yard, it was not as loud as it had been. Bethany smiled to herself. Perhaps God was working through her to spread His gospel. She would just have to continue serving Him and wait.

***

Outside the prison walls, someone else was having difficulty waiting, waiting to see if the woman he had glimpsed on the day they docked was Bethany Stillwater. Sam had devised this plan to have the female prisoners card, spin, and knit some of his wool in order to get inside the prison walls and observe the women. True, the garments they knit would advertise the beautiful, soft wool of Merino sheep, but they could just as easily do it in England. It would be simpler just to send bales of wool, not yarn or garments. But Sam wanted to get inside the prison to see Bethany, and no other avenue seemed to be open to him. The women's superintendent, and the prison director, had agreed with his plan, so now it was time to put it into operation.

Sam had talked it over with Nick and Sally, and they agreed with his plan even though they did not know the exact purpose. They both said how boredom was the main thing that started fights inside the prison and that the fights often had disastrous results. Sally especially remembered those long and lonely days without Nick, with nothing useful to do with herself. She was keen to help Sam in any way that she could, including teaching the art of making wool into yarn and knitting it into garments. They could probably sell the knitted garments in the mercantile; they would just have to speak with Joe first about having a place to display them. And while Sally would have

A JOURNEY TO JOY

liked to have the women knit things for babies and women, there were not enough of them around to warrant that kind of product. So they would concentrate on men's socks and sweaters; she was sure those would be big sellers.

They had taken a bale of fleece into the prison, along with the things Sally would need to teach the women. Sam had asked, and the prison director had reluctantly agreed, to let Sam come in the first time to introduce himself and the program. But the director made it very clear to Sam that this was a one-time visit and after this only Sally would visit the prison. Although disappointed, Sam agreed, and they set the date for the program to begin.

Finally, the big day had come. Sam and Sally arrived at the prison gates about a quarter hour prior to when they could go inside. Sam realised that Sally might be nervous about going back inside the prison and asked her if she was all right.

"I have to admit that I am nervous. The day I walked out these gates, I never planned to come back, not even to visit. But because I know something of what these women are dealing with, and I agree with your plan, I will help you. However, the sooner they learn the craft, the better." Sally gave a slight shudder.

"Perhaps there is someone here who knows the craft and can teach the other women. I never thought to ask that of the director."

"I doubt he would know that. He doesn't have much to do with the women's side of the prison. That is Mrs. Stone's domain, and she rules with an iron fist. Unless there is trouble, the director stays as far away from here as possible."

"Mrs. Stone?"

"Yes, the women's superintendent. She will be the first woman you meet today."

"Was she here when you and Nick were here?"

"Yes, I think she has been here forever. I don't know where she came from, but I am sure that she will die here."

"A lifer, huh?"

"I guess you could call her that, only please don't do it to her face."

"I won't. Nothing should jeopardise us being here. Oh, I see the gates are opening . . . After you, Sally."

"Mr. Yardley and Mrs. Tremblant. A pleasure to see you both again," said the director, a medium built man with greying hair. "I am looking forward to seeing how our mutual project comes along." Then, glancing behind him, he said, "Ah, here comes Mrs. Stone, our women's superintendent. Let me introduce you to her now."

When Mrs. Stone reached the trio, the director said, "Mrs. Stone, I would like you to meet Mr. Yardley, our benefactor in this new program. And I believe that you already know Mrs. Tremblant?"

"Yes," said the superintendent. "We have a previous acquaintance with each other. Good afternoon, Mrs. Tremblant."

"Mrs. Stone." Sally acknowledged her with a slight tip of her head.

"And Mr. Yardley," said Mrs. Stone.

"Mrs. Stone, a pleasure to meet you," said Sam, wondering if he was being entirely truthful.

"Well, now that we have the introductions out of the way, shall we go in? Mrs. Stone, are the women assembled in the yard to begin the program?"

"Yes, Director."

"Very good, then. After you, ladies. Mr. Yardley and I will follow you."

Trembling a bit, Sally moved up to walk beside Mrs. Stone, while Sam waited for a second and then joined the director in walking behind them. The two women did not speak or look at each other. As the group approached the prison yard, the director said to Sam, "Now remember, you are only to introduce yourself and your program. Then Mrs. Tremblant can take over, and a warder will escort you back to the gate. Understood?"

"I understood I was only to be allowed this one visit, Director, but I did not know that it was to be that short. Mrs. Tremblant and

I came together up the hill, and I would like to stay so I may escort her home after the session is done. Is that not possible?"

"Well, I suppose I will allow it for this one time, but only this once. Please, after you have spoken, move away from the women, and observe only from the side of the yard. That is the condition I will make if you want to stay, otherwise you will need to leave."

"I will abide by your condition, Director. Thank you for allowing me to stay today. I promise not to cause any problems."

"Just your looks, and the fact that many of these women have not seen a man for several years, is enough to cause problems, Mr. Yardley," laughed the director. "But I will allow it for this afternoon."

Embarrassed by the director's comments about his appearance, Sam did not respond. The only woman he wanted to have notice him was possibly in this group of prisoners, and he would do nothing to jeopardise his chance of seeing her again.

Then they entered the prison yard, and a titter of welcome echoed through the yard. The director strode up to the group of women seated on the ground and said, "Enough, ladies. After Mr. Yardley has introduced the program, he will move away from your group, and I want you to give your full attention to his companion, Mrs. Sally Tremblant, whom some of you might know. Mr. Yardley, if you please?"

Striding up to stand where the director had just stood, Sam said, "Ladies. Thank you for responding in such a positive way to this project. I am looking forward to seeing the results from your work in the coming days and weeks."

"Are you sticking around, Mr. Yardley?" came a voice from the back of the group.

"For the next while, yes, Miss . . .?"

"Canter, Mrs. Joann Canter."

"Yes, Mrs. Canter. At some point I will have to return home to England, but not for some time yet."

"So we will see more of you?"

"No. From now on, Mrs. Tremblant will supervise the program. I have not planned a return visit."

A chorus of dismay followed his remarks, then just as he was ready to introduce Sally to the group, the voice came again. "That's too bad, Mr Yardley. I was looking forward to getting to know you better. You should know . . . some of us in here believe your program is an answer to their prayers. Isn't that right, Worthless?" Joann said, turning her head and looking at Bethany, who had kept her head hung low while Sam was speaking.

"Not quite in those words, Canter," Bethany muttered.

"I'm sorry," said Sam, "I did not hear that, Miss . . .?"

"Miss Worthless, Mr. Yardley. Her last name is Worthless, sir," said Joann.

Sam stumbled a bit with the name. No one, no matter who they were, should be called Worthless. No one . . .

After being poked in the ribs by Joann, Bethany spoke up without raising her head. "I'm sorry, sir. I was feeling bored and useless on the day we got word about your program. I had been asking Mrs. Stone about work I could do to relieve that boredom. When we heard about your project, it seemed like an answer to my prayers. That is all."

"Thank you, Miss Worthless. Yes, God answers our prayers in miraculous ways, so I am glad He answered yours in such a way. Now, I would like Sally to come up and talk about the work itself. Sally?"

Sally moved up, and Sam stepped back, moving to the side of the yard to observe the group. Feeling like he was being watched, even though he was standing off to the side, he looked around and saw Mrs. Stone looking back at him. Standing straight as a ramrod, with her arms crossed in front of her and her eyes boring into him, Sam realised Sally had been right. This lady ran the show here, and she was not happy about this new program, not one bit. He only hoped that when Sally returned without him next week, Mrs. Stone would not take her anger out on her. Then, shifting his eyes to the back of the group where the previous comments had come from, he saw the two ladies of interest. But the one of most interest was Miss Worthless. Even now, she kept her head lowered and eyes looking straight ahead, as if she was aware of his interest and had no intention of allowing him any further insight into her life. The other woman, however, kept looking around and trying to catch his eye, but Sam refused to respond. He had no interest in her, only her companion. Why would she not have looked at him when she spoke to him? Did she have something to hide? Although her appearance was not that of Bethany Stillwater, there was just something about her, something that he could not understand, and that intrigued him. If only he could speak with her . . . that was it! It was not what she had said, but how she said it. She had Bethany's voice! Clothes and hair could be altered, but not the sound of Bethany's voice. Sam was even more certain now that this was the woman he was looking for, but how could he confirm it? And if so, why was she here?

The hour in the prison yard passed too swiftly for Sam, but not for Bethany. She could hardly wait for him, and Mrs. Tremblant, to depart so that she could get back to her cell and process what had transpired. She had felt his stare on the back of her head for the entire time Mrs. Tremblant was speaking. Joann kept nudging her to get her to turn around and glance at Sam, but Bethany resisted. It had been bad enough having to speak with him during the question time, but she was not going to single herself out for his attention anymore. That would only have landed her in more trouble with Mrs. Stone, and that was the last thing Bethany wanted. So she kept her eyes focused on Mrs. Tremblant, or on the ground, and did not look anywhere else.

When the session ended, Bethany got up and hurried across the yard towards the cell block. When she got to the entrance to the block, she did not see Sam in the shadows before he whispered to her, "Bethany Stillwater, is that you? I mean you no harm, but if it is you, even under another name, please, I need to know. I saw you when you left the prison ship, but I was unsure it was you. Even today I am not confident it is you, but your voice, your voice has not changed. It is still the sweetest voice I have ever heard, so please tell me if it indeed is you, and why on earth you are here?"

"Mr. Yardley," answered Bethany, almost in tears, looking around fearfully for Mrs. Stone. "I am not the one you are looking for. My name is Mary Worthless, and I am here doing time for theft. Now, before you get me in trouble with the superintendent, I ask that you move away from me and never approach me again. Please, just leave me alone!"

"I am sorry to have disturbed you so, Miss Worthless. That was not my intent, nor was it to get you into trouble with Mrs. Stone. Please forgive me," he said before he faded back into the shadows.

Fearing this might be the last chance that she ever got to see him, Bethany whispered his name. "Samuel Yardley, thank you for remembering me. I will remember you for the rest of my life." Then she turned and almost ran to her cell, where she flung herself down on her wooden bed, stifling her sobs with her blanket.

As her sobs subsided, Bethany started thinking. Why had she rejected Sam and his help? When she first arrived and saw him standing on the ship's deck, she had wished that there was a way she could talk to him and ask for his help. But today, when the opportunity had been right in front of her, she had rejected him. Why had she done that? Was it shame for what she had become that made her flee from him? She had done nothing to be ashamed of. She was innocent. Or was it because she did not want him to see what she had become, a prisoner with ill-fitting clothes and shorn hair? That was more likely the reason. She wanted him to remember her as she had been, and not as she was today. Then, if her dreams ever came true, someday she could meet him again in London with her head held high as they passed a pleasant moment at a gala punch bowl once more. Such a ridiculous reason, and one she was not proud of. She might never see him again. She might die in this place. And now she had ruined her chances of receiving help because of her foolish pride. Her tears flowed again.

***

When he heard her whisper his name, Sam spun around again, but she was gone. Had he heard her correctly when she thanked him for remembering her? Even though she had denied her own name, he was certain this was indeed Bethany Stillwater. But why was she here, and how was he going to help her leave this place? He was sure whatever crime they had accused her of was a lie, and that someone wanting to do her harm had sent her here. That someone was most likely her stepbrother, Howard Stillwater. His motivation would be Bethany's estate and money. Samuel would not put it past him to arrange everything that had landed Bethany in this place. But how to prove it and get Bethany released, when he was so far from England and his resources there? That was something he would have to ponder over the next several days while getting his first shipment of wool ready to sail.

Chapter 9

While Sam was busy with work, the assassin was wending his way down the coast of Africa and almost ready to round the Cape of Good Hope and enter the Indian Ocean on his way to the western coast of Australia. The weather had been favourable, and the clipper was making good time, so the assassin hoped they would land in Australia in about six weeks. He hated waiting to complete his assignments, but there was nothing else to do in this case, so he worked hard with the other crew members to make the time pass more quickly. When he was at rest, he thought about how he was going to get access to his victim, especially if, as he had been told, she was in Fremantle Prison. He did not like the idea of voluntarily going into a prison; he had narrowly escaped being sent to Botany Bay himself. And to find a way into a women's prison block, that would be even more challenging. But he had never backed down from a challenge, especially when the pay was this good. He would just have to bide his time once he got to Fremantle and use any opportunity he could to get inside the prison walls. Until then, he would just enjoy the trip.

***

Howard, too, was on the move. Soon after he made the deal with the assassin, he wondered if he had done the right thing, giving such a large amount of money to a stranger without being there to supervise his work. Suppose the assassin did as Frank had suggested he might, take the money and run off to places unknown. Howard would be out two thousand pounds with nothing to show for it. So he decided to make the trip to Australia himself, to ensure he had spent his money well. He headed down to the port office to find out what types of ships would be available to carry him south as soon as possible. He was in luck. According to the port office, there was a clipper leaving Portsmouth in one week's time, and it still had room for passengers. Howard paid the fare with the last of the money he had received from pawning Cassandra's jewels and headed home to pack. He did not tell Cassandra where he was going, only that he was going to be away on business and not to expect to see him for a while. He informed her that if she had any financial issues while he was away, she should contact Bethany's solicitor, Mr. Brown, for help as he was still handling the affairs of the Stillwater estate. Cassandra did not question him as to where he was going and when he would be back; she was just glad she would not be seeing him again soon. She agreed that she would talk to Mr. Brown with any concerns and then wished Howard a *bon voyage* before leaving his presence. That was the last time Howard saw either her, or his sons, before boarding the train to take him to Portsmouth and beyond. Soon he settled into his small cabin on the clipper and headed south, only weeks behind his hired killer.

***

Sam supervised the last of his fleece bales being loaded onto the steamship. He had enclosed a letter to his father with the shipment, detailing the agreement that he had made with the sheep farmers up north, and explaining why he was not returning home. Sam felt it was important for him to stay here, not only for business reasons but also to keep as close a contact as he could with Bethany, through Sally's weekly visits to the prison. He had divulged little to Sally, just enough so she would let him know if there was anything amiss with Bethany. That was all he could do at the present time until he received word back from his father regarding what had happened to her, and if there was any way to legally get her out of prison. Because he had decided to stay on in Fremantle, he had looked for more permanent lodging outside of Nick and Sally's house. Finding none, Sam was glad to hear they did not mind having him stay on as a semi-permanent lodger. And Sally's cooking beat anything he could cook for himself. After loading the bales of wool on the ship, it began its voyage to England. It would be a long time before Sam would hear from his father regarding his quest, so he decided to do a bit of looking around the countryside while he had the chance. He hired an aboriginal guide, Tojo, who knew the area like the back of his hand. Tojo was more than willing to show Sam the land of his birth and tell him stories of his people. Sam told Nick and Sally to expect him when they saw him, and because they knew he was safe with his aboriginal guide, they saw him off with waves and good wishes.

***

Meanwhile, Bethany was having a hard time adjusting to the new routine of spending every afternoon in the prison yard, carding and spinning wool. It was not the work that bothered her. In fact, she enjoyed being out of her cell for several hours each day, working with the beautiful fleece. No, it was that Sally Tremblant came almost every afternoon to join them and teach the less skilled women the art of creating yarn. When she had found out Bethany already had many skills in crafting wool, Sally asked Mrs. Stone if she and Bethany could spend a few minutes together each day, before the other women came to the yard, to review each woman's progress and decide which skills to concentrate on that day. Mrs. Stone had reluctantly agreed to Sally's suggestion, requesting that one warder was always present in the yard with them. Sally agreed with this demand, and so fifteen minutes before they released everyone else to go the yard, Bethany's cell was unlocked and she and Jones headed down to the yard. Jones would take up her post just outside the cell block, and Sally and Bethany would sit down in the middle of the yard to have their daily conversation.

It was not the conversation about the task at hand that bothered Bethany, but that Sally was always trying to get her into conversation about her past. Being that Sam was lodging with Nick and Sally, Bethany suspected he was behind the gentle questions such as, "Where did you grow up?" and "Where did you learn the art of working with wool?" Innocent as the questions were, Bethany wondered if Sally was gathering information that Sam could use to determine her true identity. But for her own peace of mind, she reminded herself that Bethany Stillwater was dead. Only Mary Worthless lived on in her place.

Bethany wondered if Sam had heard her last words on that day when she had fled from his presence. But even if he guessed her identity, what could he do about it, and why would he even want to help her? After all, they had only been casual acquaintances in England, having only met briefly at a few society events. And he was the second son of a duke, while she lived at the lower end of high society's strata. No, his reason for probing must be just idle curiosity, not one of wanting to help her. So she would continue to play the game of being Mary Worthless and never reveal her real name to him.

"Mary," said Sally, "you are very far away today. Are you not well? Is the heat getting to you? I imagine it differs greatly from where you came from. Uh, where was that again?"

Bethany inwardly smiled at Sally's questions but gave her no direct answers. "No, I am well, but thank you for asking. Yes, the heat can be quite oppressive, but I have learned to endure it. Sunshine and heat are preferable to the many days of rain I was used to in England."

"Yes, I remember the rain," said Sally, "and that is one reason why Nick and I stayed here after they released us from prison."

"I cannot think how hard those years must have been for both of you, and how you survived."

"By God's grace, Mary, only by His grace. Otherwise, neither of us would have lived to leave prison."

"And then to stay in the shadow of this awful place. Why did you not go elsewhere?"

"The opportunity to do good, after being shut up for so many years, appealed to us. And we found there was a need for a boarding house here. So we stayed, and I am happy we did. Because every day I can look up here and thank God for my freedom. Now I can help other women here, not only with a craft but also with encouragement as they serve out their time."

"Well, as soon as I am released, I will be on a ship heading back to England. There will be no staying here one more day than I have to once my time is up."

"Perhaps you will change your mind later and see why God allowed them to send you here. I know I am glad of your company. Our lodgers are all men, and even though most of them are very pleasant, like Sam, they are still men. You know what I mean?"

"Yes, they do have a different perspective on life, don't they?"

"They do at that, and sometimes it can be quite tiresome. But enough about men. Now I think we need to decide on today's lesson, don't you agree?"

Glad to leave the personal conversation behind, Bethany agreed, and they began to discuss the lesson for that day.

***

Trekking into the back country along the banks of the Swan River was a wonderful experience. They left the flat plateau of the village and moved up into the lowbush country. Tojo pointed out a variety of shrubs and trees as they walked. There were bottle brush and other flowering bushes that reminded Sam of the heaths of Scotland. Myrtle and grass trees were abundant as well. As they moved farther upstream, the undergrowth lessened and the huge eucalyptus, wattle, and casuarina evergreens took over the landscape. It was a whole different world to what Sam had ever seen. The wildlife was unique as well. There were the small echidnas with needle-like covering, found hiding under the bushes, along with what came to be Sam's favourite of all, the quokka. It resembled a large rodent but had a face that looked like it was perpetually smiling. They were adorable to watch. When they were in more open areas, they saw kangaroos. Tojo said they were abundant throughout the land and ranged from the small wallaby to the large grey kangaroo. But as well as the non-dangerous animals, Tojo showed Sam which ones to avoid. These were mainly snakes and spiders. There were the non-venomous carpet pythons, but there were also many varieties of snakes containing poison that could easily kill a person. They included two varieties of brown snakes one of which was the spotted brown, the western tiger which was found down amongst the reeds by the river, the dugites, and the southern death adder, which by its very name Sam knew to avoid. Spiders such as the redback tended to live under rocks, but their bite was also lethal. The only hope if someone was bitten by a venomous snake or spider, said Tojo, was that the fangs did not pierce the skin, or the venom was not injected with the bite. Otherwise, barring a miracle from God, the person would die. Sam thanked him for the lessons and said he would keep a careful watch to ensure he did not encounter any of these creatures while he was in Australia. Obviously, while beautiful, the countryside could also be deadly.

Sam was glad he had had the opportunity to get out and see some of the back country with such an experienced guide as Tojo, but after about a month of trekking he was ready to head back to Fremantle. He was worried about Bethany, and without the ability to communicate with her or even hear about her, he was left wondering how she was doing.

Over their usual breakfast of fish and fruit one morning, Sam said, "Tojo, much as I have enjoyed our time together, I think it is time to head back to Fremantle. I need to be there in case there is any urgent news from home, or if there are business questions I need to deal with. Do you mind if we head west today?"

"No, man. I figured you would soon want to turn around and go back. You're the one paying for my services, so whatever you say goes."

"Thank you, and even though it will be quite a while before we part ways, I want to tell you how incredible this journey has been. You're the best and I will recommend you to others who want this same experience.

"Thank you, Mr. Sam. It has been my great pleasure. Many men that I have guided through the bush have complained about the snakes, the spiders, and the biting insects, but you have gone along with no complaints at all."

"It's an incredible place, but I would not even attempt to venture in here without an experienced guide. From what I have seen, that would be pure folly."

"Yes, it would, sir. Much as I love my country, I know many dangers lurk in the bush, and I am always watching out for trouble. Even when I do my own walkabouts, I know there is a possibility that I may never come back to my family. But it is a risk that I will take occasionally just for the freedom of being out here by myself."

"If I were a man like you, I would do the same thing. But being a newcomer to this country, I will leave such journeys to those who know the land best."

"You are a wise man, Mr. Sam, and I look forward to perhaps having another bush walk with you someday. Now, if you are ready, it is time to head back to civilization."

"Lead on then, my man, I'm right behind you," agreed Sam as he fell into step behind the man of the bush.

***

Having travelled well with no mishaps, Sam and Tojo reached Fremantle ten days later. When they got to the boarding house, Sam wanted to pay Tojo what he owed him, but he said, "No hurry. I know you are a man of honour and will pay me soon. I need to get home to my wife and children. You can leave the money with Joe, down at the mercantile. I am frequently there getting supplies and he books my treks for me. The next time you are down there, you can give Joe the money. Again, it has been a great pleasure to spend this month with you. I hope we can do this again someday."

"My thoughts exactly. I look forward to seeing you again soon."

After a handshake the two men parted, Tojo heading to his home north of Fremantle, and Sam to his room in the boarding house.

"Sam, you're back," said Nick, spotting him when he came in the door. "Did you have a good time?"

"The best, Nick, the very best. You live in an incredible piece of the world. I can see why you and Sally did not want to head back to England after they released you from prison. Not with beauty like this at your door. How are you and Sally? Anything new since I left?"

"Nothing much. We have a new lodger; he just came in on a clipper from England. Pretty quiet fellow, I'd say. But he has only been here a day or so and is just getting his bearings."

"Quiet, huh? Nothing like me?"

"Don't think so, but it is too early to tell. Other than that, everything is about the same. Sally is still going up to the prison most afternoons to teach and supervise the women in their wool crafting—"

"And Mary?" interrupted Sam. "Is she still doing all right?"

"Far as I know. But Sally can't get her to talk much about herself, even though they have been together for weeks now."

"I'm just glad she is still okay. I have to admit, I've been worried about her."

"Some men like the solitude of the bush, but not if they have someone special on their minds," teased Nick.

"I don't know . . ."

"But I do. Besides, I've been there, and I still am that way with Sally. Speaking of . . . Sally, my love, guess who's back from his long walk?"

"Sam, you're back!" yelled Sally, rushing over to give him a big hug. "Oh, we have missed you. How was your trek? Did you have a good time? What did you see?"

"Slow down, Sally. The man just walked in the door a couple of minutes ago. Give him time to breathe before he answers all your questions."

"Of course. I'm sorry, it is just that I am so happy to see you, I got carried away."

"Wish she got that carried away every time she saw me," said Nick, "but I guess when you have been married as long as we have . . ."

"Oh, you," said Sally, giving Nick a big hug and a kiss. "You know you hold my heart; you always have and you always will, so don't be making Sam think you are jealous."

"I know, love. I was just teasing you." He leaned down and kissed Sally again.

"All right, you two lovebirds, this is too hard on a single man, so I am going to take myself off to my room and have a nap before dinner. Is that all right?"

"Of course," said Sally, before heading towards the kitchen. "And I will see what I can find in the pantry to make a special welcome home dinner for you."

"Anything you make will be great. Living off the land has been interesting, but it sure doesn't live up to your cooking."

"You are such a flatterer, Sam Yardley, but I thank you for the compliment. Have a good nap and we will see you in a couple of hours."

"Right-o," said Sam, heading up the stairs to his room. Once there, he put down his knapsack and stretched out on the bed with a gratified groan. Yes, he had missed this as well. Good food and a soft bed, what more could a man ask for? Then, thinking about the display of affection that he had witnessed between Nick and Sally, Sam decided that a loving wife to come home to would be a great thing too. A loving wife . . . Bethany . . . Those were his last thoughts before he fell into a deep sleep.

Before long it was dinner time. Sam hurried with freshening up and changing his clothes, then headed down the stairs and followed the delicious aromas to the dining table.

"My goodness, Sally, you did all this while I was asleep. You are an amazing woman."

"Careful, Sam . . ." warned Nick.

"Enough, you two," said Sally. "It's time to eat. I wonder where our other guest is?"

"Here, ma'am," said a voice from the stairwell. "I needed to wash up before dinner. Sorry if I kept you waiting."

Sally motioned the man to a seat at the table when he appeared in the doorway. "Of course not, Mr. Stone. Why, we just got Mr. Yardley up from his nap, so now we can eat. Nick, if you will ask the blessing, then we can introduce our two guests to each other after that."

Nick nodded before bowing his head and closing his eyes. Sally and Sam did the same.

Sam could not focus on Nick's prayer; his focus was on the other guest. Stone. Sally had called him Mr. Stone. Was he any relation to Mrs. Stone up at the prison? Maybe he was here to visit her? From what Sam knew of her, he could not think why anyone would make such a long trip just to visit that woman. But if not, why was Mr. Stone here, and what was his business in Fremantle? Sam aimed to find out, and this meal was a good time to start. Because his thoughts had taken him far from prayer, Sam almost missed Nick's "Amen," the signal to open his eyes again. When he did, he found Mr. Stone staring straight at him.

"Let's dig in," said Nick, and then after a nudge from his wife, he continued, "but before we do, introductions are in order. Sam, I would like you to meet our newest guest, Jack Stone. Jack, I would like to introduce to you our friend and traveller, who has just returned from six weeks in the bush, Samuel Yardley. There, now that the introductions are over, let's eat. Sam, why don't you start with the meat, and you can start the potatoes, Jack?"

After they have passed the food around and everyone's plate was full, Jack said to Sam, "Mr. Yardley, is it?

"Yes."

"What part of England do you hail from, sir?"

"London. And you, Mr. Stone?"

"The same. Your name seems quite familiar to me. Have we ever met before?"

"Not to my knowledge, but Yardley is not an uncommon name."

"True, but I keep thinking that I at least know of you, even if we have not met previous to today."

"I cannot think where that might have been, but I am also curious about your name. There is a Mrs. Stone who is the superintendent of the women's block of Fremantle Prison. Are you perhaps some relation to her and are to visit her?"

"Mrs. Stone? Well, that is coincidental. No, I was not aware of any relatives here in Australia, but it might be worth a trip to the prison to see this lady and find out who she is."

"It is not easy to gain entrance to the prison," said Sally, who was listening intently to their conversation. "And Mrs. Stone rarely leaves the grounds. She has quarters there as well, so we do not often see her here in the village."

"Still, it might provide some entertainment for me whilst I am here. How do you suggest I might gain an interview?"

"By being a newly landed woman convict. Otherwise, you might start with the director of the prison, Mr. Stanley. He might help you gain access to Mrs. Stone. But I warn you, she is not the sociable type."

"Thank you for your warning, but I would like to meet her. I will try to contact her by speaking with the director first. You said his name was Stanley?"

"Yes, that is his last name. I do not know his first name."

"No matter. When do you think it would be a good time to go up to the prison?"

"If you were trying to see a prisoner, then your only chance would be a week Thursday, in the afternoon. That is the monthly visiting day at the prison. But because you would like to see Mrs. Stone, you could go anytime, I suppose."

"Do the prisoners get many visitors on that day, Mrs. Tremblant?"

"No, because they have all been sent here from England and most of their families live far away, they do not see many visitors. Occasionally, a family member might visit, or even move here for the prisoner's term, but that is rare. So, visiting day is more of a gesture than a reality."

"How sad."

"Yes, it is. I have heard that Britain may soon stop transporting convicts to Australia and keep them in Britain. That would be much better for the prisoners and their families, I think."

"Indeed, it would. Well, enough about prisons and prisoners. Such a dreary topic. Perhaps we should let Mr. Yardley tell us all about his recent trek into the bush. Would you do that for us, Mr. Yardley, and brighten the mood around the table?" asked Jack.

"I would be happy to. But I will say one thing about the prison, before I move on to tell you about my trip. While it may seem *dreary* to you, to talk about the prison, for those who are living there, or have lived there, it is much more than that. It is a horrible place that no one, no matter what they have done, should have to endure. Even for the worst of crimes, I suspect that being hung, so that your punishment is over swiftly, would be preferable to a living death, which is what they are experiencing in Fremantle Prison today."

"Such an emotional response, Mr. Yardley," said Jack. "Do you perchance have someone near and dear to you living up on the hill?"

"No, but I have been inside the prison walls, and I know about the living conditions there. So if indeed Mrs. Stone is related to you, perhaps you could use your influence to better the conditions for the women in the prison."

"That would be presumptuous of me, as I have yet to meet the woman. But I will see what I can do. Now, your story, please?"

Sam relaxed back in his chair and related his adventures to his interested audience.

While he did so, Jack eyed him carefully. He knew that Sam's last name rang a bell with him, but for what reason? What was it? He pondered on this as he listened half-heartedly to Sam's tales—until Sam started talking about all the dangerous animals, from spiders to snakes, he and Tojo had seen. That caught Jack's attention. He thought about how he might use this new knowledge in his plans. Perhaps Mr. Sam Yardley could be useful to him in locating some of these creatures in the surrounding area.

"What are the chances of encountering these creatures here in Fremantle?" he asked Sam. "Do they live here as well, or just in the bush?"

"They are everywhere, Mr. Stone. But most of them are very shy and avoid contact with humans. So you are unlikely to encounter them unless you search for them."

"That is true," agreed Nick. "Sally and I have seen few of these snakes or spiders, even though we have lived here for over fifteen years. The main thing to do to avoid contact is to make lots of noise if you venture into the trees and not to be turning over any large rocks with your bare hands."

"Thank you for that advice," said Jack. "Any snakes or spiders I should particularly know about in this area?"

"Spotted brown snakes and redback spiders," said Sally. "Snakes like to heat their bodies in the sun, whereas spiders will hide under rocks, just as Nick said. So always be aware of your surroundings, especially in the bush."

"I will heed your advice." And I will search those very areas as soon as I can, in the event I need these creatures to do my work for me. It appeared Jack might not need Sam Yardley's help after all. What a pity. He had not had a kill in months, and it would have been nice to hone his skills before completing his task at the prison. Ah well, another time and place, perhaps.

***

The next day, Jack headed up to the prison to see if he could speak with Mrs. Stone. If it was Agatha, his long-lost sister-in-law, that would be a lucky stroke for Jack, as she could be his ticket into the prison. Agatha had disappeared years ago, right after her husband had died of a heart attack on the way home from the pub with Jack one evening. Jack had half-heartedly looked for her until another young woman had appealed to him, then he lost interest in pursuing Agatha any further. But if this was Agatha, he could use some lies to convince her to assist him, or he might have her arrested for poisoning her husband with deadly nightshade, which had caused his heart to fail.

When Jack got to the prison gates, he asked the guards if it would be possible for him to see the director. When he gave the guards his name, they startled for a moment, before leaving to call the director from his office. Shortly thereafter, the director appeared at the gates and said, "I am Director Stanley. I understand that you are John Stone. What can I help you with today?"

"Thank you for seeing me, Director. I was wondering if it might be possible for me to see Mrs. Stone for a few minutes."

"Mrs. Stone? Are you a relative of hers? You have the same last name."

"I do not know, Director. Yesterday, by chance I found out that we bear the same last name. I have looked for my late brother's wife for many years. She disappeared after he suffered a fatal heart attack. The doctor thought an ingestion of deadly nightshade might have caused it. Because Agatha vanished before they could question her, no one knew for sure. Not that I am accusing her of anything, you understand . . . and it was so long ago, I would not press any charges, if indeed your Mrs. Stone is Agatha. I would just like to meet her. That is all I wish to do. But if that is not possible . . ."

"No, no, no, I did not mean that you could not see her, I was just curious as to your reason, Mr Stone. Please, come inside. Tom, would you go and bring Mrs. Stone to my office?"

"Yes, sir, but what if she won't come, Director? You know how she is at times."

"Tell her it is a direct order from me. She cannot refuse a direct order, Tom."

"Yes, sir, I will, and I will bring her back right away," said Tom, before heading off across the prison yard to the women's cell block.

"Please, come with me to my office. We will wait for Agatha—I mean Mrs. Stone, there."

Jack's heart leapt when he heard the director say the name Agatha. Could it actually be her? Had she got this far away from Britain? But she had no money, so how could she have paid for passage down here, and how did she get this job? Questions running through his head, Jack decided to wait until she came to the director's office, and then he would know for sure. He just needed to be patient.

And then she was there. Jack heard her voice before she even entered the office. It was Agatha. He remembered her strident voice and how the sound of it had always grated on his nerves. "You wanted to see me, Director?" she asked as she strode into his office. "This had better be important, as I am—" She stopped midsentence and stared at Jack. Was it truly him? But why was he here in Australia? And why did he want to see her? With Jack it could only mean one of two things: money, or intimate relations. That was all he ever cared about back home. And she doubted that now it was the latter, so it had to be money he was after. But she had no money, so he was in for a huge disappointment.

"Agatha, dearest sister? Are my eyes deceiving me?"

"No, Jack, it is me."

"But we had given you up for dead, my dear. Have you been here all this time?"

"Yes."

"But why? Our family has missed you so since the sudden death of my brother."

"I had my reasons. Now, if you will excuse me, I need to get back to work. Was there anything else, Director?"

"Wait, Mrs. Stone. Don't you wish to speak with your brother further? As he cannot go into the women's cell block, you could use my office."

"Please, Agatha," said Jack, "it has been so long since we saw each other. Just a few more minutes of your time, my dear."

"Oh, very well. But only a few minutes. Thank you, Director, for the use of your office. We won't be long."

"Take as much time as you need. I need to run into the village for a few things, so I won't be back for a while. Enjoy your visit with your brother. It was nice to meet you, sir." The director picked up his hat and coat and headed out the door.

"Well, well, well . . . little Agatha, alive and well, and living in Australia. Who would have thought it?"

"Cut the chatter, Jack, and tell me what you came for."

"Why, to visit you, my dear sister-in-law. What else?"

"You did not know I was here, so you must have come because of one of your schemes. If you are looking for money, you are out of luck. I have none. And if you are looking for the other, forget it, and go back to England. I will have naught of you."

Jack laughed. "You think that I want that of you, Agatha? What a foolish notion. And no, I do not need your money, but I could use your assistance."

"I knew it. Jack and his schemes. You have not changed one bit. No, I want nothing to do with whatever you are planning, Jack, nothing at all."

"Not even for a share of the money that I will receive when I complete my job here?"

"What money? What job?"

"I won't tell you unless you agree to help me, Agatha. That is my deal."

"Does it involve anything criminal, Jack? You have always lived on the edge of the law. I am surprised they did not transport you here or to Botany Bay."

"Well, some might say that it is a crime, but I look at it this way. The person I am looking for will not continue suffering here for the next several years after I complete my work. And that might be more of a blessing than a curse."

"You are going to help someone, I presume a woman, because you are talking to me, to escape this prison?"

"Yes."

"Are you crazy? No one escapes from Fremantle Prison, and even if they did, they would have no place to hide before we found them again."

"I was not speaking of that kind of freedom."

"You mean . . . no, you can't be meaning . . ."

Jack raised an eyebrow.

"There is no way that I am going to help you murder someone here in Fremantle Gaol. If they caught me, I could be hanged for assisting you. And even if I were not, I draw the line at murder. So goodbye, Jack, and have nice trip back to England." She turned to open the door.

"Not even for £500, Agatha? Not even then?"

"Did you say £500?"

"I believe I did."

"Who would pay you that kind of money to murder someone in a prison?"

"Someone who needs her out of his way so he can inherit her estate."

"Who is that? Who is the target?"

"Uh-uh. No more until you agree."

"I need to think about this. I can't decide right at this moment."

"Okay, I will give you until visitors' day, Agatha. If you agree, I will need a visitor's pass to come back and see you to make our plans. If not, I will have to come up with something else, and you will be out the money I promised you. So think about it, and I will wait for your answer. I am staying at the Tremblant's boarding house, you can send your answer to me there. Such nice people . . . especially the missus."

"Don't you dare touch Sally Tremblant, Jack. If you do, I will not help you, and I will tell the director what you have just said to me. Leave the Tremblants alone."

"And what about the handsome young Mr. Yardley? Am I to leave him alone as well?"

"No, you can do what you want with him. There is something about him that bothers me, but I can't put my finger on it."

"I felt the same way on meeting him last evening, but for the present I will leave him alone as well. He may be of some use to me, and if not, I can always dispose of him later. Until we see each other again, dear sister, stay well. And silent." He headed out the door.

Agatha sank into her chair. Jack was here, and she knew he meant what he said. He was here to murder one of the women. But which one and why? Could she dare help him and get away with it? Still, £500 could get her away from here. She was so tired of this place; she needed a new start and a new life.

***

Sam was at loose ends. He had concluded his business; he could do no more now but wait on a reply from his father about their enterprise, and that would take months. He was tired of walking so did not even have the energy to walk down to Joe's place and chat with him. Sally was busy in the kitchen and Nick was working with the books for the lodge. Sam did not know exactly where the other lodger had gone, but their conversation last evening had not made Sam anxious to spend a lot more time with Jack. But what to do now?

Finally, he decided to go down and beg a cup of coffee from Sally, and if she was not too busy, have a visit with her. He wanted to find out more about what was happening at the prison. When he got down to the kitchen, he found Sally rolling dough for some type of tasty delight.

"What are you making?" he asked.

"Oh, I am just making up a batch of sweet rolls. They need to rise for about an hour. Would you mind watching them for me while I run down to Joe's to pick up some things? I won't be more than about half an hour."

"I'll make sure they do not run away. It's better than sitting in my room and staring at the ceiling. But only if I can beg another cup of coffee from you before you go."

"Of course, you are always welcome to help yourself. I just made a fresh pot, it's on the back of the stove. We'll have sweet rolls later today, but I only have this window of time to run to the mercantile. You're sure you don't mind helping me out? I could ask Nick, but he's busy with the books, and I hate to disturb him."

"No problem. You run along and I will grab a cup of coffee and sit here until you get back."

"Thanks. Do you need anything from Joe's while I'm there? I could save you a trip."

"No, not for right now, but thanks for asking."

"Okay, then I will be back soon."

When she was gone, Sam poured himself a cup of coffee before settling into a kitchen chair to watch the rolls rise. *I don't know if this is any better than staring at the ceiling in my room, but at least the aroma of the coffee and rolls are stimulating my senses.* And so, he waited . . .

*****

About a quarter hour later, Sam heard the front door open. Nick greeted Jack. "Was your trip to the prison a success?"

"It was," he heard Jack reply. "It turns out your Mrs. Stone is my sister-in-law, Agatha, whom we had long ago given up for dead."

"Really? That is quite a coincidence. You were able to speak with her today?"

"I was, and I hope to have a longer visit with her on visitors' day, if she agrees to see me again."

"Why would she not? I would think that she would be thrilled to see a member of her family after such a long time away from you."

"We did not part on good terms, so I think she is wondering if I am still the man I was when I was much younger."

"And are you?"

"Absolutely not," said Jack. "I have given up the ways of my misspent youth and am a different man now."

"Glad to hear it. But you may have to do a lot to convince Mrs. Stone of the changes in your life. She is not a very trusting woman, at least according to my wife."

"Your wife knows her well?"

"Too well. She spent ten years under the eagle eye of your sister-in-law at the prison."

"Oh, did she work as a warder?"

"No, she was a prisoner, as was I. We spent those ten years in Fremantle Gaol, together yet always apart."

"Really? I would not have taken you or your wife for the criminal type. What happened that they sent you here?"

"We were not, and are not, criminals. In fact, it was our landlord who should be called criminal for his actions toward us. But because he was of the noble class, and we were only lowly tenants, his word was better than ours. And when we could not pay our taxes one year because of a bad crop, he took it upon himself to send us to prison and grab our property for himself."

"I can't imagine such a man. Do you recall his name? Perhaps I know of him."

"I will never forget his name. It is Howard Stillwater, and if you ever chance to meet him, walk away, or you will be the worse for it. I warn all our lodgers in the same way, Jack, so just be prepared."

"I will heed your word, Nick," said Jack. "And if ever I meet him, I will do as you say."

"They gave me the same warning, Jack, when I first heard Nick's story," said Sam, coming into the room. "It is a terrible thing what some members of the nobility will do to their tenants."

"Are you quite familiar with the ways of the nobles, Mr. Yardley?"

"Yes, I have worked among them for several years, Mr. Stone, but fortunately, the ones I know are not of the same ilk as Howard Stillwater."

"Have you ever met him?"

"No, but I have heard of him."

"And you are of the same opinion of him as Nick is?"

"Oh, yes."

"When, and where, did you hear about him?"

"You are very curious about my past, Mr. Stone."

"It is just that I feel I know of you, and yet I do not think that we have ever met prior to this time."

"I do not know why you would think such a thing. Are you also in business?"

"Yes, to a degree."

"And what type of business, may I ask?"

"Providing a service that few else want to do."

"And that is?"

"I am afraid that I am not at liberty to disclose that to you. It is a very confidential business."

"I see . . ."

"No, I don't think you do. But your manner of speech, and your familiarity with Mr. Stillwater, has answered my question as to your identity."

"And that is?" said Sam, dreading the next words out of Jack's mouth.

"You are Samuel E. Yardley, second son of the Duke of Yardley, are you not? And if so, why are you living here and deceiving these dear folk?"

Chapter 10

Sam drew a deep breath after Jack revealed his identity.

"Sam, is this true?" asked Nick.

"Yes."

"But why would you not have told us right from the beginning who you were? Do you have something to hide from us?"

"No, Nick, I do not. There were a couple of reasons I did not inform you of my identity. First, you had painted all the upper class in the same brush as Howard Stillwater because of your terrible experience with him. Even though that is not true, in your mind you believe the worst of all the nobility. Second, it was a chance for me to escape all the formalities of being a duke's son and just be myself for a time. I have enjoyed that tremendously over the past few months. But if this revelation has hurt you to where you no longer wish my company, I will pack my bag and head down to Joe's to see if he will give me a bed at his place."

"No, no, of course not, Sam, or should I call you Lord Yardley now? I am just in a bit of shock, but it does not change who you are, or our relationship. I have got to know you as Sam Yardley, and regardless of your background, I wish to remain your friend."

"Thank you, Nick. I feel the same way. Please, continue to call me Sam. That is my name and I want you to use it, not my title."

"Well, isn't this sweet?" said Jack. "The noble and the working-class man, calling each other by their given names. This would not be the case in England, would it, Lord Yardley, even in your father's dukedom?"

"No, I suppose it would not, Mr. Stone," said Sam. "But this is a new country, with new ideas and new customs. We would do well to take some of this back to England with us when we return home. But what did you expect to achieve by revealing my name and circumstance to Nick?"

"Well, I expected my revelation would cause him to boot you out onto the street and have nothing more to do with you, after his previous misfortune with nobility. That is why I am surprised, and disappointed, in how he has reacted to my news of your heritage."

"After living here for these many years, I have learned to judge men by their character, not their heritage," Nick replied. "As I said earlier, I have learned about Sam's character over the past few months. While the disclosure of his title took me aback, it was only for a moment, and then I remembered what kind of man he was. While you, sir, have revealed characteristics I am not pleased to see. Therefore, I am wondering if you are someone to be trusted. I will reserve judgment until I get to know you better. We will say no more about this, although I hope that you are not planning to keep this secret from Sally. Are you, Sam?"

"Absolutely not. I was trying to find a way to reveal myself to you and Sally prior to this conversation, but I could not come up with a suitable plan. So Mr. Stone, you have helped me, and I thank you for that. And now, gentlemen, speaking of Sally, I promised to watch her rising rolls in the kitchen, so I had better get back there and do what she asked of me," he said, before heading in that direction.

"And I must get back to my books. I do not know why you thought to make such a statement about Sam, but if you wish to stay here, you will refrain from any similar behaviours. Do I make myself clear?"

"Very clear, Mr. Tremblant. I see I made a mistake in assessing your character and I apologise for that. I will try to restrain myself from any further misdoings."

***

Sally returned home shortly thereafter and found a very silent household. Noticing that Nick was still working on his books at the front desk, she went over, and after kissing him, said, "Why, it does not look as if you have made much progress with the books, my love. Are there problems in the accounting?"

"No, love, but I have had little time to deal with the numbers whilst you have been gone."

"Oh, and why is that?"

"I've been discussing some issues with our two lodgers."

"And that has caused you some distress?"

"Yes, and no."

"What does that mean?"

"Yes, it has distressed me to a certain degree, and no, the results, mostly, are most satisfying."

"Nick Tremblant, whatever do you mean?"

"Why don't you go in, tend to your sweet rolls, and ask Sam about our conversation?" He pushed her gently towards the kitchen. "I do need to finish with my work here before our noon meal."

"Very well," said Sally, "but if I am not satisfied with Sam's explanation, I will come back to see you." Then she opened the door and went into the other room.

***

Upstairs, Jack was fuming. He had thought that revealing Sam's identity, knowing how Nick felt about English nobility, would cause a deep rift between the two men. But instead it had backfired, and Jack had almost had himself thrown out of the boarding house. How dare Nick Tremblant, a nobody and an ex-convict, humiliate him like that? What difference would a couple more killings make? He was here for one, so another three did not matter to him. No one put down Jack Stone and got away with it. No one, not even a duke's son!

A little while later, there came a knock at his door. "Yes," he answered.

"Mr. Stone," said Sally's voice. "It is lunch time."

Turning on the charm, Jack went over to the door and opened it. "I'm sorry, Mrs. Tremblant, but what did you say? When you called me, I was trying to fix a crease in my blankets."

"I said it is lunch time, if you care to join us."

"I don't think that would be a good idea today. I had some unpleasant words with your husband and Mr. Yardley earlier this morning, so if I come down, the atmosphere might not be very congenial. Perhaps, if you would be so kind, you could bring me up some lunch after you have finished eating? I would be much obliged," he smiled.

"I suppose so, but we rarely feed guests in their rooms. And yes, I heard about what went on while I was away, and I have to say that I am very displeased with you, sir. So perhaps it would be best if you ate alone, at least for luncheon, and then we will see about dinnertime."

"That would be most kind of you. I will try not to cause any more upset while I am here as your guest. I promise you that," lied Jack.

"Very well then, I will bring you a tray in about a half hour."

"I shall await your return, Mrs. Tremblant," said Jack, before closing the door against her and going back to lie down on his bed. *Yes, I shall wait for your return, Sally, and the treats that you will bring me.* He laughed to himself.

***

The men went back to the front desk to finish Nick's paperwork; Sam having offered to help him with the task to give himself something worthy to do. This followed a congenial luncheon downstairs where the Tremblants had plied Sam with question after question about his background. Sally, with some misgivings, fixed a lunch tray for Jack and headed upstairs with it. She had not told Nick and Sam about what she was going to do, for fear that it would cause more conflict, but now she was wondering if she was doing the right thing. She had not liked how Jack looked at her earlier, having seen that look before from some of the male warders at the prison. None of them had ever gone beyond a look, but it caused her limbs to tremble. And Jack would be closer to her than the guards ever were when she handed him the tray. Perhaps she would just put the tray down outside his door, knock and let him know it was there, and then run back to the safety of her kitchen. Yes, that is what she would do. She would not give him any opportunity to touch her; she would just stay far away. Having made that plan on the way up the stairs, she walked over to Jack's door, put the tray down, but just as she was about to knock, the door flew open. Jack grabbed her and pulled her inside with a hand over her mouth, saying, "Thank you for coming, my dear. I knew you would. No woman could ever resist my charms."

Struggling against him as he pulled her towards the bed, Sally managed to loosen his grip on her mouth and bite down hard on his hand before kneeing him in his groin, as Nick had taught her early in their marriage in case she ever needed to defend herself.

"Ow! You little termagant! You will pay for that!" said Jack, as he sucked on his injured hand and folded up in pain on the floor.

"Leave me alone, Jack Stone, and leave here immediately, or I'll—"

"You'll what?" he groaned as Sally moved back to the hallway.

"I'll tell the constable what you tried to do. He will arrest you and put you in jail until the next ship leaves for England. Then they will throw you in the hold, and you'll stay there until you reach Britain.

After that, I don't care what happens to you. Just stay away from me . . . Oh, by the way, your tray is out here. Enjoy your lunch."

***

Nick wondered where his wife was. Not finding her in the kitchen, he called up the stairwell. "Sally, are you upstairs? I need to have a word with you." When he got no response to his call, he climbed the stairs and headed to their room. The door was closed, so he opened it slightly and saw Sally in front of her dressing mirror. He could see that her hands were shaking as she tried to comb her now unbound hair. His worry turned into fear, and he rushed into the room and over to the bed. "Sally, my love, are you all right? What is going on? Why are your hands shaking? Why is your hair down at this time of day?"

Sally tried to laugh, but it came out as a whimper. "Nick, so many questions. Which one should I answer first? I am fine. I came in here to fix my hair; for some reason it came undone. Don't worry, I am not ill. Did you need to see me?"

"Yes, I had a question for you about something I found in the books, but it can wait. Are you sure you are all right? You look rather pale. Perhaps you should lie down for a rest. You are always working too hard, love. Yes, that is it. You just stay up here for the next hour, and I will take care of things downstairs. All right?"

"No," Sally answered. "I am fine, and I don't need to rest. As soon as I fix my hair, I will come downstairs with you. Please don't fuss, love."

"Okay, but if you feel the need for a rest later, just let me know. Please?"

"I will. Now, what did you need to ask me?"

"It was about a certain entry in the ledger. I can't quite make out the amount, and I need you to look at it."

"I will," said Sally, her hair back in place. She opened the door and scanned the hallway for any sign of Jack. Seeing none, she stepped into the hall and then started down the stairs, followed by a still mystified Nick. *Women,* he thought, *can one ever figure them out?* Shaking his head, he headed toward the lobby behind Sally.

After deciphering the ledger amount for Nick, Sally said, "Now, I need to go to the prison. Did you need me to do anything else for you before I leave?"

"No, I was going down to Joe's to pick up supplies, but that could wait. Are you sure you want to go to the prison today, Sal?"

Thinking that he, and possibly Sam, might leave her alone in the house with Stone, she said, "I don't want to miss any days with the women. They depend on me coming to see them, and I don't want to disappoint them. I keep thinking of all those long hours I spent in my cell with nothing to do, and so I want to relieve some of that boredom for the women."

"Okay, but on one—no, actually two, conditions, will I let you go. One, you let me drive you there before I head down to the mercantile for supplies and then pick you up in a couple of hours. And two, I want you to leave early if you start to feel unwell. Will you do that for me, my love?"

"Yes, Nick, I will. And Nick . . ." she said, as he turned to go downstairs and get the mule and cart ready.

"Yes?"

"I love you, my husband. I hope you know that and never forget it."

"I love you too, Sally," said Nick, a little perplexed at her words. Not that she did not regularly tell him of her love for him, it just seemed odd that she had to reassure him right now. But he decided to accept her words at face value.

Before heading out to the shed to harness the mule to the cart, Nick noticed Jack coming down the front stairs. He was carrying his knapsack. "Leaving us, Mr. Stone?" Nick asked.

"Yes, after all that has happened today, I thought perhaps it would be better if I found a bed at the mercantile for the rest of my stay. I am heading there now."

"That is a good idea. Say, you would not know anything about what happened to my wife when she brought your tray up, would you?"

"No, what happened?"

"Nothing really, she is just not quite herself. She was fine at lunch, and now she is not."

"No, I'm sorry, but I don't know anything about her."

"Just wondering. But she insists she is well enough to go to the prison, so I'm off to hitch up the cart and take her there before going down to pick up supplies."

"You're headed to Joe's after you drop off your wife? Would it be too much to ask for a ride down the hill?"

"It's a nice day for a walk, so I am going to decline your request," Nick said as they got to the bottom of the steps. "I would like to fare thee well, but I can't seem to get those words out of my mouth. So goodbye, Mr. Stone. It has been very interesting getting to know you, but I hope our paths never meet again."

Feeling rebuffed again, Jack thought, *oh, I think we will, Mr. Tremblant, in fact you can count on it.* "I'm sorry you feel that way," he said instead. "I did not mean to cause any upset. I thought you would be happy to know who the real Mr. Yardley was, but apparently you don't care. So, I will take my leave of you now, and wish you a good day." He adjusted his knapsack on his shoulder and started his walk down the dusty hill.

"What was that all about?" asked Sam, coming out onto the step behind him. "Where is Stone off to now?"

"I don't know what is going on, but I can only say I am glad to see the back of that man and hope to never see him again."

"I echo your feelings, but is there something else I should know? It would give me great pleasure to go and beat him into the dust."

"No, but thanks for offering," laughed Nick. "According to Sally, everything is fine. I just wish that I believed her."

"Sally? What has happened to Sally? Did Stone have anything to do with it? Now I do want to run down and pummel him."

"Sally is fine, my friend," said a soft voice behind them. "And if her dear husband would get the mule and cart and take her to the prison, she would be much obliged."

"Sally, I'm sorry, I did not see you. You do not look well. Are you sure you want to go up to the prison today?'

"I'm fine. Now please, both of you, just leave it alone. Please?"

Before Nick headed over to the stable to hitch up the mule and cart, he gave Sam a look that said, *See?*

Sam interpreted the look to mean, *you try to find out what I cannot*, so he thought he would give it one more try.

"Sally," he whispered, his fingers crossed behind his back. "If you want to tell me what happened, I promise not to tell Nick."

"Hah! How long would you keep that promise if there was anything to tell, Sam, which there is not. So please, just stop asking. Please?"

"Very well, but I have to say one thing. Your husband is very worried about you and thinks that you are not being honest with him."

"Sam, enough! Leave it alone!"

"All right. You know best how you are feeling. But I am here if you need me."

"I know, and thank you," she said as she saw Nick approaching with the mule and cart. "Now, if you will excuse me, I need to get up to the prison. I will see you later." She hurried down the steps.

After Nick helped her up into the cart, he looked at Sam, but Sam just shrugged his shoulders and shook his head. So Nick clambered up into the cart and headed off to the prison.

***

When Sally arrived in the prison yard, Agatha Stone took one look at her and knew. Jack had not kept his promise. He had messed with Sally. Had he also hurt Nick? Before this afternoon was over, she would get her answers, and then on visitors' day she would deal with Jack.

When Bethany saw Sally, she gasped. "Sally, you look so pale. Are you all right?"

Sally half laughed before saying, "That is what I kept hearing from Nick and Sam. I guess I need to buy some rouge for my cheeks. I am fine, but thank you for asking."

"Sam is back? Is he well?"

"Very well," said Sally, glad to have the focus off herself. "He just got back yesterday. It exhausted him to do all that walking but he had a marvellous time and saw all kinds of wildlife."

"It must have been wonderful, Sally. The only wildlife I see here are rats and other vermin which I would rather not see at all."

"I know what you mean. When I was here, I lived in almost constant fear of being bitten by a rat, or a snake, or even spiders. Until one day, God spoke to me and told me not to fear because He was looking after me, and He would never allow them to bite me. After that, even when I saw them, I was not afraid anymore. And I never was bitten, not even once. God kept His promise."

"That's good to know. I am not sure I have your absolute faith in His promises after what happened to me, but I am trying harder to believe Him."

"The key to faith is not to try harder, but to just let go and let God do His work in you, and through you. Sometimes we get in God's way because we want to take control and try harder for Him. But He does not need that from us; He just wants us to abide in Him and let Him do all the work through us."

"Well, thanks for your sermon of the day, but I think we need to talk about wool and crafting. Mrs. Stone is standing in the yard watching us, which is odd, because she rarely comes out here in the afternoon. However, if she thinks we are just visiting, she might end the program, and that would hurt more than just me."

"Sorry. Sometimes I just get carried away with God's goodness and faithfulness to me. Oops, there I go again, off on another one. Yes, it is odd that Mrs. Stone is here. I wonder why. Uh oh, speak of the *devil* woman. Here she comes."

"Sally, Worthless, what topic do you have for the women today? You seem to be having quite an intense conversation. Do you mind telling me what it was about?" she asked, moving her stick from one hand to the other.

"We were just trying to decide on a topic, ma'am," said Bethany, hoping that the superintendent would believe her. "Perhaps you could suggest something?"

"Me? Whatever gave you the idea that I knew—know, anything about wool crafting, Worthless?" asked Mrs. Stone in surprise.

"Well, you seem to be quite knowledgeable about a lot of things, ma'am, and so I was wondering if you had ever done anything with wool?"

"Actually, I have. Before my husband died, we had a few sheep that he used to shear each year. He would then give the fleece to me to card, spin, and knit into garments for him. But it has been such a long time since I did any of that, I don't know if I could help you."

"I am sure you could, Mrs. Stone. We would welcome your assistance. Some women are quite the novices with wool, so we would greatly appreciate your expertise," said Bethany.

"Are you trying to butter me up for some reason, Worthless? I have much better things to do with my time than sit around in a hot yard working with wool."

"No, ma'am, I was just inviting you to join us. But as you say, you have much better things to do with your time. I'm sorry I bothered you with my suggestion."

"Well, maybe someday, if I don't have a lot to do, I might come out for a little while and check on your progress. After all, the success of the program lies upon my shoulders, and I would hate to see it fail."

"That would be fine, ma'am."

"All right then, I see the other women coming now, so I will head indoors. Be sure and keep them busy, Mrs. Tremblant," said Mrs. Stone before turning and heading into the cell block.

"Well, I never . . . Mary Worthless, you are quite something."

"I did not even know what I was saying. It just started coming out of me and I could not stop it."

"I believe *it* was the Holy Spirit speaking his words through you. Congratulations, you just put my words into action and see what happened. The *Stone* cracked."

Bethany giggled. "The proof of the pudding is in the eating, Sally. I will believe it when Mrs. Stone does come out and join us someday. That will be my proof."

"She will probably frighten all the other women away if she does, but then you and I can stay with her and keep chipping away at the *Stone* via the Holy Spirit."

"Stop it now, Sally Tremblant, before I keel over laughing. You are too much, my friend, too much indeed."

Sally closed her mouth. *Yes, we are friends, Mary, and soon you are going to confide in me just who you are and how you came to be here. I just know it for a fact, my dear.*

The afternoon passed swiftly for the women, and soon it was time for Sally to pack up her things and head home. After saying goodbye to Bethany and the other women, Sally started to head towards the gates when she heard Mrs. Stone call her name and come towards her.

"Sally, may I speak with you for a minute?"

"Yes, but only for a moment. Nick will be outside to drive me home, and I don't want to keep him waiting."'

"Can you come down to my office? I would like to speak privately with you."

"Your office? Can we not speak here? There is no one else about at the present time."

"Very well, but we must keep our voices low. I don't want anyone else to hear what I am saying."

Curious, Sally agreed.

"Uh, this is very hard for me to ask, Sally, but did your pale face today have anything to do with Jack Stone, perchance?"

"Why would you want to know that?"

"Because I know his history with women, and even though he says he has changed in the past twenty years, I do not quite believe him."

"If I said yes, would that make a difference?"

"Possibly."

"Then yes, it did."

"I knew it. Sally, I am so sorry. I should have warned you about him the moment that I again laid eyes on him, but I was hoping he had changed. Thank you for telling me. I will use this information to make sure that he never makes you feel this way again."

"How are you going to control his actions?"

"That is within my power, Sally, don't you worry about it."

"Well, as he is no longer lodging with us, I doubt I will have any further contact with him, but I thank you for your concern, ma'am. Now, I must be going."

"Yes, yes, of course. I don't want to keep Nick waiting. I just wanted to confirm my suspicions. I hope you feel better soon and never have to experience this kind of thing again."

After saying that, the two women parted, Mrs. Stone to go to her office to ponder how to deal with Jack, and Sally to go out to where Nick was waiting to take her home.

***

Once Jack reached the mercantile, he sat down on his cot and opened the invitation to visitors' day. It read: *This notice allows Jack Stone to visit his sister, Agatha Stone, on the next day of visiting at Fremantle Gaol. Signed, Director Stanley.*

Yes, thought Jack, *I am in, and can now look around the prison, find my target, and devise a plan to get rid of her.* He lay back on the lumpy cot and, with a smile of satisfaction, closed his eyes and contemplated how next to proceed with his plan.

Jack had his scheme in place by the time visitors' day arrived. He had found his venomous companions quite easily on one of his walks and secured them safely until he needed them. Today they would do his work for him, and no one would ever suspect him of murder. It was almost too perfect a plan. He was too brilliant, even if no one else agreed with him. His plan was that he would meet Agatha in the prison yard and then go with her to her office. There, he would get the keys to the cells from her, whether she gave them up willingly or he took them by force. Either way was fine with him. Then he would take the keys, and when he found his target's cell, he would leave her a little gift in her chamber pot. Something she would discover the next time she had to relieve herself. And that would be it. By the time she discovered the present, he would be long gone from the prison. Perhaps he would even leave a present for Agatha, as thanks for her part in his plan. That would leave him with no witnesses to his crime, and he would not have to share any of his fee with her; he could keep it all for himself. The more he had thought about it, the better it sounded to him. A spotted brown snake was curled around his waist, with its mouth tied shut so it could not bite Jack, and the redback spider was secured in a small tin can Jack had found in the trash heap behind the boarding house. This he was keeping in his coat pocket.

***

There was one glitch in Jack's plan. He had assumed all the women prisoners would be in the prison yard during visitors' day and that none would be in their cells. But because Bethany was not expecting any visitors that day, she had asked to be excused from going into the yard that afternoon. There being no reason for her presence, they granted her request, so she was spending the day in the cell block. The only person she expected to see that day was Jones when she brought Bethany's lunch. Bethany was looking forward to a day of peace, without the constant chatter of her fellow prisoners.

**

When Jack arrived at the prison gates, he showed his visitor's invitation, and after a brief pat-down by the guards to make sure he was not carrying a weapon, he could go inside the prison. Once there, he headed straight for the prison yard where he knew he would find Agatha waiting for him. As he approached the yard, he saw her stiff and upright figure observing the activities in front of her. When she turned her head towards the gates and saw him sauntering in, Jack thought her posture stiffened up even more, and her grim mouth turned into a scowl. When he reached her side, he said, "Why, Agatha, my dear, aren't you happy to see me? After all, you offered me an invitation to come and see you today."

"Happy is never the word I would use regarding you, Jack Stone. But I am glad that you accepted the invitation. You and I need to talk."

"So we do, dear Agatha, so we do."

"But not here. I don't want anyone to overhear what I have to say to you, so we need to go to my office for a private conversation."

"Exactly what I was thinking. We must be thinking the same thoughts today."

"I would never lower myself to think as you do. That would put us in the same class of people, and I hope I never sink that low in my life."

"I am deeply cut by your words," he smirked. "What have I ever done to you that would make you say such things to me?"

"You are well aware of how I have always felt about you, and my feelings have not changed since the last time I saw you."

"Neither have mine. Shall we continue this delightful little conversation in a more private setting?"

"Yes, come with me," said Agatha, before turning towards the hallway that led to her office.

"After you, my dear," said Jack, following her down the hall. He patted his midsection as he felt movement around his waist. *Soon, my pet, soon. You will be free to act very soon.*

Arriving at her office, Agatha reached down and unlocked the door with one key that she had hung on a chain around her waist. She pushed open the door and walked in, standing to one side to allow Jack entry before she closed the door and locked it again. She did not want the door to crack open, as it often did, and allow any passer-by to overhear what she had to say to Jack. These words would be for his ears only.

"Why, Agatha," laughed Jack. "I did not know that we were to be that private for our little chat. But you know me. I am willing to be as close with you as you want me to be."

"Get your mind out of the sewer. I only locked the door because I do not want anyone to overhear what I have to say to you, not for any other reason. You disgust me."

"Once again, I am dreadfully hurt," said Jack, putting a hand over his heart. "But if talk is all you want, then I am all ears."

Agatha moved to the other side of her desk and motioned Jack to sit in the chair on the other side of the room. Then she said, "I have been thinking about what you said the other day and the answer is no. I will not help you to complete your task. While sharing your fee sounded tempting, I cannot stoop to assisting you with murder. So, once we have finished talking, I will escort you to the front gates and say goodbye to you forever."

"I am sorry to hear that," said Jack, as he soothed the movement around his waist with a pat. "I was hoping we could be partners in this venture. It would make my task so much easier. But if you do not assist me, I will have to do this on my own."

"You will do nothing here except leave after we talk."

"But if you will not help me, what is there to talk about?"

"Your conduct with Sally Tremblant, that's what."

"Oh, so little Sally told you about our brief encounter, did she?"

"No, she did not have to tell me. But when she came here the other day, looking so pale and distressed, I knew you were up to your old tricks, even after I warned you to stay away from her and her husband."

"Yes, unfortunately she was not willing to play games with me and she ended up being hurt. But it was all her own fault, not mine. If she had been willing . . ."

"Ha! Just as I suspected. Well, you will not get away with it this time. I've had it with your shenanigans. I plan to tell Nick what happened, and I look forward to seeing him serve you justice before sending you back to England on the next ship."

Too bad you are not going to get the chance to tell anyone about my plans, thought Jack, as he once again smoothed a hand over his abdomen. But how was he going to release his *pet* in the office without Agatha being aware of his actions?

Agatha herself presented him with the opportunity. She got up, walked to the door, and unlocked it. When she turned her back to him, Jack reached under his tunic and unwound the spotted brown snake from his waist. He stood up and placed the snake on the chair before tossing his cap on top of it and saying, "Well, I guess we have nothing more to say to each other, so if you don't mind escorting me to the gates . . ."

Not looking back as she opened the door, Agatha swept an arm forward to indicate that Jack should precede her out of the room.

Once he had, she closed the door and locked it again. Then she and Jack started heading back down the hallway towards the gates.

"My cap," exclaimed Jack a moment later. "I forgot my cap. Would you mind if I ran back and got it? I'll meet you at the gates in a minute. Oh, I guess I will need your keys to let myself into the office. I'll give them back to you when I get back to the gates. Please?"

Agatha sighed. How long was it going to take to finally get rid of him? But she said, "I'll come back with you and open the door. I don't trust anyone with my keys, especially you."

Jack nodded and they briskly walked back to Agatha's office. She unlocked the door and said, "Hurry up. I haven't got all day."

Knowing he had to move fast, Jack opened the door and cautiously looked around. He saw a slight movement under his cap, and after looking back he saw that Agatha had her back turned towards him. He picked up her stick that was hanging on the wall next to the door, and with it he reached out and levered his cap off the chair, revealing the coiled snake. Using the stick again, he reached under the snake's head and pulled off the tied cloth from around its mouth. Not having time to do anything else, he pushed the snake off the chair towards the opposite wall. Gathering up his cap, he then rehung the stick before walking out and closing the door. Turning to Agatha with a smile, he said, "Thanks, Agatha, I need my cap to bear the heat here. It sure is a hot country, isn't it?" Then he walked down the hallway and back to the front gates with her. When they got there and found a small line of visitors waiting to exit the prison, he said, "You don't need to stay with me. I'll be fine waiting here to exit by myself."

"I know that, Jack. You always seem to land on your feet, no matter what trouble you get into. I would advise you to seek a berth on the next ship back to England, otherwise your luck might just run out and you will end up in here, not as a visitor but as a prisoner. Goodbye, and may our paths never cross again."

"Goodbye, Agatha, and may you find what you are looking for in this place of horrors," replied Jack, before he turned away and looked out the gates. He heard her footsteps as she walked away. Once he could no longer hear her footsteps, he glanced back to make sure she was out of sight before slowly edging away from the line of visitors and into the shadows. None of the guards appeared to be watching his movements, so once he was out of their sight line, Jack crept back to the prison yard. He kept to the shadows until he was again in the hallway leading to Agatha's office. Seeing no one about, he strolled down the corridor, and then, after another quick check of the hallway, tested the door lock. It was open, so Jack carefully opened the door while whispering Agatha's name. When he got no response, he eased the door open, and after checking to make sure the snake was not close to the door, he stepped inside and looked over at the desk. What he saw filled him with satisfaction. Agatha was slumped over, her head resting sideways on the desk surface. She was not moving at all. The venomous snake had done its work swiftly. Soon Agatha would be gone.

Seeing the chain of keys was on the same peg as Agatha's stick, Jack reached over and grabbed it. He quickly stepped back into the doorway when he heard a hissing sound from under the desk. After one last look at Agatha's body, Jack closed and locked the door before pocketing the key chain and wandering back down the hall. He felt no remorse for what he had done; Agatha had had an opportunity to share in his fortune, but when she turned him down, she brought about her own misfortune. And he was richer for it. That was the way of life, at least to Jack's thinking. And now on to the task they had sent here him to do . . .

Chapter 11

While Jack was cautiously making his way towards the women's cell blocks, Sam and Sally were approaching the prison gates hoping for a visit with Mary. Although they did not have a visitors' pass, they hoped that, because Sally was a frequent visitor at the prison, they could get in without one. They were allowed in with no searches or questioning when they got to the gates and the guard recognized Sally. They then proceeded to the prison yard hoping Mary would be there, but there was no sign of her amongst the prisoners and their visitors. Sally saw Jones standing off to the side of the yard, so she approached her and asked if Mary had been down this afternoon.

"No. Because she had no scheduled visitors today, she stayed in her cell and has not come down."

"Would it be possible for you to go up and let her know Sam and I are here and would like to visit with her?"

"I suppose I can do that for you. I just need to let Smith know I will be gone for a few minutes, and then I will head to the cell block."

"Thanks. We appreciate your help."

"It's not a problem. I'll be back with Mary in a few moments." And Jones headed off across the yard to speak with the other warder.

"While we wait, we might as well find a shady spot to sit in," said Sam. "It is hot in here today."

"I agree. I see a spot over there by the wall that is shaded. It might be cooler, not much, but at least it is in the shade."

Moving over to the spot with Sally, Sam pondered what it must have been like for her to live like this for ten years. "How did you survive all this, Sally?"

"One day at a time. You learned to live only for that day, and when it was over and you were back in your cell, you thanked God for getting you through another day. But if I had not had God on my side, I don't know how I would have survived, especially knowing Nick was just on the other side of that wall and we could not be together. My faith brought me through, and nothing else."

"Still, those must have been extremely hard days for you."

"Oh, they were. I am not denying that fact. But at least I had hope, which many of my fellow prisoners did not have."

"Yes, hope is a mighty factor in surviving any trial."

"Without that hope, many of the women I knew did not survive. The graveyard beyond this wall is full of those who died without hope."

Sam shook his head at her words.

"That is why I come back, not only to teach but also to bring a bit of hope to the lives of the women who are living here."

"I am sure you are a great inspiration, letting them know there is life after this place. Oh look, here come Jones and Mary. Perhaps we can bring some of that hope to Mary today as well."

"Mary," said Sally. "I hope we did not disturb you, but Sam wanted to come and visit you, to see for himself how you are doing."

"Sally, Mr. Yardley," said Bethany in response. "I am doing fine, as you can see. Thank you for coming to see after my welfare. How are you, Mr. Yardley? I heard from Sally that you just returned from a six-week adventure in the wilderness. Did you enjoy it?"

"Very much so, Miss Worthless. I saw and learned a lot of things while I was away. Perhaps someday I can come back on a longer visit and fill you in."

"I don't see that being a possibility, but I am sure Sally can tell me of some of your adventures when she next comes to the prison."

"It would be better if you heard them firsthand," said Sally. "Sam would be more than willing to come back on the next visitors' day. Wouldn't you?"

"Absolutely, although I do need to think about heading back home soon. I sent a letter to my father with the last ship that left for England, but I am sure that he is eager to see me in person and hear about the business opportunities here."

Hearing his words, Bethany thought about telling him her true identity. But what if he rejected her because of what she had become? That would crush all her dreams, and besides her faith in God, that was all she lived for. Without her dreams of a future outside these prison walls, she would wither up inside and her spirit would die. No, it was better to keep her identity a mystery and live out her sentence, before going back to England. And who knew, if God was gracious, Sam might still be single when she arrived home and her dream might still come true . . . So, she said, "I am sorry to hear that I might not see you again, Mr. Yardley. It has been a pleasure meeting you, and if our paths do not cross before you leave, have a safe voyage back to England." Bethany turned to walk back to her cell.

"Wait, please, Mary, Miss Worthless! Have I offended you? I had hoped to visit with you for a bit. I see they are serving cold lemonade. May I get you a glass to quench your thirst?" asked Sam.

"No, you have done nothing to offend me, Mr. Yardley. I just did not think we had anything more to talk about. But yes, a glass of lemonade would be lovely, thank you."

"Sally?"

"Yes, please. That would be wonderful, thank you."

"I will be right back with our drinks, ladies. Please excuse me for a moment," said Sam, before he headed over to the table for their lemonade.

"Such a gentleman," laughed Sally.

"Yes, but he has always been that way," said Bethany, without thinking of what she was conveying with her words.

"What do you mean, Mary? 'He has always been that way.' Did you know Sam when you both lived in England?"

Realising what she had just said, Bethany scrambled for words. "No, I did not know him, but everyone knew of his family. They were in the upper crust of society, and we were not. So I am sure that he learned to be a gentleman from the time that he was very young."

"I see . . ." mused Sally.

Hoping she did not *see* too much, Bethany was thankful Sam was returning with their lemonade and that Sally did not have time to ask her any more questions about him.

Reverting to their previous conversation, Bethany said, "So, Mr. Yardley, what was the most interesting or exciting thing that you saw on your recent trek?"

"That is a hard question, Miss Worthless. Everything was so different from what I know, so it is hard to choose. But if I had to, I would say seeing the quokkas. They were fascinating. They appear to smile all the time. Perhaps you could say they are the happiest animals on earth. Apparently they belong to a group of animals called marsupials. They carry their young around in a pouch for a few months after it is born, then it crawls out to live on its mother's back for another couple of months, and finally it is off on its own. Add that to all their cuteness, and well, I guess I would have to say that they are at the top of my list."

"They sound wonderful. I would love to see one someday," said Bethany.

"Perhaps you will once you get your release from here."

"I don't know. By then I will probably board the next ship back to England and never look back."

"I hope you don't," said Sally. "I know I had that very thought many times while they imprisoned me, but once I was free and living in the village with Nick, I changed my mind."

"Yes, but your circumstances differed from mine. I just want to get home to make sure that my stepbrother receives justice for what he did to me."

"Who is your stepbrother, and what did he do, if I can be so bold in asking?" said Sam. "Perhaps I could help you once I return to England."

"Thank you, but no, Mr. Yardley. This is a family affair, and I would not want to draw you into our troubles."

"Well, if you change your mind before I depart, please let Sally know, and she can pass the information along to me."

"I don't think your services will be necessary, but I will keep your offer in mind, thank you. Now, please, tell me more about your adventure."

The conversation continued in a more lighthearted manner as Sam told story after story about his recent trek into the wilderness. But soon the visiting time was over, and Sally and Sam had to leave. Bethany waved them off at the entrance to the prison yard before heading back to her cell.

***

While Bethany had been out, a visitor had accessed her cell and left an unwanted surprise in her chamber pot. This time, instead of a snake, Jack left a deadly redback spider in the pot, knowing that when Bethany lifted the lid of the pot, the spider would immediately attack her and Jack's task would be completed. While he was there, he searched for any personal items that would identify his victim, but finding none, he decided Mr. Stillwater would have to take his word that he had completed the job. He could not stick around to make sure Bethany died, but he had a fair certainty that his plan would work. So, as soon as he had deposited the spider in the pot, Jack left the cell, locking it behind him with the master key he had "borrowed" from Agatha. Keeping again to the shadows, he crept down the hallway, and once he was in the prison yard, he sauntered casually towards the front gate where more visitors were departing. In the yard, he almost bumped into Bethany, who was headed towards her cell block. Jack kept his head low, murmuring a quick apology, and twisted away from Bethany and quickened his pace. Even though she did not know him and was hopefully soon to be gone, Jack did not want to take the chance she could identify him, in case the spider did not do its lethal work. Bethany acknowledged his apology and continued her way down the hall to her cell block without a backward glance.

As Jack was counting himself lucky that she took little notice of him, he found a more unpleasant blow waiting for him at the prison gates. Sam and Sally were still standing in line to make their way out of the prison. Deciding a direct approach was better than hiding in the shadows, Jack hailed the pair as he neared them. "Well, hello," he said. "Were you two visiting someone here today? I spent time with my sister-in-law. It was nice to see her again before I left for England. And who were you two visiting, if I may ask?"

Sam felt Sally shudder when she heard Jack's voice. Even though she had said nothing about what happened earlier with Jack, Sam knew it had been very upsetting for Sally. Sam said, "We were visiting a friend. You do not need to know who that friend is, Mr. Stone. Good day to you." Sam turned his back on Jack and gently propelled Sally forward in the line.

"Well, I see that the friendliness of the people here has not rubbed off on you, Lord Yardley," said Jack with a sneer. "I was only trying to be friendly, nothing else. But I see you have no plans to return the favour. I will bid you good day as well and find my place at the back of the line." Then he, too, turned and headed to the back of the line, fuming at the arrogance of the pair in front of him.

"Are you all right, Sally?" asked Sam.

"Yes, thank you, Sam. I was just shocked to hear him call us. That is all."

"I did not like running into him again. I find him most unpleasant."

"Me, too. Thank you for turning him away."

"I hope this is the last time we ever see, or hear, that man again."

"Fremantle is a small village. Until he boards a ship to go back to England, I daresay we may see him again."

"I hope I don't end up on the same ship with him. But if I do, maybe I can accidentally push him overboard . . ."

"Sam!"

"I was only teasing."

"I, too, have to admit that the idea is tempting."

"Sally Tremblant!"

They looked at each other and laughed, putting the thought of Jack Stone far behind them, while the man in question fumed as he waited for his turn to leave this place. He could not wait to shake the dust of Australia off his feet.

***

When Bethany arrived back in her cell block, she found Jones there waiting to unlock her cell and let her in. After locking the cell door behind her, she said, "I will be back soon with the dinner trays. Do you need anything before that, Worthless?"

"No, I think I will just lie down again until dinner arrives."

"Okay, I will see you in a little while."

After she left to check the other cell doors to make sure that they were all secured, Bethany decided she needed to use the chamber pot before laying down. Crossing over to the darkened corner where the pot was, she rearranged her clothes and then bent down and lifted the lid of the pot. A dark shadow leapt out and fastened its sharp fangs to her hand. Bethany screamed with pain, shook the shadowy creature back into the pot, and slammed the lid again. Feeling the venom shooting up her arm and already feeling dizzy, she stumbled across the cell until she reached the bars. She screamed for help before collapsing into an unconscious heap on the floor.

***

"Worthless, would you shut up? Some of us are trying to rest," came Joann's voice from down the hallway. When Joann did not hear any response from Mary, she called again, "Worthless! Mary! Did you hear me?" Now, sensing that something was wrong, Joann called out again. "Jones! Anyone! Mary is in trouble. We need help right away!

Realising Joann was serious, the rest of the cell block residents took up the call as well. The noise became loud enough that they could hear it all the way down to the prison yard where Jones was conversing with Smith.

"What is going on down there? What is all the noise?" Jones shouted down the hallway as she and Smith hurried back.

The yelling continued until she reached the cell block. "Stop all this noise! What in the world is going on?"

As soon as the prisoners heard Jones's voice, they all quietened down so Joann could speak to her.

"Jones, it's Worthless. Please check on her. She is not answering me. There must be something wrong with her."

"Canter, I just saw her a few minutes ago and she was fine," said Jones as she headed towards Bethany's cell. Looking through the bars, she saw her crumpled on the floor. Jones grabbed her key and opened the cell door. She ran over to Bethany and turned her on her back. As she did so, she saw Bethany's right arm. It was swollen and had red streaks running from her wrist all the way up her arm. Her face was white, and when Jones touched it, it was cold as ice.

"Mary!" she shouted. "Mary, can you hear me? Worthless, please answer me if you can hear me?" There was no visible response to her calls. Turning to Smith, she said, "We need help here right away. I can't get Worthless to wake up. Please run and get Mrs. Stone, or anyone who can help us. Mary's life depends on it. Go now!"

The other warder did as Jones had asked, while she kept tapping Bethany's hands and face, hoping she could get her to wake up. What had happened to Mary in such a short time? She had been fine just a few minutes ago. Why would she not wake up? Then she looked more closely at Bethany's right wrist and saw the puncture marks where the spider's fangs had dug into her flesh. Mary had been bitten, but by what, and was it still lurking in the cell? She took a quick look around and when she saw nothing alarming, she picked up Bethany's limp body and brought her out into the area between the cells.

From her cell, Joann saw Bethany's apparently lifeless body and called out to Jones, "What's wrong with Mary? She's not d-d-dead, is she? Please tell me she's not dead. Please . . ."

"No," replied Jones. "Her heart is still beating, and she is breathing, but I do fear for her life. She is so cold, and I can't get her to wake up. I don't know what to do to help her. Did anyone see or hear anything that might have caused this? It looks like something bit her on her wrist, but I don't know what it is. Until we know what bit her, we can't help her."

"We can pray, Jones," replied Joann in a soft, broken voice. "That is what she would tell us to do. We can pray."

Several other women agreed before Joann started her petition for Mary's life. "Uh, dear God, it's me, Joann Canter. I know we were best friends many years ago, but I've kind of put you out of my life because of what happened to me. Today, God, I am not asking anything for myself, but only for my friend, Mary. You know her very well, God, and I know she is a special daughter of yours. God, Mary is very sick, and we don't know how to help her get better. If it is Your will that she gets well, God, then please help us find a way. But if You want to take her home to heaven, I guess that will be okay too. We will miss her a lot, but at least she will be out of this place, God, and with You. So I'm leaving it up to you, God, and asking that You do the best thing for Mary. Amen."

A chorus of soft amens echoed down the hallway after Joann's prayer. But Mary's condition did not change.

Then Smith came running back to the cell block, accompanied by the prison director.

"Jones," the warder yelled. "Mrs. Stone, she's . . . she's dead!"

"What!"

"It's true," said the director. "I checked her myself. She is dead, and now we have a young woman who is at death's door as well. What is going on?"

"I don't know," replied Jones. "But at least Mary is still alive and maybe we can help her. Do you know anything about bite marks, Director? I found these marks on Mary's wrist, but I don't know what caused them." She lifted Bethany's right wrist.

"I've seen those marks before, on a dead man. A redback spider bit him. But I've rarely seen venomous spiders in the prison. How would it have gotten into Mary's cell, and where would she have encountered it?"

"I did look around the cell but could not see anything, Director. But it is quite dark. Maybe the spider is lurking in a dark corner. Or maybe it ran away . . ."

The notion of a deadly spider running loose in their cell block immediately caused panic with the other prisoners. They all started yelling at Jones to let them out of their cells and into the hall. The director agreed, and Smith used her master key to open the cells before gathering the prisoners together in a spot away from Bethany.

Joann came forward then and said, "You know, I think I heard someone in Mary's cell while she was down visiting. I thought nothing about it at the time, but maybe someone came in and put the spider in Mary's cell to harm her."

"But why, Canter?" asked Jones. "We have all grown to care about Mary. Why would anyone want to kill her?"

"Perhaps it was not anyone from the prison, but someone from outside," said Joann. "Remember, it was visitors' day, so maybe it was someone who came in as a visitor."

"Everyone who came in had a pass, Canter," said the director. "Except for Sally and Sam, and I am sure that neither of them would have any reason to harm Mary."

"No, but wait, Director," exclaimed Jones. "Didn't I hear Mr. Yardley say he had recently returned from a six-week bush walk, and that he had learned a lot while he was out there? Maybe he could help Mary now, with what he learned. Can someone go and get him? Please?"

"That's a great idea, Jones. Smith," the Director said to the other warder, "run down to the gate and get a guard to chase down Mr. Yardley and bring him back here right away."

"Yes sir," she said. She took off running down the hallway towards the prison yard and gates.

"Is there anything else we can do for Mary while we wait, Director?" Jones asked.

"Not that I know of, Jones, we can only wait and pray. That is all we can do."

"We'll do that," said Joann as she turned and went back to the group of women huddled together. She dropped on her knees, closed her eyes, and started once again to ask the God of Heaven to heal Mary. The other prisoners did the same, sending a chorus of requests upward on Mary's behalf.

***

Meanwhile, the message of need was swiftly communicated from one guard to another, who took off running down the hill towards the village. In the distance he could see two familiar people, and so the guard ran even faster to catch up with them.

Once he reached Sam and Sally, the guard was so out of breath he could hardly get the words out that he needed to say to Sam. But he tried desperately to convey the message that he had received. "Mr. Yardley . . . need . . . your . . . help . . . badly. Back . . . at . . . prison. Please . . . come . . . with me . . . now. Can't wait!"

Sam looked at the anxious, panting man with alarm. "Why? What is it? Who sent you for me?"

"The director sent . . . needs you . . . help Mary. Come . . . now. Please!"

"Mary. Mary Worthless? Why? What's wrong with her?"

"Bit bad. Think it was a . . . spider. Won't wake up. Please come now!" the guard said as he pulled on Sam's arm.

"Yes, of course, I'll come. Sally?"

"Oh no, Sam, this could be bad. I'll run home and bring what supplies I can that might help her."

"Thanks," said Sam, "but if it is a venomous spider who bit her, our best bet for healing is from God. Start praying hard for her, Sally, very hard."

Sam turned and ran back up the hill towards the prison, his heart sinking within him. He had learned a lot about venomous snakes and spiders while he was trekking with Tojo, but he had also learned that once a person had been bitten, there was not a lot that could stop the poison from spreading rapidly through the body. Only the person's state of health and God's willingness to keep them alive would stop them from dying. So, with every panting breath that Sam took, he prayed God would spare Bethany from death, even if it meant she continued to live in the prison for the next several years.

Coming up to the prison gates, a warder from the women's section of the prison met him. She told him that he should accompany her up to Mary's cell block. They took off at a rapid pace across the yard and through the hallway towards the cell block. As they approached, Sam could see Jones and the prison director kneeling beside a still body on the floor and a group of women on their knees, huddled in a back corner. Recognising Bethany as the body on the floor, Sam rushed over to her and dropped to his knees as well.

"Thanks for coming, Mr. Yardley," said the Director. "If there is anything that you can do . . ."

"I understand a venomous spider bit her, is that correct?" asked Sam, watching Bethany take quick shallow breaths of air.

"We believe so," said the Director, picking up Bethany's arm and showing Sam the fang marks on her wrist. "No one saw what happened, and we have not found the spider yet, so we are uncertain it is a spider bite."

"It looks like something bit her. Was she in her cell when it happened?"

"Yes."

"Doing what?"

"We don't know. Probably just resting on her bed."

"I'll bet she was using her chamber pot," came a voice from behind them. "I heard a loud clanging just before she screamed, so maybe the spider was in the pot and when she opened the lid, it jumped out and bit her. Maybe it is still there," said Joann.

"That's a thought, Canter," said Jones. "If we could get some light and check the pot, then we might know for sure."

"Be careful," said Sam. "Some of those spiders can jump a long way and move quickly."

"I'll get Stone's stick and use it to open the pot. It has quite a reach and I guess Mrs. Stone has no need of it now."

"Why's that?" asked Sam.

"She's dead."

"What? Mrs. Stone is dead? How? When?"

"Today. She got done in by a snake bite."

"Mrs. Stone died of a snake bite? Where?"

"In her office."

"So, Mrs. Stone dies of a snake bite and a poisonous spider has probably bitten Mary. Do these things happen frequently, Director?"

"Never before in my history here has something like this happened, especially on the same day."

"Then it is either a very rare coincidence—or someone made it happen," said Sam. He bent down again to check that Bethany was still breathing. As he did so and felt her soft breath upon his cheek, he whispered into her ear, "Bethany. Bethany Stillwater. I know this is who you are, no matter how hard you try to deny it. You need to fight this poison and come back to us, Bethany. We all care for you and need you here. Please don't leave us, Beth. Please don't leave me alone."

When his gentle words did not receive a response, Sam felt his eyes fill with tears. At this moment he realised how much Bethany meant to him, and no matter how long it took, he would fight to get her freed from here and back home where she belonged. But she had to want to come back to the land of the living, and at present it did not look like she was trying very hard to do so. So Sam would just keep working to persuade her to come back to him.

A short time later, while Sam persisted in calling out to Bethany, he heard a loud crash and then several thumps coming from a cell.

"I got it," exclaimed Jones. "That big old spider will not bite anyone ever again."

The director got up and went into the cell. Looking at the dead spider, or what was left of it, he confirmed it was a deadly redback spider. Mary's chances for survival were not good. He left the cell and came back to tell Sam the bad news.

"Well, at least we know what we are dealing with," said Sam. "It's not good news, but Mary is still alive, and that is good news. We just need to keep her still and pray for her recovery. I don't know what else to do."

The director agreed and then told the warders to put the women back in their cells now that they knew there was no further danger. They did so, and the hallway slowly emptied of women. Before she went into her cell, Joann came over to Bethany and said, "Worthless, you got to keep fighting. I don't know what I'll do if you die. You brought me back to God, and if you don't beat this thing, I won't have a chance to tell you. So please, Mary, fight, fight, fight. This is a fight you must take on; you must win." Then she was gone.

Sam bent once more towards Bethany's ear and said, "I see why God brought you here, Beth. You have done good work, but I don't believe that your work is finished. So, as Joann just said, you must keep on fighting this evil poison in your body and beat it out of your system. If not for your sake, for ours, dear Beth. Come back to us now, I beg of you."

***

Bethany floated on that plane between earth and heaven. She could see the bright lights of heaven and wanted so badly to go there. But something kept dragging her back. She kept hearing her name, her real name, being called from afar. But how could that be? No one in that place knew her real name. No one except . . . but he could not be there, in her prison cell with her. No, it must be just a dream. A beautiful dream, but not reality. She turned her eyes toward the light and tried to move toward it, to get rid of the awful pain she was experiencing. She could almost hear her parents' voices; she was so close and yet still so far away. Why couldn't she go to them?

"Because it is not your time yet, my child," said the voice of ultimate Love. "Soon, but not today. Your work for Me on earth is not yet done. When you have completed your work, you will come home and live here with Us forever and ever. But not today, my child, not today."

Then the voice and the light started fading away, and the dark-ness and the pain engulfed Bethany once more, until she once again heard the other voice say, more clearly now, "Beth, come back to us now, I beg of you." And she opened her eyes.

Chapter 12

The first thing Bethany saw when she opened her eyes was Sam's blue eyes only a few inches from her own.

"Sam?" she whispered. "Where am I? Why are you staring at me like that? Are you . . . are you . . . crying? Has something terrible happened?"

"These are happy tears, Beth," he whispered back to her, not ashamed of the wetness of his cheeks. "No, something wonderful has happened. God has granted us a miracle. He has sent you back to us."

"Sent me back? Where was I? I don't understand."

"A poisonous spider bit you, and we did not know if you were going to survive. But we started praying, and God has answered our prayers. You are alive!"

Then Bethany noticed the other people huddled around her: the director, Jones, and Smith. They were all smiling at her, but their cheeks were wet with tears. Then Bethany heard a chorus of joyous voices coming from the surrounding cells as the good news about her miraculous recovery spread quickly from cell to cell.

"Mary, don't you ever scare me again like that, you hear me?" called Joann. "I almost died from fright when I thought you were dead. But God was good and answered our prayers."

"Director, where can we take her to recover?" asked Sam.

"Well," said the director, "I don't think this will be the best place for you to recover, Mary, but you are still a prisoner. I don't know where we can put you. I don't have the staff to look after you properly, especially now that Mrs. Stone is gone."

"Mrs. Stone is gone?" said Bethany. "What do you mean? Where did she go? I saw her earlier today, if today is still visitors' day. Is it, Sam? Is that why you are still here? I am so confused."

"Yes, it is still visitors' day, Bethany. I don't wonder that things are very confusing for you right now. Mrs. Stone . . . she, too, had a horrible experience, with a spotted brown snake, but she, unlike you, did not recover from her bite. Mrs. Stone is dead, Bethany."

"Dead?"

"Yes."

"But how . . .?"

"We don't know, but that is not something you need to worry yourself about at the present time. You need to concentrate on getting better, and I agree this is not the place for you to do that. Director, would you be agreeable to me taking Bethany down to the Tremblants' boarding house and letting her recover under Sally's care? I promise I will act as her warder and not let her escape while she is recovering."

"I suppose that is a reasonable thing to do under the circumstances, Mr. Yardley. But why do you keep referring to Mary as Bethany? They registered her as Mary Worthless; I thought that was her real name. Is it not?"

"No," said Bethany. "Sam is right. My real name is Bethany Stillwater, but when they convicted me of theft and sent me down here, they changed my name to Mary Worthless. I don't know the reason for the name change except that perhaps my accusers did not want anyone to find out where I was and try to free me."

"I see. But Mr. Yardley keeps referring to you by your first name. Were the two of you acquainted with each other back in England?"

"Barely," replied Sam. "But I hope that if things go as planned, we will become good friends in the coming weeks and months."

Bethany blushed. Could he mean—? But no, she was still a prisoner, and would be for many years to come. So, what was he saying?

"This, however, is not the time to talk about Miss Stillwater and my past relationship. I see Sally coming now with bandages and blankets, so I would like to wrap Bethany's arm up and then transport her to the boarding house. Are you agreeable, Director?"

"Certainly. I, too, think it would be the best place for Mary—I mean, Miss Stillwater, to recover."

"Excellent, then let us make Bethany comfortable for the move, and we will be off," said Sam, as Sally reached the group. "Sally, a miracle has occurred. Bethany is back in the land of the living. But she needs time to recover. The director has agreed she can do so at your boarding house. Are you able to look after her there?"

"Yes, of course," said a stunned Sally, who had been expecting to see a dead body or at least one that was unconscious. But to see Mary awake and aware of her surroundings, that was indeed a miracle sent by God. But wait, had Sam just now referred to her as Bethany, and not Mary? Was this the young woman Sam thought she was? If so, that was another miracle in itself.

While Sam wrapped Bethany's arm and then secured it across her chest with the bandages, he filled Sally in on what they had discovered since they'd left the prison only a short time ago. Sally could hardly believe what had happened to Mrs. Stone, especially after what Bethany/Mary had just experienced. Was this only a coincidence? If it wasn't, there was someone out there who thought they had got away with murder twice. When that person realised Bethany was still alive, he or she might try to murder her again. But how were they going to prevent that from happening when they did not know who had committed the crimes?

Once Sam had finished wrapping Bethany's arm and chest, he cocooned her in a couple of blankets Sally had brought with her. Then he lifted her into his arms and walked out of the cell block. Bethany heard choruses of "Get well, soon, Mary" and "We love you, Mary" coming from the cells as she passed by them. When they got to Joann's cell, Bethany asked Sam to stop for a moment so that she could speak to Joann. "I'll be back soon, Joann, and when I return, we need to talk about what has happened to you through all of this. I'll be praying for you, Joann, and look forward to seeing you soon."

"Don't come back too soon, Worthless," replied Joann in a choked-up voice. "Take all the time you need to recover before you come back to this. But I'll miss you."

Bethany also teared up when she heard Joann's words, but then Joann turned and moved towards the back of her cell, where Bethany could barely see her. Knowing that there was no point in lingering there, she nodded to Sam, and they left the cell block behind, heading for the prison yard and ultimately the gates of the prison. The director met them there to assure there was no problem with Bethany leaving with Sam and Sally. "Take care, Miss Stillwater," he said, "and don't come back until you have recovered. I trust you and Mr. Yardley completely."

"I will not try to escape. You have my word on that."

"Well, be off," harrumphed the director. "I see Nick is here with a cart for you, so I won't delay you. Godspeed in healing, Miss Stillwater."

Nick and Sally made a nest of the extra blankets in the back of the cart. When they finished, Sam laid Bethany in the nest. "Close your eyes and rest, Beth," he said. "Sally and I will walk on either side of the cart down the hill, so if you are uncomfortable, please let one of us know straight away so we can help you."

"I'm sure I will be fine, but thank you for your concern. A rest will be good. I am suddenly very weary."

"As long as it is not a heavenly rest, Beth," he said. "I'm all right with you taking a nap. I am sure your body is worn out after everything that has happened."

"Sam, while I was unconscious, God said my work on earth has not yet been completed. I don't plan to drift off again to the heavenly plains anytime soon."

"That's good news. Now, I think Nick is ready to go, so I'll let you start that nap now."

Nick was indeed ready to go, and he gently snapped the reins to turn the mule around and head back towards the village. As promised, Sally walked on one side of the cart and Sam walked on the other, both keeping a close eye on the sleeping Bethany inside the cart.

***

As they walked past a grove of trees, unseen eyes followed the cart and its occupant. The bundle of blankets was so still it appeared they were taking the body to bury it in the village graveyard. Once that was done, all he had to do was dig up the corpse, hack off the little finger as proof of the success of his mission, and head home to collect the rest of his money. Jack rubbed his hands in glee. Now his next task would be to find the first ship travelling back to England. After that, he did not know what he would do. He was enjoying the heat and sunshine here, so maybe instead of staying in England, he would head out to live on a warm southern island somewhere, where nobody knew or cared about his past. But first he needed to assure himself that his target was indeed dead and bring back the proof to her brother. So, as they passed him, Jack followed them down the hill, keeping to the cover of the trees so as not to be seen by wandering eyes.

Just before they reached the boarding house, Sam looked out over the harbour and said, "Oh, there is a ship docking. I hope it has come from England and my father has sent a reply to my question about Bethany and her trial. I'm hoping he knows of some way she can be acquitted."

"Did you want to head down to the mercantile now and see if there is any mail for you?" asked Nick. "Sally and I can get Bethany settled, if you want to go now."

"No, it will be a while before they unload. I can wait until Beth is resting before I check for any mail."

Stopping the cart in front of the boarding house, Nick tied the mule to a hitching post, while Sam reached into the back of the cart and picked up Bethany in her bundle of blankets. "Beth," he whispered. "We are at the boarding house now. Sally has run ahead to prepare a bed for you, and then I will carry you upstairs so you can rest awhile longer. How do you feel?"

"My arm hurts," said Bethany, "and I am still exhausted, but other than that, I am doing all right."

"I'll check your arm once we get you into bed. If it is hurting too much, I'm sure Sally has something that will help to ease the pain."

"It is just uncomfortable, so I will try to rest without taking anything, at least until most of the poison has left my body."

"That's a good thought, but be sure to let us know if the pain becomes unbearable."

"I will."

"Good. Oh, I see Sally is back at the door, so she must have your bed prepared. Are you ready for me to lift you up?"

"Lift away, Lord Yardley."

"Shhh! I would like to be just plain Sam."

"You will never be just plain Sam, Lord Yardley. You are much too handsome for that," replied Bethany.

"Now I know you must be delirious with pain, Miss Stillwater," smiled Sam. "But I will not contest your statement at this time; we can discuss my best features at a later time when you are feeling more yourself."

Then he gathered her up in his arms and carried her into the house, following Sally up the stairs to the bedroom at the head of the stairs.

"Sally, isn't this yours and Nick's room?"

"Yes, but I changed the bedding this morning, so it is clean. Besides, it will be easier to care for Bethany here than in a room farther down the hallway. Nick and I will do fine in one of the smaller rooms for the time being."

"That's very thoughtful of you, Sally. It will be good to hear her more easily when she is stirring and needing help. You are sure that Nick won't mind giving up his room?"

"No, he will be fine. Now, it is time for you to leave so I can get Bethany out of these grimy clothes and into a clean nightgown. But before you leave, would you help me remove these bandages? That will make it easier for me to help her change, and we can take another look at her injury while we do so."

Sam agreed and helped Sally remove the bandages from around Bethany's arm and chest. They both inspected the wrist wound and right arm; it did not appear to have worsened in the last hour. In fact, the red streaks seemed to have lessened in colour, and the wound itself was less red and swollen. Bethany told them the arm was uncomfortable but not painful, so they decided not to give her anything for pain now. Then Sam left and closed the door behind him, to allow Sally and Bethany the privacy they needed to change her clothes. Sam headed downstairs to the kitchen where he found Nick making coffee, and they settled into a couple of kitchen chairs to discuss the incredible events of the day.

***

While helping Bethany change into one of her nightgowns, Sally said, "After all this time of calling you Mary, I don't know what name you would prefer. I was not there when your true name was revealed, but we can speak about that later. I am just so thankful God spared you, and that we can share this time together outside of the prison."

"Please call me Bethany. That is my name, and now that everyone, including the director, is aware of it, I don't want to go back to being Mary Worthless."

"I can see why. That was a terrible name. I'll be thrilled to call you Bethany from now on."

"Thank you for that and all your kindness to me," said Bethany as she indicated the nightgown and the bed. "You don't know how it feels to have a clean nightgown and an actual bed to sleep in. Oh, I guess you do. I forgot you were in my position several years ago."

"It seems like an eternity ago, but I remember how I felt when I got out of the prison garb and into actual clothes again. And the bed, oh, I remember how good the bed felt to my aching back. That is why I decided these things should be of first importance on your road to recovery. Now, I will head downstairs and let you rest further. There is a glass of water here at your bedside. Do you need anything else at the present time?"

"I hate to ask this of you but before this all happened, I was going to use the chamber pot in my cell. Would you mind? I never got a chance to use it before the spider bit me."

"Of course I don't mind. I should have thought of that myself, without you having to ask. Please, don't be shy around me. Ask for anything you need," said Sally as she pulled out the chamber pot from under the bed and helped Bethany to use it, before tucking her back under the blankets.

"There. Anything else?" asked Sally.

A sleepy shake of Bethany's head was her answer, so Sally left the room, and after leaving the door ajar, headed downstairs to join the men in the kitchen.

***

He kept to the shadow of the trees behind the boarding house, watching to see what was happening. Jack was surprised the cart had stopped here instead of going down to the village cemetery. Did this mean his victim had survived? Impossible. Unless Sam had not been correct about how deadly the spider's venom was to humans. Jack needed to be sure. He had to get into the boarding house and see the condition of his victim for himself. He had seen movement in one of the upper bedrooms. From his previous experience of staying there, he determined it must be Sally and Nick's room. He watched as Sally came over to the window and closed the drapes, leaving them just cracked open a bit. Not enough for Jack to see what was going on in the room, but he could see whenever shadows passed by the crack, and the shadows became more frequent as time passed by. How was he to get in there without being noticed? Then he saw a wooden trellis that ran up the side of the building, right beside his former window. *How convenient,* he thought. *I will just climb up the trellis, open the window, and climb in. Then, when I am certain I am the only one moving around upstairs, I will check out the body in the Tremblants' room. If indeed it is my target, and she is still alive, I will dispose of her once and for all before exiting as quietly as I came in. That will complete my work. I will have my proof of her identity, and then I can leave this place for all time.*

Jack waited until the shadows ceased moving past the window, and then he dashed to the house. Testing the trellis for weight, he found it to be solid, so he swiftly made his way up to the bedroom window. When he got there, he found the window was cracked open, as if to welcome him in. He pushed upward on the window sash until it was wide enough for his body, then entered the room, landing with a soft thud on the floor. He waited by the window to see if anyone was coming upstairs to investigate the noise, but when no sound was heard on the stairs, he crept across the room and slowly opened the door. Looking down the hall, he saw no one, so he left the room and tiptoed down the hallway until he came to the far bedroom door, just above the stairs. He could hear voices below him in the kitchen and listened carefully until he had identified the voices of Sam, Nick, and Sally. *Good,* thought Jack. *That accounts for all of them; there should be no one else in this bedroom, except perhaps my target, which will make my job that much easier.* With that thought in mind, he opened the door and crept inside.

Chapter 13

⟋⟍

"Did you hear that?" asked Sam.

"No," said Nick. "What did you hear?"

"I don't know, but it sounded like something fell in an upstairs bedroom. Did you hear it, Sally?"

"No, but I doubt it was anything to worry about. The old timbers in this house sometimes move and make strange noises. Perhaps that is what you heard."

"No, it was not a creaking sound. It was definitely a thud. If you don't mind, I think I will run up and check on Bethany. Perhaps she knocked something off the table beside her, or she needs some help. I'll be right back." Sam pushed back his chair from the table and headed up the stairs.

"He's sure got it bad," chuckled Nick.

"What do you mean?" asked Sally.

"Didn't you see the look in his eyes? He's a man in love, even if he doesn't quite realise it yet. Yep, he's sure got it bad."

"You mean the look that you used to get when we were young and first married?"

"What do you mean when we were young? I still feel the same way now as I did the day I married you. Perhaps even more so."

"I know. I was only teasing you. It is the same for me. I love you more and more every day we are together. I thank God every day that He preserved us through those long years apart, so that we could be together again until He calls us home."

"My thoughts exactly."

The mood was shattered when Sam came racing down the stairs. "Sally, didn't you say you had left the door ajar so we could hear Bethany if she woke up and needed anything?"

"Yes, why?"

"Well, the door is shut and locked now."

"That can't be," said Nick. "The only way to lock the door is with the key that is inside the door. Unless Bethany got up and locked the door—"

"Someone has to be in the room with her," said Sam. "Do you have another key for the bedroom?"

"Yes, I have a master key that fits all the locks. It's in my desk." Nick got up and ran to the other room.

"Oh, Sam," cried Sally. "What if—"

"Don't," said Sam. "Don't say it."

"I'm going to run down and get the constable," said Sally, tears streaming down her cheeks.

Nick returned with the key, which Sam quickly grabbed. "Hold on for a second," said Nick. "You need a weapon."

"I'm never without one," said Sam, pulling up his pant leg to reveal a sheathed blade. "I'm ready. Are you?"

Nick nodded, revealing his own weapon, before the two men ran up the steps.

***

As he heard the footsteps descending and then quickly coming back up the stairs, Jack looked around the room for a place to hide. He had not yet completed his task, but he had wanted to identify his victim first. He had just moved over to open the drapes a bit more, to get more light in the room, when he heard Sam come up the stairs and try to open the door, at the same time calling Bethany's name. Then he heard him run back downstairs. Jack needed Bethany as a shield to get out of here. It would be better to hide on the other side of the bed, with his knife close to her throat, when the other men entered the bedroom. That way he would be ready to strike quickly. Jack was crouching low on the far side of the bed with his knife out when the lock clicked and the door opened.

"Stand up and surrender yourself," commanded Sam. "We know you are in here, and there is no way out except through this door, and we have no intention of letting you leave this room. Stand up and surrender!"

There was no response to his command, except for Bethany stirring and opening her eyes. "Sam?" she asked. "What's going on?"

"Bethany, I need you to move over to this side of the bed. Now! Just do as I say. Move!"

"I . . . what?"

"Come over here, now, Bethany!"

As Bethany realised the urgency in Sam's voice, she started to wiggle her way across the bed. Then something pricked her throat, a hand grabbed her, and a voice close to her ear said, "I would not move if I were you, Miss Stillwater. It is better for you to stay still if you wish to stay alive."

Then Jack stood up and faced Sam across the room. "Well, it appears we are in a bit of a muddle, Lord Yardley. You wish for this young woman to stay alive, and I need her dead so that I can collect my fee from her brother. What shall we do to solve our problem?"

"Easy enough, Mr. Stone. I will pay you double whatever you were getting from Howard Stillwater if you move that blade away from Miss Stillwater's throat. Then you can disappear with the money and never surface again, either in Australia or in England."

"Much as I would like to take you up on that offer, I am a man of honour. I never fail to fulfil my commitments to my clients. So, unfortunately, I am going to decline your gracious offer. Now, if you do not wish to see Miss Stillwater murdered in front of you, I suggest you move away from the doorway and let the two of us leave by the front door."

"Sam," said Bethany. "Please do as Mr. Stone says."

"How touching, Miss Stillwater," said Jack. "Now, are you going to move or not, Lord Yardley?"

"I'm going," said Sam, stepping out of the doorway and moving slightly to the side. "You are free to leave."

"Thank you, and if your friend Nick is beside you, I would advise him not to try anything either. This blade will remain at Miss Stillwater's neck the entire time. Say your farewells, Miss Stillwater. You will not be seeing Lord Yardley again."

Frightened, but determined not to have Sam harmed, Bethany got out of the bed on Jack's side, walked beside him around the bed and then out the door. As they reached the door, she looked up at Sam, and with tears in her eyes, bid him a silent farewell. Then she moved past him, and as she did so, she felt the knife at her throat move slightly and then heard it fall to the floor behind her. Jack's grasp on her first tightened and then fell away before he crumpled to the floor in a heap. Turning back, she saw a long blade protruding from his upper back. Bewildered, she turned back to Sam, and from the corner of her eye, she saw Nick stand up from his crouch beside the bed. He must have thrown the blade from there. She realised that while she had been getting out and moving around the bed, Nick had slithered under it. Then, when they were in the doorway, with their backs turned to the bed, Nick had crawled out and thrown his knife into the assassin's back. Suddenly, her legs felt like they could not hold her up any longer and she started wavering.

Seeing her start to fall, Sam reached out and pulled her into his arms. He said, "I think Beth has had enough of this excitement. I'll take her down to my room and put her on my bed. I don't think that she will rest if she stays in your room."

"That's a good idea. She doesn't need to see this."

Sam agreed, and after carrying Bethany into his room, laid her down on the bed. "Are you cold?" he asked as he noted her shivering.

"Freezing."

Sam grabbed the coverlet at the end of the bed and pulled it up over Bethany's shoulders. Once Sally got here, he would grab the extra blankets they had used to transport Bethany down from the prison, but he did not want to leave her alone, not even for a moment.

"Sam?"

"Yes?"

"Is it over? Am I safe now?"

"You are safe from any further attacks from Jack Stone, yes, but unfortunately we still have to deal with your brother. Jack was only Howard's henchman; Howard is the one who now needs to be caught and punished, Beth. But as he is thousands of miles away at the moment; you don't need to worry about him at the present time."

"First, framing me for a theft I did not commit, then trying to have me murdered? How far has Howard sunk? If I had known what he was prepared to do to get more money from the estate, I would have either given him what he needed, or paid off his debts myself. At first I was enraged and only wanted revenge, but now I feel only sympathy for him. He has become a sad and desperate man, nothing like the older brother he used to be."

"I did not know of him when he was a young man, but if he was a kind and loving older brother to you, then he has definitely changed, and not for the better. He is desperate and doing everything he can to find money to pay off his gambling debts. Even before I left England to come here, it was well known how deep in debt Howard was, and the people that he was getting loans from, well, let's just say they are not patient about getting their money back or the methods they use to retrieve it."

"What can I do to help him from here, Sam? I could send a letter to my solicitor and ask him to pay off Howard's debts. Even though it will take a long time for the letter to reach Mr. Brown, I know he would respect my wishes. Yes, I shall write to him immediately."

"That is very forgiving and kind of you, Bethany. Perhaps, once Howard's debts are paid, he will revert to being the man you once knew him to be."

"I hope so. I would love to have that brother back again. I also pray that he will find help for his troubles with gambling so he does not end up like this again."

"I do too, Bethany. Now, I hear Sally coming down the hallway. She is going to stay with you while Nick and I talk to the constable. All right?"

"All right."

"Try to sleep, Beth. I know that today has been horrendous for you, but your body needs sleep to recuperate. Or at the very least, close your eyes and rest."

"I'll try. That is all I can promise. Nothing more than that."

Seeing Sally in the doorway, Sam said, "Please try to get her to close her eyes and rest. She will probably want to talk to you about what happened this afternoon, but she needs rest more than anything."

"You are right, Sam," said Sally. "Rest, and no talking. Got it."

"And good luck with that," said Sam with a wink, before he closed the door and headed out to meet with Nick and the constable.

When Sam arrived at where the body lay in the hallway, Nick had already uncovered it and the constable was crouching down beside it and examining the knife wound in Jack's back.

"I've already filled Joe in on what happened," said Nick when Sam joined them. "But he might have a few questions for you as well."

"I'd be happy to help in any way that I can, Joe."

A JOURNEY TO JOY

"Thanks. But from what Nick has told me, it is quite straight-forward. I would not have reacted in any other way, considering the circumstances."

"Then you will not charge Nick for what he did?"

"No, absolutely not. Your choices to save the young woman's life were very limited, and you both did what you had to do to rescue her. No charges will be laid against either you or Nick. You have my word on that."

"Have you finished examining the body, Joe? Can we move it out of the hallway now?" asked Nick.

"Yes, we can move it. I am sure Sally would like us to get it out of the house as soon as possible. But I am wondering where we can store it until we get a grave dug?"

"We can store it in the shed as long as it is not there too long."

"I'll commandeer a couple of men in the village to dig the grave right away, Nick. In this heat, we don't want to have a body lying around above ground for too long."

"Thanks, Joe."

"Anything else, gentlemen? How is the young lady doing?"

"She is upset, with everything that has happened to her today. Especially finding out her brother is behind all the attempts on her life."

"Her brother?"

"Yes, well, her stepbrother, but she grew up with him in the family, so she considers him her brother."

"And he lives in England?"

"Yes, in London. Why do you ask?"

"No reason, except that I had a dapper-looking fellow stop in the mercantile this afternoon looking for accommodations. He did not give me his name, but he was just off the ship from England. I directed him here, Nick, as I thought I still had Mr. Stone as my guest. But there was something odd about his manner, and his dress was totally out of place for around here. I told him he should remove his coat, vest, and cravat so he would be more comfortable in the heat, but he said that a gentleman never did that in public. Each to his own, I suppose, but I repeat, he certainly was odd."

"Could you describe him?" asked Sam.

"Certainly. He would be about five foot four inches, overweight, thinning brownish grey hair . . ."

"Sounds like Howard, wouldn't you say, Nick?"

"I haven't seen him in over fifteen years, but the height and weight match my memory of him."

"You think that this might be the young lady's brother?" Joe asked.

"It could be, or it might not be," said Sam. "There are a lot of *gentlemen* wandering around London who would match that description. But it would be worth keeping an eye on him."

"Will do. Well, if there is nothing else, I'll head down and get those grave diggers working. Unless you need me to help you with the body."

"No, Sam and I can handle it. Thanks for coming up, and for your quick understanding of the situation. Really appreciate it."

"No problem. Goodbye for now," he said, before taking the stairs down to the kitchen and then heading out the front door.

***

Walking back down the hill, Joe met the English gentleman struggling to make his way up the long hill. He was red in the face and sweating profusely as he made his way up the long incline. Upon seeing Joe, he stopped and said, "Oh, hello again. I was wondering how much further it is to the boarding house, sir?"

"You are just about there, but from the look of you, I would advise you to rest a bit in the shade before you make the last climb. It looks like the heat is getting to you, and if you don't take it easy you may not make it the rest of the way."

"If it is only a short piece, I am sure I can make it, but thank you for your concern, sir."

"All right, but as one who has lived here for many years, I only wanted to give you some advice. By the way, I don't think that I caught your name when we were speaking earlier. I am Joe, the local storekeeper, constable, ticket agent, etcetera. I do pretty much everything here in the village. And you are . . .?"

"Just a weary traveller, sir, who would like to get some rest if you don't mind. Perhaps later we can get more acquainted, but right now I only want to find some food and rest. If you will excuse me?"

"Certainly, sir. Only trying to be friendly. Well, I won't keep you then. I hope you can find what you are looking for at the boarding house. If not, I now have an empty cot in my lodging; my previous lodger has just died, so he won't be needing that cot anymore. Please keep that in mind if they have no space for you at the boarding house. Good day to you, sir," said Joe, tipping his hat before he turned and headed down the hill. Yes, that fellow was worth watching. He was strange and secretive about his identity. That did not bode well for his reasons for being here. Best to keep an eye on him. Joe turned his attention back to the task at hand, finding the men to dig a grave for Mr. Stone's body.

***

Nosy copper, thought Howard as he continued up the hill, gasping for breath with every step he took. *Why can't everyone just mind their own business? I never have this kind of problem with people in London. Maybe the heat here just makes everyone a little bit crazy. Yes, that must be it. Why would anyone want to live here for any length of time?* Then Howard saw a large house just ahead of him. When he approached the house, he saw two men in the distance carrying a large, wrapped bundle down to a type of shed. Not wanting to talk to them, Howard walked into the house and gave a sigh of relief at the coolness in the foyer, created by a large fan in the ceiling. He tugged at his cravat and loosened it slightly so that he could breathe easier. He was still sweating, and he had a strange ache in his chest, but at least he was cooler. Seeing a desk at the far end of the foyer, he walked over there and sat down on a nearby chair after ringing the bell to attract the landlord of the place. And then he waited. After several minutes of waiting, Howard became impatient, and he got up and rang the bell again. What kind of establishment was this when no one answered a ringing bell? More evidence of the kind of people who lived here.

Just then, one of the two men Howard had seen earlier walked into the lobby. "Hello, sir," he greeted Howard. "Welcome. What can I do for you today?"

"I'm here to inquire if you have any spare rooms for rent, sir? I understand you are the only boarding house in the vicinity."

"That is correct, sir. We rarely get visitors here, except for those who come to see their relatives in the prison, but lately we have had quite a rush of people looking for rooms. Are you here to see someone in the prison, sir?"

"Perhaps . . ."

"Have you been to Fremantle previously, sir?"

"No, why do you ask?"

"Because you look somewhat familiar to me, and I have not left this place in over fifteen years."

"I don't think that we have ever met before, my good man. Now, do you have a room for me, or do I need to go back down and stay in the village? I understand the shopkeeper has just had a cot become available."

"Ah, yes, because of the unexpected death of the fellow we just carried out to the shed. Perhaps you saw us carrying out our task."

"I did not know what you were carrying, nor do I care. Now, do you have a room or not?"

"I do not, but you are welcome to stay and rest in our public lounge until you cool off. You look a bit dishevelled and hot. May I offer you a cold drink as well? Sam and I were just about to have one; you are welcome to join us."

"Sam?"

"Yes, my friend who was assisting me with the body. But you, having come from England, may know him as Lord Yardley, son of the Duke of Yardley. Are you acquainted with him?"

"I know of him, but I do not believe that our paths have ever crossed, sir. Why do you ask?"

"Because we are wondering why you are being so secretive about your identity, Howard," came a voice from behind him in the lobby.

"Secretive?" sputtered Howard, turning to face his inquirer. "I don't know what you mean, sir, and you must be mistaken about whom you think you are speaking to."

"I don't think I am mistaken, Howard," said Sam. "And I do not believe that Nick is mistaken either, are you, Nick?"

"No, Sam, his looks may have changed, but his voice and his uppity manner have not. This is the man I knew, the man who threw Sally and me into prison for missing one small payment on our land. One tiny, measly payment that you could not wait on for a few months, wasn't it, Mr. Stillwater?"

"I don't know what you are talking about, sir. You say that your name is Nick. What is your last name?"

"Oh, I am sure that your memory is not that poor, Stillwater. Think back sixteen years and the name Tremblant might ring a bell. Do you know me now?"

"Tremblant? Nick Tremblant? Tenants of one acre of Stillwater land?"

"Now you remember, don't you?"

"But-but-but what are you doing here, after all this time?"

"Making a life for myself and my wife, which you stole from us when you sent us down here to rot in Fremantle Prison. Ten years of hard labour for me and ten years for my lovely wife, who did nothing to deserve it. You robbed us of ten years of marriage and the chance to have a family. If God had not convinced us of the need to forgive you, I would have taken the next boat back to England and seen that you paid for what you did. But during those ten years in prison, I found Christ, as did Sally, and He commands us to love our enemies, and not hate them, or pay them back for what they have done. So we stayed and made a life for ourselves here, and we have never gone back to England. Now I ask again, what are you doing here?"

"Nothing that has anything to do with you, Tremblant. But I see I am not welcome here, so I will take myself off and stay in the village while I conduct my business." He got up and started stumbling towards the front door, the aching pain in his chest intensifying with every step he took.

"Sit down, man, before you fall down," commanded Sam, shoving Howard back down onto a chair. "Now, if you are here to see your sister Bethany at the prison, as I think your intent might be, I have to tell you she is no longer there."

"No longer there?"

"No, she is not."

"Then she is . . . gone?"

"Not exactly."

"What do you mean, not exactly?"

"She is not dead, though your hired assassin tried twice to make it so and failed. In fact, it was he that we just carried out to the shed. Would you like to come with Nick and me to identify his body?"

"My hired assassin? What are you talking about, Yardley? You think I hired Jack Stone to kill my sister? Are you crazy, just like everyone else in this place?"

"Funny, I don't believe I had mentioned his name, had I, Nick?"

"No, you had not."

"Then how would Howard know his name if he did not hire him to murder Bethany?"

"I don't know, Sam. It seems quite impossible to me."

"Me as well. Perhaps Howard would like to clear up the mystery for us. Howard?"

"I, uh, heard the name of the assassin from the constable. He told me about him when I met him on the hill. He offered me a cot in his house. That is where I heard the name."

"No, you knew Jack's name when you hired him many months ago in London, Howard," said Sam. "Jack confessed you hired him before he died."

Howard's heart was racing now, and his chest felt like something was squeezing it tighter and tighter. He could hardly breathe, but he would not stay here and have all his sins laid out in the open. He had to get away, now. So he stood up and started stumbling towards the door again. The door kept wavering in his sight, but he kept moving. He had to get out; he had to get away.

Once he was out on the porch, he half fell down the wooden steps. His accusers were following him, telling him to confess all to God and ask for His forgiveness. But Howard could not, he had done too much; his sins were too great. If only . . . But it was too late. He collapsed onto the ground and felt his life ebbing away. The darkness was overtaking him, and there was no shining light at the end of his tunnel. His time on earth was over, and he headed towards the Heavenly Judge.

Rushing down the steps, Sam turned over Howard's body and checked for signs of life. There were none. Howard had gone the way of all men. Another body to bury today. Another soul lost for eternity.

"Is he?" asked Nick.

"Yes."

"That is the third one today, if you count Mrs. Stone. I'd better go down and tell Joe."

"Yes, and I will go up and tell Bethany and Sally."

"After that we will meet back here and take his body to the shed to join Stone's."

The two men separated, each to his own task, while Howard's body lay motionless on the ground in front of the house.

Chapter 14

Sam made his way up the stairs. All he had to tell the ladies was bad news, so why hurry to tell them that another man had died in his presence? At least this time neither he nor Nick had anything to do with the death. Howard had brought it all on himself.

When Sam got to Bethany's room, he knocked and Sally came to the door. Seeing who it was, she let him into the room. Sam walked over to the bed where Bethany was sitting up, propped up by many pillows. He sat down on the side of the bed and took a deep breath.

"What is it, Sam?" said Bethany. "What has happened? Please tell me nothing is bad. I don't know if I can handle any more bad news today. Where is Nick?"

"I am not sure how to tell you this, Beth, but there has been another death just now."

"Another death? Oh, please God, tell me it isn't Nick," cried Sally.

"No, Nick is fine. He has gone down to the village to speak with Joe and let him know that there will be one more grave to dig today."

"Then who is it?" asked Bethany.

"It's Howard."

"Howard? But how could that be? He is in England, isn't he? Why would he be here?"

"It was Howard. He came in on the last ship and came up here looking for lodging. Nick and I both recognized him. He came looking for you to make sure that Jack had done his work. But his heart gave out, and he died just below the porch steps. I'm so sorry, Bethany. I know you still cared for him, even after what you found out about him. There was no easy way to tell you of his death. Please tell me what I can do, or say, to help you with this news. Please?"

"I don't know what to say, Sam. I'm having a hard time believing you. I do, but I don't want to. I want to believe Howard is still in England, and that he had nothing to do with all of this. But I know in my head that is not the truth; I am just having trouble with my heart believing it as well. Yes, I did still love him. He was my brother. We had our disagreements, but he was still family. At least now Cassandra can have a better life, as can the boys. But I need some time to digest what you have told me. Would you mind leaving me alone for a bit?"

"Of course not. I will be right downstairs if you need me."

"And me as well," said Sally, giving her a hug. "Call if you need anything. I'll be in the kitchen making us all some dinner."

"Thank you both for your understanding. I appreciate it. Yes, I will call if I need anything in the next while," said Bethany. She turned her head towards the window and tried to stifle the sobs that were collecting in her throat. Once she heard the door close and the footsteps recede down the hallway, she let the sobs come forth in full strength until there were none left. Howard was gone, and she had never had the chance to say goodbye. She would have to live with that thought for the rest of her life, but she would now focus on caring for Cassandra and her nephews, to make sure that none of what Howard had done had any repercussions for them. She needed to get to England as soon as possible to tell Cassandra what had happened, and that she would not be alone in bringing up her sons. But how was Bethany going to get to England? She was still a prisoner here. Only a judge in England could overturn her sentence and acquit her of her crime. Would she have to wait in prison for another year or so until Sam could get her free in England and then come back and free her here? That would ask a lot of him, but he had said that he would do anything for her. So now was the time to take him up on his promise.

After about an hour of not hearing anything from Bethany, Sam could no longer stand it. "I'm going to go up and check on Bethany," he said to Sally and Nick. "She said she needed some time to grieve alone, but I am having trouble keeping my promise. I will also check to see if she wants any dinner, Sally, and if she wants it in her room or if she wants to come down to the kitchen to eat with us. I'll be back with her answer."

"That's a good idea. I'm happy to fix a tray for her, but it might be good for her to eat with us as well. Just let me know."

Sam left the kitchen and headed up the stairs and down the hallway, towards his old room. He knocked quietly on her door. "Bethany, are you awake?"

"Yes, Sam, come in," was the reply from the other side of the door.

Sam opened the door to find Bethany sitting up in bed. She greeted him with a small smile on her face, although her eyes were still red and swollen from crying.

"How are you doing?"

"Better, thank you. I needed that time alone to work through my feelings, but I am more at peace now."

"That's good. Do you want to come down for some dinner, or do you want me to bring a tray of food up to you? Either way will work for me and Sally."

"I think I would like some company while I eat. Though I'm not exactly dressed for the dinner table," she said, indicating the night-gown she was wearing.

"Well, even though everyone else will wear their finest attire, young lady, I suppose under the circumstances, we will allow you to come as you are. But only this once, mind you. Don't let it happen again."

"Yes, Lord Yardley. I will adhere to your dinner dress requirements after this day. I will remember your edict."

He laughed, and then, after wrapping a light blanket around her shoulders, he picked her up and carried her downstairs to the kitchen, to the delight of Nick and Sally. Sam placed her gently in a chair at the table and then pushed it in for her. "Is that all right for you?"

"It's fine, thank you," she replied.

Having received her approval, Sam went to a chair next to her and sat down, while Sally and Nick finished putting the food on the table before they, too, took their places.

"Now that everyone is here," said Nick, "let us thank God for bringing us through this trial-filled day and for the food that He has supplied for us." Then he closed his eyes, and the others followed suit, before Nick prayed, "Dear Heavenly Father, thank you for what You have done for us this day, for Bethany's miraculous recovery from the spider bite and for protecting her from further harm. The events of this day have also saddened us with the lives that were lost, and we pray for those who mourn, Lord. May You comfort Bethany with Your love in the death of her brother, as she thinks about the impact this will have on his family. Keep them in Your care, Lord, even though they are far away from us this night. Now, I thank You providing this meal and bless the hands that prepared it. I pray this in Jesus's name. Amen."

As Nick ended his prayer, a chorus of amens went around the table, and then everyone opened their eyes. "Well, just reach out and help yourselves," said Sally.

"Everything looks great, Sally, thank you; much better than what I would have been getting for dinner at the prison tonight, were I still there," replied Bethany. "So I am going to relish every bite."

"I don't know if I would even call what they serve for meals up there food," said Nick. "Unless it has changed drastically since I was last their guest."

Bethany laughed. "No, it probably has not changed in the past years, Nick. But it has sustained me, and I guess that is what is most important in a prison setting."

"Well, here's hoping you never have to go back and eat that food again, Bethany," said Sam.

"And how will we prevent that, Sam? My understanding is that the Director only allowed me to stay with all of you while I recuperated from my spider bite, and then I am to go back to prison."

"Perhaps with all the information that we have gathered today, the director will change his mind and release you from your sentence."

"I don't know that he has the power to do so. I think that my acquittal will have to come from the judge in England before they can release me from prison. Besides, the sentence of theft still stands, and now only Cassandra can attest to my innocence in that regard."

"Do you think that a letter from Cassandra would suffice?"

"A letter? I suppose it might help, but I have not received anything from Cassandra since I came here."

"Well, I meant to keep this until after dinner," said Sam, "but a letter arrived for you on today's ship. It went up to the prison and Jones received it, but when she saw they addressed it to you, she sent it down here with a guard. It arrived just a short while ago, but I did not want to disturb your time alone, so I was waiting to give it to you after dinner. Would you like it now?"

"No, I can wait," said Bethany. "If it is good news, it will wait, and if it is more bad news, I can wait. Let's just enjoy our meal before I open the letter."

"Hear, hear, Bethany!" said Nick. "I agree with you, and do not want this splendid meal spoiled by the news in that letter."

Sam and Sally agreed, and the four friends put aside thoughts of the letter and the past day, falling into light-hearted conversation that eased their minds and souls.

After dinner, they gathered in the lounge for tea. Sam, sitting beside Bethany on the settee, handed her the promised letter. She looked at the handwriting and the return address and said, "It looks like Cassandra's writing, and that is her address, so this must be from her. But why is she writing to me?"

"Well, there is only one way to find out," said Sam, "and that is by opening the letter and reading it."

Bethany continued to just hold it and stare at the envelope. "I'm scared to open it," she confessed. "Would you do it for me, Sam?"

"Are you sure?"

"Yes, please."

"Very well." He took the envelope and pried open the seal on the back of it. Then he withdrew the letter and started to hand it to Bethany to read.

But she shook her head and pushed back his hand containing the letter. "No, read it out loud for me, please."

"But what if there is private information that your sister-in-law only wants you to see, Bethany? Shall I skip any sections that look like they are only meant for your eyes?"

Bethany shook her head again and said, "I can't think what that might be, Sam, and because you are all my dear friends, I don't mind if you hear everything that is in the letter."

"All right," said Sam, before he cleared his throat and read.

Dear Bethany,

I know that receiving this letter from me must come as a great shock to you, but I had to write and tell you how sorry I am that I consented to be a part of Howard's scheme. I should have stood up to him and refused to lie about you stealing my necklace. Even though I knew the truth, I was willing to lie to the judge. Oh, Bethany, can you ever forgive me for that? My only excuse, if there is one, was that Howard threatened he would divorce me and leave me with nothing if I did not go along with his plan. He also said that he would sue for custody of the boys, and if he was successful I would never see them again. If there is one thing I love, it is my four sons, and I could not bear to be without them, Bethany. So I agreed to Howard's scheme, and watched you being judged and found guilty of a crime you did not commit before being shipped off to Australia.

The weight of my sin has laid heavily upon my soul ever since that dreadful day. And so, now, after many months of agony, I am going to go to the judge and recant my statement. Hopefully they will acquit you of your crime, and you will be free. If I am found guilty of perjury, then so be it; I may have to go to prison myself for a time, but at least my conscience will be clear and I will be free of my misery. My only prayer is that once you are home again and if I am in prison, you will look after my boys. I do not want them growing up under Howard's hand. If you can forgive me enough to do that, I would be eternally grateful to you.

I hope this letter finds you in the best health that you can be under those very trying circumstances. Howard will be away from home on business tomorrow, so I will make sure I post this letter while he is away, and you receive it as soon as possible.

Once again, my best wishes to you, my dear sister-in-law.

I hope to see you again once they have freed you from your prison and you return home to us.

Your loving sister,

Cassandra

Finishing the letter, Sam looked over at Bethany. Tears filled her eyes and her hands started shaking. "Is it true, Sam? Is it really true?" she asked. "Will Cassandra be able to free me with her confession to the judge?"

"I expect so, Bethany. There would be no reason for the judge not to believe her, especially if she tells him that they, Howard and Frank, coerced her into lying. I don't know what the consequences will be for Cassandra, but I know what it means for you. You are going to be free, and soon. No more prison meals for you, my dear. You are going home!"

"Yes, but when will this all take place? We are so far away from England, and it takes so long for messages to travel back and forth. I may need to stay in prison until the notice of my acquittal comes from the judge in England, and that could take months yet."

"Not if I have anything to say about it. Tomorrow morning, with your permission, I am going to take this letter up to the director and let him read it. Then I am going to petition him, based on this letter and his mercy, to free you from the prison. If he still requires that you stay in my custody until the letter of acquittal arrives, then I am agreeable to that, and you can stay with me until you are free."

"But Sam, I thought you were planning to leave for England on the next ship travelling that way? How can I stay with you and yet be here at the same time?"

"There is no reason you have to stay here, Beth. You can travel back to England with me."

"Go back to England with you? Now? But . . . but . . . but . . . what about propriety? I cannot travel back with a single man as my only companion."

"You can if that man is your husband."

"My . . . my . . . my husband? You? You . . . would marry me, Sam?"

"Only if you consent, Beth," said Sam, getting up and kneeling before her. While he was doing so, Sally nudged Nick, and they melted out of the room.

"I would love to marry you, but you need to marry someone with a large dowry and a high social standing. Even with my estate restored to me, I have neither of those two qualifications."

"Bethany Anne Stillwater, do you love me?" asked Sam, looking up into her beautiful brown eyes.

"Yes, I do," she replied.

"And I love you with all my heart, Beth. And that is all the qualification you need to be my wife. Nothing else, my love."

"But what about your father? And your family? Won't they want you to marry someone from the peerage?"

"I am the second son of the duke. Fortunately for me, my older brother is well, and is continuing to produce more sons to secure the dukedom. I also received a letter today from my father, and he informed me that Rupert's wife just gave birth to their fourth son, God bless her. So unless something drastic happens to Rupert and his sons, I have very little chance of becoming the Duke of Yardley, for which I am very grateful. He also said he had been looking into your plight, both on my recommendation and my mother's. They both believe they unjustly convicted you and wish to help free you. My mother has always had a soft spot for you, Bethany, and before everything happened was always nudging me in your direction. I am sure it will thrill them to receive you as their next daughter-in-law. With all those factors in mind, I choose you, Miss Stillwater, and ask again if you will join your life with mine, as long as God gives us breath."

"Then, Lord Samuel Edward Yardley, I do consent to be your wife and to live with you for the rest of my life," replied Bethany, happy tears now filling her eyes.

Sam whooped with joy, bringing Nick and Sally back from the kitchen. "She said yes!" he exclaimed. "She said yes!"

Before they could reach them with congratulatory hugs, Sam pulled Bethany's head down and kissed her tenderly on her lips to seal their engagement. The kiss was brief, and it was all Bethany could do not to pull Sam back for another one.

Then it was time for celebration. Sally brought in a cake with their tea, and the couples sat for many hours rejoicing and making plans for the days ahead.

***

The next day, after Sam had seen the director and received approval for his plan of taking Bethany back to England as his wife, he tracked down Joe, who was licensed to perform weddings in the area. He was more than happy to hear Sam and Bethany exchange their vows, with Nick and Sally standing as witnesses for them. Bethany shed a single tear as she was getting ready for the ceremony; it was not how she had envisioned her wedding day to be. But then she cheered up when she thought of her groom; he was not who she'd thought she would marry. He was so much more, and she could hardly believe that in a couple of hours she would be the wife of a lord. Not that it mattered one iota to her, except for the fact that the lord was her love, Samuel Edward Yardley, son of the Duke of Yardley, her fantasy prince.

After the simple wedding ceremony was over, and the feast Sally had whipped up for the occasion was consumed, the bride and groom retired to the small back bedroom of the boarding house to spend their first night together as man and wife.

Epilogue

Three years later. . .

"Look, Sam, I can see the prison towers," said Bethany. "I can see them. We are almost home!"

Sam laughed at the joyful expression on her face. "Darling, I don't know of another woman who would get excited about seeing prison towers and call it home."

She smiled and gave him a little shove. "Oh, you know what I mean. It's not the prison, it's the fact that they stand on the headland of our new homeland."

"I know, love, I just had to tease you a bit. And yes, I can't wait to get *home* as well."

It had been a long three years since Bethany and Sam had left Australia, but now, except for occasional travels back to see relatives in England, they were looking forward to settling down and starting a family in their own sheep station.

Bethany thought back over the past few years. They had left here two days after their wedding, amidst tears of farewell and sorrow from their friends, both at the prison and in the village. Bethany had promised her dear friends at the prison that she would be back, and that as soon as she was, she would visit them again, and often. It was hard to leave them, but even harder to leave Nick and Sally, whom she counted now more as family than as friends. But as she was leaving with the love of her life, her new husband, the leave-taking was not as painful as she'd thought it would be. They had had a smooth journey back to England with no mishaps, so the newly married couple could revel in their love for each other. Once they reached England, and after they had established themselves in Sam's London townhouse, they went to see the judge who was reviewing Bethany's case. It was not the same judge who had sent Bethany away. Judge Henley and Frank Walden had been disbarred after several counts of misconduct had been filed against them. The present judge was very cordial to Sam and Bethany; he told them that after hearing Cassandra's confession on that day many months ago, he had had no problem with signing the papers of acquittal for Bethany. With those papers and others safely in hand, they headed over to see Cassandra and her boys. The judge had only sentenced Cassandra to probation for her perjury after hearing her story, so Cassandra and the boys had continued to live in the London townhouse. All Howard's gambling notes had been paid off, thanks to Bethany's generosity. The plan was for them to move out to Stillwater Estate as soon as Cassandra's probationary period was over. They could get away from the city and give the boys an opportunity to grow up as gentlemen in the countryside. Cassandra had wept profusely when Bethany presented her with the good news and a key to the estate.

Then it had been time to meet the Duke and Duchess of Yardley, along with the rest of Sam's family. Upon their arrival in London, Sam had sent a note to his parents, letting them know of their arrival. Bethany's knees had trembled before meeting his family, but it had surprised her when the duchess readily and warmly welcomed her into the family. One of the first things she did, upon meeting Bethany, was apologise to her for her inaction at the time of Bethany's arrest and incarceration. She even asked Bethany's forgiveness for her sin of omission, which of course Bethany gave her. The duchess told her of her involvement with Bethany's charity but was quick to assure her that now that Bethany was home, she could take back the leadership of the committee. Having heard from Mrs. Hayward about what a good job the duchess was doing, Bethany was hesitant to do so. She and Sam were planning to move back to Australia to live, so she did not want to disrupt the present workings of the committee. She was content to work under the leadership of her mother-in-law and leave her to steer the charitable group. Sam had not disclosed their future plans to his family, so Bethany concentrated on commending the duchess for her good work, and asked her to continue in her present role, which she readily accepted.

Regarding her release from prison and exoneration by the judge, Bethany thanked the duke and duchess for their work on her behalf. They were modest in accepting her praise and said they were pleased everything had worked out for the best, including Sam and Bethany's marriage. The duchess informed Bethany that she had dreamed of having Bethany as a daughter-in-law and was thrilled to hear of their recent vows. She was sorry they had not been there to attend their wedding but agreed that marrying in Australia before their long voyage home had been the right thing to do. She was hoping Sam and Bethany would allow her to throw a big party on their behalf, to welcome them home and celebrate their marriage in style. Although Bethany cringed at being the centre of attention at such an event, she smiled and told the delighted duchess that would be a great honour. The duchess would start planning a gala right away. Once she moved away from Bethany, Sam came over. Upon hearing the news about an upcoming party, he reassured Bethany that when they moved back to Australia, there would be no big galas to attend in the backcountry. So she only needed to endure this one, and then the parties would end. Bethany gave him a grateful kiss for this timely reminder.

After greeting the duke and duchess, it was time to meet the rest of the family, starting with the oldest brother, Rupert, and his wife, Hannah. Seeing that Hannah was again with child, Sam had winked at Bethany, and she had had a hard time containing her laughter.

After that initial meeting, Bethany and Hannah spent many hours together playing with the boys and the baby, while Sam spent time with his father and Rupert doing the business that would prepare the way for them to move back to Australia.

And at last, the day had come for them to set sail back to Australia and their new home. Again, it was a hard day, leaving loved ones behind, but Sam and Bethany knew that this was the right decision for them. So they left on their journey to their new home, with Bethany knowing that when they arrived, they would soon be a family of three. She did not share that information with Sam before they left, because she knew he would delay their trip until she had delivered the baby in England, but midway through the journey it became clear to both of them they would soon be parents. As expected, Sam fussed a bit about her not telling him before they left England, but he soon settled down to enjoy this new stage of his life and was very excited the first day he could feel the baby moving in Bethany's belly. Fortunately, Beth had shared the news with Hannah before she left, so she had a trunk full of maternity clothes and baby things ready for her new adventure. They were going to stay with Nick and Sally until after the baby was born, and then head up to the newly named station, the Yardley Downs, just north and west of Geraldton. And now they were almost home . . .

Sam wrapped his arms around his wife's expanding waist and said, "What a different arrival this is for both you and me, love. When we arrived here previously, everything was unknown to both of us. You were heading to a life of misery while I was looking for business and adventure. Miraculously, God brought us together, out of the storm and into a life of joy and happiness, that can only get better during our years together. They say home is where the heart is, and my heart will always be with you, darling, wherever we may be."

Bethany leaned back into Sam's embrace and moved his hand to where the babe was kicking. It was true. Out of her misery had come the joy of her life, and now she was going to spend all the rest of her days with the man she had only dreamed about marrying. God had worked everything out in her life, just as He had promised to do for all His children.[4] Her life as a prisoner, and now as Sam's wife, proved that no matter where you were placed, life was a journey to joy.

End Notes

1. James 4:17 (King James Bible; All following citations are from this version)

2. Isaiah 40:31

3. Matthew 5:44

4. Psalm 23: 1-6

5. Romans 8:28

I hope you enjoyed Bethany and Sam's story. If you have any comments, I would love to hear them. You can reach me on my website **www.nancyireneyoung.com**.